. . . Nyla stepped up to Karp's desk, picked up a photo and looked at it closely. Karp watched her. She forced herself to contain her revulsion—in black and white photos, blood was black, but no less gory. She put the picture down in front of the Chief and kept her finger on it.

"You'll talk to Mitch Masters and Ritchie Dennis?" Her eyes told him she was afraid of nothing.

"And with the footwear specialist," Lucy added, hearing her voice break. She wanted to turn all the pictures over.

Karp didn't answer. Nyla leaned in close to him. "Don't underestimate us, Chief . . ."

Works by Vicki P. McConnell also available from Naiad Press:

MRS. PORTER'S LETTER

THE BURNTON WIDOWS

Vicki P. McConnell

Illustrated by Janet Fons

THE NAIAD PRESS INC.

1984

Printed in the United States of America
First Edition

Cover design by Tee A. Corinne
Interior drawings by Janet Fons
Typesetting by Sandi Stancil

Library of Congress Cataloging in Publication Data

McConnell, Vicki P.
    The Burnton widows.

    I. Title.
PS3563.C344B8 1984   813'.54   84-3440
ISBN 0-930044-52-5

DEDICATION

This book is dedicated to my mother, Dorothy Rose Mitchell McConnell, who told me every person should follow her own dream. For her, Druscilla Ketcham and I have built the limestone castle.

This book is also written in memory of our special loved ones who have gone before us, in the death of love or even in death. Like Nyla Wade, I believe we find them anew.

KUDOS AND KARMA

"Like lovers with karma, I cast out my netting," quotes Nyla Wade from a sonnet in these pages. There were many in my net who helped in the karma of this book and to whom I offer kudos.

DEIRDRE REILLY as proof reader and cherished friend.

JANET FONS for her care in Oregon so I could see and work, and for bringing my characters so gloriously into view.

KATHERINE FORREST for hot shot editing.

GAIL BOOMS VILA for castle research and writing, and for her precise intellect about the artistic process and its hard choices.

LIV EDWARDS for the critical idea of the echo.

DOROTHY LA FLEUR for growing me up, giving me answers, and convincing me there *is* a light at the end of the tunnel.

ROBERTA PARRY for inspiration—she has, as my grandfather would say, a flower and a metal in her—yellow roses and gold.

NANCY WHITE for a crucial conversation about Lesbian consciousness in fiction and avoiding exploitation.

RONNIE STOREY for sending me *On Becoming a Writer* and for showing me the art of quilting.

SANDY JONES's loyalty; WOOD's call to writers to take risks; CORONA's rescuing my manuscript in San Francisco; GAIL McLELLAND getting me through the first readings; DONNA and L giving me their desk.

PETE FELTEN helping me research Kansas limestone quarrying and building; RANDY and WARREN for special research; BILL K. for research and for showing the sweetness and caring that inspired the character of Perry Day Truman.

FRANK GIULIANO for finding out the starting date of the Civil War when I was crazed to know it, and for listening.

Authors JOANNA L. STRATTON and LILLIAN SCHLISSEL for their inspiring books, *Pioneer Women* and *Women's Diaries of the Westward Journey.*

The 1982 Denver chapter of the FEMINIST WRITERS GUILD, for sharing the delightful exercise, "How to Write a Sex Scene in Twelve Minutes."

The WOMEN who have taken the risk to write or call me to say they liked my work.

KATE WARREN for patiently posing in photographs crucial to the illustrations.

My sister DENISE McCONNELL, for patiently photographing Kate in the OKC heat, sharing my process especially when I get scared, and reminding everyone how long it takes to write a single book.

TWO OTHERS have made this book possible: my grandfather, NOLY MITCHELL, a person who speaks in a language all his own. And LOTUS, who reached through time to find me and speak the language of passion, dreams, life.

CONTENTS

PRELUDE

Ritchie Dennis had been squatting on the road since afternoon. He liked this road high up on one of the bluffs, away from traffic. In the darkness he watched lights go on and off in the houses of Burnton. He moved his feet in the gravel, listening to the crunchy sounds and how they filled up all the space around him. The bluff was at his back and he leaned against it, looking at the stars. They stayed on all night, not like the house lights. He liked to watch one for a while and then another. But now maybe it was time for a walk. He was a little stiff from sitting; he would go visit his friend. Even though she barked at him, he still liked her.

There were no cars on the road as Ritchie walked down from his view of the town lights. Clumsy and timid, he picked his way carefully, frowning and straining to see where to place his feet. Sometimes the gravel was loose and would make him slide.

"Who's that?"

The voice came out of nowhere and so startled Ritchie that as he turned to locate the voice, he lost his footing. Waving his arms, he grunted and fell in a heap. "Who there? No nishmon! No Ritchie onesome!"

Steps shuffled in the gravel and the boy saw the dark silhouette of a man.

"You know me, boy. Get up and get home. It's not safe out here. They can hook a wave onto you easy because they can see in the dark and we can't."

"Who there? No nishmon!"

"Get on up."

As Ritchie got himself up off the road, the old man scanned the sky. "Ricks," he said. "Ricks."

"Go see dog now. See dog." When Ritchie started away, the man grabbed the sleeve of his coat with a gloved hand. He smelled strongly of household cleanser and tobacco. "You leave that dog alone. Now get on home."

Val wanted to dry Joan's hair; they were playfully arguing near their bedroom window when Ritchie passed on the road and Dobro started to bark. Joan pulled up the shade.

"Anyone out there?" Val asked.

"Someone on the road. Looks like . . . it *is*, it's Ritchie. Dobro's loose. I've got to go put her on the chain."

"She won't bite him unless he comes into the yard."

"*Maybe* she won't. But maybe he *will* come into the yard."

Her caftan flowing out behind her, Joan went down the hall to the front door and turned on the porch light. "Hush, Dobro! Ritchie? Ritchie Dennis, is that you?"

A neighbor's porch light came on. Loamie Newsome called, "You having trouble, Joan?"

The boy on the road stood stock-still, as if the lights had paralyzed him. Joan went to the doghouse and put Dobro on her chain. Loamie could hear the chain rattle and Joan saying, "Easy girl, it's not the bogeyman. It's just Ritchie Dennis."

When Joan turned around, the boy had not moved. What could be wrong with him? Usually he babbled and stumbled toward her. She was somewhat afraid of his size but usually managed to keep him safely away from the dog. Dobro, no matter what reassurance, would never allow him to pet her.

"G'won home, Ritchie. Shoo, scat!" Loamie was on her porch in fuzzy slippers and a laughable hairnet that squashed her ears flat against her head. She held a broom. Dobro growled;

Loamie shooed. Still the boy didn't move.

Joan called to him again. "Ritchie, are you all right? Are you hurt, son?"

Valerie was at the door and came into the light, wearing a caftan matching Joan's. "What's going on out here?" She had never seen the boy out this late before; he stood just beyond the shadow of the porch lights, his huge size eerie and distorted in the darkness, his arms hanging limp at his sides.

Loamie warned from her porch, "Don't let him get too close, Joan. He's not right, you know. He might get ahold of you."

Ritchie took a step and the three women jumped. "Don know who say. Fall down when he say. Sky man. Star man!" The boy pointed toward the sky. "Who say?" Then he put his arms straight in front of him and turned to Joan. "Hans," he said, still questioning, shaking his head. He rolled one fist into the palm of the other hand and said again, "Hans, hide hans. Sky man, hide hans."

Loamie retreated back behind her screen door. Dobro's growl signaled a definite desire to bite.

"Go home now, Ritchie. It's all right. No more sky man. Go on."

The boy looked at Joan, then at Val. Then slowly, still rolling one fist in the other hand, he started on down the road.

As Loamie's porch light snapped out and Dobro's growling faded, Val looked out into the side yard and driveway. The moon was what her husband used to call a cloud moon: its light was diffused by traveling clouds, bright moments of moonlight paling so that night seemed deeper and blacker than usual, almost thick in its blackness. He would never sail in cloud moon, claiming it was an omen of coming bad weather; the truth was, the strange night color unnerved him. Now Val understood why. She was grateful for the protective dog. Just before Val shut the door, Dobro gave the cloud moon her own judgement—a short bark like a terse aside about the bother of strangers on the road.

"I saw the bouquet," Val said, joining Joan in their bedroom. "I just love it when you give me toothbrushes."

"Now it's a luxury. Then, it was our little safeguard."

"Ah yes, a way to hedge questions from Stan."

"Just sometimes when you were over a lot, and especially when you stayed all night. I didn't want him to ask too many questions about the extra toothbrush. So I changed them often and started making my little bouquets, a whole vase full of brightly colored toothbrushes. Of course the kids loved it."

"I loved it too—the intrigue, the danger of discovery! And you."

They kissed, Val touching the back of Joan's neck and feeling her way into the marvelous head of thick greying hair, Joan touching the extra bit of Val's lip that she could only touch with her tongue, and feeling it stir her deeply.

"My sweet bush." Val tugged gently at Joan's hair.

"My eternal romantic." Joan's lips were fervent.

"Now that we have our own home, do you ever miss the intrigue?"

"Joan, it's like the boats. I loved sailing but Richard was so much of that memory and I'm glad he's gone from my life. So sure, I loved our intrigue but you and I were apart. Now we have each other and anyone who would look at this life and long for the old intrigue—well, that's the fool who hasn't been there."

Again they kissed and stroked each other, embraced and held one another, rocking slightly. Compared to all the years before when they had struggled in different directions, their nine years together seemed to roll away like recent history.

"You still bothered by Joyce's phone call, honey?" Val asked.

"A little." Joan gave her a peck on the lips. "But I'm not going to be anymore, darn it! She and James are adults and they've got to solve their own problems."

"I saw you rubbing your shoulder. How about a massage?"

"My favorite thing. I submit willingly, gratefully!"

"One quick surprise goes in the oven for you and then I will place my magic hands upon you!"

After Val put the biscuits in the oven, she stood for a moment in the kitchen. She felt as well as heard the surf, a vibration and a sound so constant it faded into the background.

Yet it was its own distinct being at night, so much of the reason she loved their house by the sea. When they made love with the sound of the ocean all around them, she became the water, able to flow over Joan's every part at once, her all-skin self. Together in that vulnerability between them and the vastness and terrible beauty of the ocean outside of them, she knew they were more terrifying and beautiful than any other part of nature. Sometimes when she climaxed she became the rush of the sea between rocks and waves splashing salty—ferocious and gentle.

"Want some air, honey?" she asked, returning to the bedroom.

"Yes, let's do."

Val opened the door at the end of the hall outside their bedroom, the door that abutted the beach front. The yard, which ran only about ten feet before a fairly steep drop to the beach, contained a humorous touch: Druscilla Ketcham had inlaid a limestone walkway, just as if a sidewalk into an abyss made perfect sense.

Val took from her caftan pocket the silk scarf she'd been wearing that afternoon and tied it around her neck. Joan watched with a look of delight and surprise. She had lit three lavender candles by the bed and now sat up, holding out her arms to Val.

Val slid across the end of the bed and in between those arms; she ran her hands lightly over Joan's arms on the outside of the caftan, then slowly slipped her hands underneath the fabric and began to massage her shoulders. Joan could feel herself relaxing from the warm touch, from Val's closeness. In a few minutes, she leaned her head back slightly and eased the caftan down off her shoulders; it slid with a soft brush into the bedcovers. Val's fingertips brushed her lightly all over. Joan caught her breath as Val's moist lips, her breath, were hot against her neck. Her hands moved to cast away Val's caftan and reveal slender, strong shoulders, the ones that could lift her in a fierce embrace, the ones rounded where she rested her face to sleep safe. Stroking those shoulders, she took her favorite journey, in the mist of their eyes upon each other: naked arms, breasts, legs, running her two index fingers down the front of Val's thighs. Val's breath jerked when Joan leaned down and flicked the skin on the front of her legs with her tongue. They knew the journey together and lay back on the bed; Joan's teeth grazed the skin of Val's hip bones and Joan felt a hot palm flat against her lower back.

Joan relished her command, made love in no rush as she savored her lover, moved slow when Val appealed, "Eat me, eat me soft." The journey was familiar but never the same except in its reward, that drop from the present as if out of the sky into limbo, the womb with resounding walls, the self given up and claimed from any further waiting.

Tender time, their afterglow. They held each other closer, longer than is allowed by all that women are taught. They marveled again at themselves and had shy moments. They played with their fingers wrapped together, wiggling and winding. They looked at the shape of their hands in candlelight. They saw the shadows of the room ease around their bareness. They thought of no one outside themselves nor of any danger.

"Your treat from the oven is ready," Val whispered when it seemed they had been lying silent, their legs overlapping, for hours.

"Burned by now, don't you think?"

"No less than perfect. It's our anniversary."

Val got up and headed for the kitchen dressed only in her silk scarf. Joan retrieved a box from under Val's pillow and placed it on top. It was deep purple, wrapped with a black cloth ribbon. Pulling the covers up around her, she propped herself against her pillow just in time for Val's return. "Being fed in bed, the ultimate decadence."

Val saw the purple box. "More surprises?"

Careful not to tug at the ribbon, Val slipped it off the box. Inside, surrounded by lavender tissue paper, was a gold bracelet: two strands of delicate chain connected at each end with one small gold link.

"It's gorgeous, Joan."

"It's a lot like us—two strands connected by one strong link. I've been so happy, Val, being us, making that link."

Joan fiddled with the clasp until the bracelet was on Val's wrist. She ran her fingers over it, feeling the chain and Val's skin.

"You may be wondering about *your* anniversary gift," Val said, getting up and going to the closet. "It was too big to put under your pillow. I never wanted to do this but you bugged me long enough so I've granted you your wish." She scooted back hangers and dragged out a large, flat package wrapped in brown paper.

"Oh Valerie, it isn't . . . you didn't . . ." Joan excitedly began tearing away the brown paper. "You did it! You sat for Lea Hemingway!"

There indeed was Val's portrait, painted by the San Francisco artist Joan had long admired. Val had posed nude, reclining languorously on the limestone ledge beneath the blue window. In the portrait, she held a bouquet of white rhodies.

"My goddess, what a portrait! I love it, Val, I love it so much! And you!"

They hugged around the portrait and then Joan put it down and they hugged again, laughing and hopping back onto the bed.

"I've got another surprise for you, Val. A crystal for your collection in the window. We can hang it together tomorrow in the sunlight."

"Wonderful!"

Lifting up a napkin, Val revealed four biscuits. "Your feast, before it gets cold." She broke a biscuit open and Joan saw the flaky layers still steaming from the oven.

"Want one?" Val asked, spreading them with lemon curd. Joan nodded vigorously. "Well, not just yet." Val put the biscuit back on the plate and ran one finger underneath the scarf at her neck. She untied it and drew it by one end down her body and into her lap. Joan watched the scarf flow over Val's skin. Val waited another moment. She held Joan's eyes with her own. Joan waited too, relaxed against the pillows. Then Val picked up the scarf by both ends and held it in front of her, a blindfold. Joan leaned forward and offered her head as Val tied the scarf loosely around her eyes. Part of the scarf trailed down her back when it was tied; Val touched it down this length so that Joan felt her hand through the silky fabric.

Placing an extra dollop of lemon curd on the hot biscuit, Val fed it slowly to Joan, watching the wafer-thin layers of bread disappear. She wiped Joan's lips, then kissed them, then fed her another biscuit. She could feel the ocean's soft thuds on the beach, coming right up through the floor, through the bed, up inside her and through her body. She could smell the tangy lemon smell and taste it when she kissed Joan.

"Enough?"

"Just enough."

Val moved the tray onto the floor, then eased the covers back away from Joan, who was still blindfolded. Val massaged her—first her feet, then her calves, then her thighs. She eased her hands over Joan's abdomen, rippling the skin with her fingers. Taking a nipple into her mouth was like eating a flower, the flesh soft as a petal.

"Tell me what you would do for me in this world, Joanie."

"Whatever you asked me to do, Val, anything."

Val slipped the blindfold off Joan's head. She untied the scarf and sat up on her knees, dangling it, and touching Joan with the silk. Joan lay still and felt the silk against her skin. When Val ran the scarf up her arm, Joan took hold of the end of it and tugged. Val tugged back. For a moment, they tested the bond between them with the scarf, each of them pulling with an equal tension.

"You touch me," Joan said soon. "Touch me."

"You, me, and the cloud moon," Val whispered at some unknown hour in that night, no time kept by lovers. Joan did not answer. She was already asleep, her face itself a clouded moon, her chin dipped against Val's shoulder. The scarf that had been a momentary blindfold was wound loosely around Joan's wrist. Even after nine years, the way each traded the other her power to love, give, release, give up complete and total sovereignty, still amazed Val. She smiled, shifted to feel Joan's chin against her like the moon on her shoulder.

The surf broke just at the end of their yard. It wooed with its constancy; Val listened, slowly giving way to the vibration. She and Joan joined in dreams and followed each other with every turn and shift, body-to-body warm, only their faces wearing the chill sent in from the ocean through their open back door.

ONE

Enter Nyla Wade

"Setting off on a little adventure, searching for something, aren't you?"

Nyla Wade smiled, thinking of her father's words over the telephone when she'd given her parents the news of her job in Oregon with the Burnton *Beckoner*. As she pulled her over-heating Mustang off to the side of the road and felt the air's coolness masked by bright sun, she smiled again. Traveling toward the ocean seemed absolutely right. *No,* she told her father in her fantasy, *I'm not searching so hard anymore. I've found quite a lot already. I'm a lesbian and a writer, and if I seek anything, it's a way to be both all of the time. I passed long enough for a partial person when I was trying to be a wife and a heterosexual.*

Her furniture, including her priceless golden oak roll-top desk, had gone on before her, piggy-backed in a huge van with a Denver family's belongings on their way to Portland. All she had with her were clothes, her typewriter, and the antique lamp with the pale peach-colored shade she'd bought in Denver. She'd finally junked Mike's old dust-burner lamp.

Oh yes, Mike—he'd actually shown up to bid her farewell, insisting they have a special dinner at that place where they went on their honeymoon, Maxwell's. He'd wanted to cram a

1

lot of revelations into a short time. Over salad, that he'd been neglectful. With the entree, that he'd been selfish. For dessert, that he'd been too judgemental. With brandy, that he wished he hadn't been so late in his realizations.

"So I'm a swell gal after all," she concluded from what he hadn't said directly. She stared down Highway 107, ruminating on what she hadn't said to him.

I wanted to growl at him for his stupidity—the place he picked, the dinner, his timing, his comments. Instead I pained him more. I didn't say anything—no response from me, no reward for his coming to his senses, no ataboys. When I left him he didn't see me stop at the door to take one final good look at him. All I could think was it could have been worse and at least I kept my own name. And thank God Mike's doctorate wasn't in Literature or English or anything remotely connected—he might well have ruined me as a writer entirely. I had to do one last ornery thing before I left town: send him a gloxinia at his office, those flowers that always embarrassed him with their erotic beauty. They're my favorites, of course. Maybe the only thing we ever shared was our love of F. Scott Fitzgerald.

The Mustang seemed to be cooling down; she reached in the car window and touched the fringe on her lamp, thinking again of that day she and her best friend, Audrey Louise Landry, had found it. Audrey Louise wanted her to buy a couch but instead they both fell in love with the lamp, which had been virtually hiding in the chaos of a little antique shop. Along with the lamp, they'd found the desk and within it, Mrs. Porter's letters, and at the end of that adventure, Nyla Wade had found herself.

The worst parting was leaving behind this friend and soulmate, even though they'd argued in fun a few days before the move, Audrey Louise making her fork over a commission on the $500 from the unusual freelance job she'd done for Sara and Nikki. "I put up the notices you said would never get you any work," Audrey Louise crowed, "so pay up, sister!" And then at the last minute when the van was picking up Nyla's furniture, Audrey Louise had shown up with her brother Larry

2

driving a truck loaded with—what else—the long lost couch.
"For your new life." Audrey Louise had nudged her and
winked. "And your new seductions. The hideabed is so handy."
Count on Audrey Louise not to fuss about Nyla's declaration
of lesbianism, though she did make Nyla promise not to recruit
any nubile Landry relatives.

The parting shot for Nyla's life in Denver was her goodbye
to the people at Kinter Paint Company, especially Gigi, the
trademark koala bear. The poor bear had sat on Nyla's lap,
diapered and sad-eyed, drooping against her like a lost soul.

So this is the historic Gold Coast, Nyla thought as she and
the cooled-off Mustang headed up the highway, passing through
North Bend and Bunker Hill. She longed for a double scotch
rocks in an ice-cold glass. Robert Frost had written that nothing
ever stayed gold. Maybe he'd never seen the Gold Coast. Anyway, she didn't believe every poet—Hold fast to your feeling
of possibility, she told herself as she headed toward her future.

She'd stayed overnight at the Moosehead Lodge in Jackson
Hole and over a perfect brunch, a perfect moose had loped
past the lodge windows on the banks of beautiful Lake Jenny.
What a picture postcard place, with the Tetons rising up from
the lake waters in such majestic beauty they seemed staged
on a set. Outside the lodge, a class of oil painters tried to
capture the scenic beauty on their canvas. Nyla stared at their
mountains made in paint, and then at the real ones, wishing
she could meet the Indian princess who named them "Great
Breasts." Breasts—"love food of the goddesses," she'd written
in her journal, and found herself scanning sweaters and T-shirts
and halter tops that passed by. She would spot a pair in a
crowd and in her mind could trace them ever so lightly with
her tongue, could feel her palms heat up as she imagined tender
stroking. Not just breasts, but all the woman curves tantalized
her thoughts: cheeks, shoulders, and bottoms, those oh-so-
round and touchable pleasure places. In her dreams, gloxinias
covered everything and she ate them.

> "Myself my mystery
> Like lovers with karma, I cast out my netting."

3

She remembered the phrase from a sonnet read by a feminist poet at Womanbooks in Denver only a week ago. It's no mystery to me anymore, she told herself, and now she was casting out her net toward the ocean and a vastness of discovery in a new place and new loving. Of course, she had partly liked the line from the sonnet as much for the poet—small and feminine, her curly black hair a sensual wreath over blazing dark eyes, the hottest woman she'd seen since Sara. There had been a beckoning to the touch in the lavender silk blouse she'd worn, and Nyla had hardly been able to take her eyes off the poet during the entire reading.

She laughed at her memory. Yes, she *had* been able to take her eyes off that poet and that slit of silk dipping so sweetly between her breasts. Long enough to cruise the entire crowd of breasts. *Here are some of the best feminist breasts in Denver and I am nuzzling them to my heart's content!*

In Jackson Hole, she'd thought about the poet again, having herself a perfect sexual fantasy just before her perfect brunch. Her poet lover was a poet in bed and that black hair a net of rapture to her fingers. She'd traced a sizzling sonnet of her own on her fantasy poet's thigh . . .

A low whine from the Mustang let Nyla know she was pumping the gas pedal too hard. "Mercy," she breathed, feeling herself blush. She reminded herself to keep her eyes on the road.

"Always questing," a recent how-to-write book she'd read pronounced some writers, and she, Nyla Wade, filled the bill. In her heart of hearts she knew she was no journalist but an always questing fictionalist, and probably even in this safe Oregon town she would get into trouble trying to mix the two—or worse, by being "investigative."

The feminist poet and her sonnet echoed:

> "Myself my mystery
> Like lovers with karma, I cast out my netting
> To the sea of my past
> To a sea plain clear as glass.
> There in waves of mirrored waters
> My fins emerge, my soul floats free."

4

My soul is finally floating free, of old molds and an old marriage. Now my lovers will be in vital ways a mirror image, our love as fluid as those mirrored waters . . .

Nyla Wade smiled at the sign announcing Burnton, Oregon, in eight miles.

If my taste in poetry has not changed over the years, at least my preference for poets has improved.

TWO

A Woman's Fortress

As she drove into Burnton, Nyla decided to take a quick tour. The main street, Copeland, forked at one end onto Beach Loop and Old Town Drive. The latter was a short street with recently remodeled shops along it: Cranberry Sweets, the Wharf Restaurant, Sam's Fresh Fish, an art gallery and knick-knacks place, a gourmet brunch shop, and at the end of the street in a marble-columned building, the Burnton Historical Society. The wharf backed Old Town, and about three hundred yards away an abandoned boatworks sat out in the water with some of its pilings rotted so that one end of the lonely pier dipped into the waves. Just past South Jetty Road the mouth of the Coquille River could be seen, and less than half a mile further was Bullards Island and on it the Burnton lighthouse.

The Beach Loop took her past four or five small motels, Burnton's community hospital, and a residential section. Then the road curved past a park and several miles of unpopulated beach. She caught glimpses of grey-blue ocean and jutting shore rocks while she drove. She could hardly wait to pull over and take a sprint down to the surf, to feel that sand between her toes.

When she passed a dense break of trees, a boy jumped out at the edge of the road, yelling and running straight toward

7

the moving car, his eyes wide, his hands waving. She jerked the wheel and slammed on the brakes. The boy smacked the side of the car with both hands, then ran back into the trees laughing, his huge shoulders shaking, his head bobbing back and forth. "Some jokester," she grumbled.

She'd squealed the car to a halt just at the bottom of a hill, and now as she looked up ahead on the road, she caught her first sight of a limestone castle.

Completely out of context with the modern wood-and-brick beach homes, it loomed over the town on its bluff like a mausoleum refusing to be part of a cemetery. Yet there was nothing gloomy about the house; it beckoned to her. She headed toward it, not quite believing what she saw, but swerving around bothersome street construction to bump up over the curb so that she could turn up the road to the castle. Three mud-covered bulldozers were parked off to one side; they made her think of the tiny rusted shovels she'd seen in the graveyard in Fleming, Colorado, during her search for the author of Mrs. Porter's letters.

The castle was two stories high with turreted towers at each corner and a huge stained-glass window over the front second-story terrace. From a distance, the window suggested a cathedral. It shone bright blue in the sun, its design accented by golden panes depicting wheat—two shocks on either side and four stalks in the center. In a driveway with no cars, a doghouse sat incongruously, no faithful pooch at home.

A castle right here in Burnton! The perfect house for a gothic plot, she decided as she walked up under the carriage-way. She imagined the creak of leather and the jangle of harnesses. *Who stepped lightly here, polished boot upon gravel, bringing serious business to this grand place?*

A peek into a first floor window revealed only that it was shuttered. She ran her fingers over the carving around the front door, amazed by the delicate strokes in the stone. She touched a slender feathered tassel of wheat carved into the yellow rock, and felt a shiver.

She walked around the castle to the side facing the ocean. Three limestone squares had been carefully inlaid into the ground, even though the stretch of yard from the back door

8

to the beach was less than five steps and ended in a steep incline. Nyla was amused by the silly sidewalk. The limestone castle's architect had had a wry sense of humor.

The back windows were also shuttered. *Too bad a place this grand is all closed up. Maybe only summer people live here.* She remembered the Chamber of Commerce brochure. Summer was short here, not a real season like in the Midwest, just the two warm months of August and September before the Cranberry Festival. *Perhaps the owners aren't in for the season yet—even such a short one.*

Heading back to her car, she wondered who had sat in those turreted bay windows, ocean musing; what festive music had flowed around every stone for dancers waltzing on the covered porch. No clues echoed from the past. She turned around to drive away and noticed a sign in red letters with an arrow pointing toward the castle. It read: FUTURE SITE OF SEASCAPE.

After a stop at the Sea Galley Restaurant, she got her bearings quickly enough and headed for the Burnton *Beckoner* newspaper office. The small office front bore the masthead of the paper, a quill and lighthouse.

Before she got out of the car, she took a deep breath and gave herself a pep talk. *No question of failure here, my girl. Your college advisor, Dr. Walter Peistermeister, believes in you. The even more esteemed Dr. Julia Ramsey of New York University's School of Journalism said she knew of no one better to fill the job. So they both know you've got it, Wade. Know it for yourself.*

She went into the office, her first real live press room since college days.

A thick-chested man of about fifty with glasses pushed up into stiff grey hair read copy to himself at a green metal desk. His blue pencil scratchings were vigorous. He hadn't looked up when Nyla entered, so she scanned the room. It was surprisingly empty of noticeable newspaper activity; no cut-and-paste layout in progress, no file clippings posted, no wire service chatter. A long counter separated two other desks from the editor's and the area near the front door. A door behind these desks led to another room. On the wall hung a single Chamber

9

of Commerce plaque. No Honorable Mention awards for stories of merit, not even a newspaper association membership certificate. She was disappointed. But maybe the room behind the desks harbored the gritty command center of *Beckoner* reporters, the hub of journalistic fervor she had hoped for and expected.

"Can I help you, Miss?"

When the man at the desk stood up, he reminded her of Hopfrog: burly of torso but short in the legs department. His forearms were thick as hams and she guessed they were tattooed. Could this possibly be "Gruff" Hamilton?

"I'm Nyla Wade. I just drove in from Denver and—"

The man scooted his chair back with a kick. "I've been expecting you, Nyla. Welcome to Burnton." He shook her hand firmly. "Gruff Hamilton, *Beckoner* editor. How was your drive? Some day it'll be all superhighway instead of that irritating switch-over to two lane every hundred miles. The washout in the redwoods near Newport, still pretty bad?"

She'd missed the washout altogether and was somewhat embarrassed by her lack of observation, but before she could answer, Hamilton said, "Walt Peistermeister thinks you're a crackerjack writer. Pegged you best in his class. Sent me some of those *Brush Stroke* issues. I liked the article about the Fleming cemetery. And your copy for the bear—real creative."

"Yes, Gigi . . . " She thought again of the bedraggled koala.

Hamilton indicated the chair in front of his desk. He leaned over muddled piles of paper. "Well, you haven't exactly hit the big time, Nyla, but our weekly paper'll keep you busier than a monthly newsletter. You'll cover school board meetings, maybe the city commission, and coordinate our Langlois and Coquille stringers. Hell, you'll cover sports when I can't. And all the society stuff Jean doesn't handle. She's our other full-time reporter. Today she's over in North Bend." Hamilton leaned back into his chair and stretched out his arms. "This town's no hotbed of excitement, but like every town we have our politics, our parades. The Cranberry Festival coming up is a big deal, Cranberry princesses and cooking contests for everything from cranberry pudding to cranberry pizza. There's the annual puffin migration and grey whales swimming to Baja. We've got bikeathons, walkathons, telethons, class reunions, fifty-year anniversaries, not to mention your basic local crime beat.

"As for the press room, you're in it. Jean and I do the layout back there in the *real* press room." He pointed over his shoulder. "We've got an old Goss and we run all our own papers. Open that door and take a look."

Sure enough, there was the hulking Goss press with a stack of papers next to it and inking supplies on a nearby table.

"Do you roll 'em and toss 'em too?" Nyla asked, still staring at the press.

Hamilton rose from his chair and hiked up his pants. "Just about." His tone was defensive. "I'm a third-generation newspaperman in this town. My grandfather started the paper in eighteen sixty-five and my uncle took over when he died. Now I'm publisher and editor. I write most features, take most photographs. I choose type and rough the layout. Practiced my writing skills in the U.S. Navy on everything from PR for USO tours to regulations manuals. Trial by fire—figuring creative ways to write up brasswear polishing and seasickness remedies."

Hamilton was flexing his tattoos; she found him entertaining.

"So I ended up back here in Burnton running the family newspaper. This isn't *The New York Times* but it's more interesting than the military scoop any day."

Vaguely she sensed he might like her to say, "Yessir!"

"You may see this as a three-hick newspaper in a three-hick town with no hopes for a Pulitzer, Nyla, but it's *my* three-hick paper."

"Some three-hick town. You've got a castle to boast."

"Yes, the Ketcham house up on the bluff at Land's End—a house with a lot of history attached to it. Not all of it good. No one's lived there the past year, it's tied up in inheritance litigation. A lot of people hope it'll be torn down. Everyone wants the Seascape group to start building."

"What's Seascape?"

Hamilton grinned at her. "Your first day on the job and

you want me to tell you everything?" He went over to the counter and grabbed a stack of newspapers. Then he rummaged in one of the piles on his desk, poking a pencil over one ear as he did so. "I'll give you the rest of your week's assignments in the morning. You'll be on tap tomorrow night for a school board meeting. Our deadline's Tuesday noon for the Wednesday edition." His bifocals slid down onto his nose and he grinned again. "Your big debut's next Wednesday. Burnton's own Nyla Wade."

She grinned back at Hamilton. "Will I have an assigned route to toss, too?"

For a moment, the squatty editor with the beefy forearms gauged Nyla Wade just-blown-in-from-Denver. Then he smiled. "Not just yet. But miss a deadline and you better watch out."

"Do you always assign story ideas? And what about features—can I propose my own?"

Gruff raised one eyebrow at her. "You can *propose*," he allowed.

"Then how about a feature on the Ketcham castle before it's torn down—you run one lately? On the history of the house, I mean? Or an angle like its architecture, its period significance? I could do something with lots of local color. The bricks in that castle don't look like native stone to me."

"They aren't. In fact, there isn't much *native* about that house."

Hamilton pulled the pencil from behind his ear and pointed it at the stack of back issues. "Do your homework first. In your spare time you can worry about that castle. Go on over to the Historical Society if you want to learn more about it." The editor peered through his glasses, a sharply focused look at Nyla. "As a matter of fact, you'll learn quite a lot when you go over there."

When she left the *Beckoner* office, Nyla Wade was congratulating herself, rubbing her hands together in anticipation of the castle feature. Ole Walter Peistermeister always did credit her for jumping right into a story. But she resisted the temptation to speed back to Old Town Drive and the Historical Society. A more pressing matter was at hand: a roof over her head. "Avoid the Loop motels," Hamilton had advised her, "those are tourist traps. Try the Shady Stay. Peeling at the edges, maybe, but it won't peel back your budget."

There was no one at the Shady Stay front desk. She rang the bell. She looked into a sitting room to the right of the lobby and saw a smallish man sitting on the sofa. Again she rang the bell. Again no one answered. The little man stood up. He walked toward the desk in a shuffle; his clothes appeared to float over delicate bones and shoulders. He looked about eighty. His nose was shaped like an old-fashioned plow blade. Yarn was wrapped around the templates of his glasses and a baseball-style cap was squashed down over his ears. He wore rubber-soled boots that stuck to the linoleum with his first steps. He didn't smile.

"Jefferson is out awhile." The man's eyes covered the room nervously and he wouldn't quite look at her.

"I need a room. Can you help me?"

Without hesitating, the man reached into a box of keys. "Number fourteen is empty." He looked into her eyes. "I ran a fan in there to empty it out. Shouldn't be any waves left."

"What?"

"No waves left," he said again.

Extending a hand, she introduced herself. "I'm Nyla Wade. I've just moved here from Denver."

The old man didn't take her hand but kept looking into her eyes.

"What's your name?" she asked.

"Mitch Masters," he said in a dull voice. Still he held her eyes.

The hotel was quiet, the man strange and intense.

"I'm the handyman." He stuck his hand out abruptly. She shook a rough workman's glove. "You have bags?"

"Oh yes, but I can get them."

"That's a good room, number fourteen."

"Yes, I'm sure it is. Do I need to sign a register?"

"I'll tell Jefferson. I'm waiting for him." The old man's eyes wandered the room again, and he seemed to be muttering to himself.

"Say, since I'm new in town, can you tell me anything

about that house up on the hill—the one built out of stone? You know, the castle."

Mitch Masters narrowed his eyes. "The widows' house," he said. "I used to do their plumbling. Always full of sand. But good copper pipes."

"Do you know when the house was built?"

"Eighteen hundreds. That stone's from Kansas. I came from Kansas too, you know." For the first time he smiled and then giggled in a girlish, squealy way that surprised her. He was getting stranger by the minute.

"When I first came here, I didn't know nothing about fishing. That's where all the jobs were, on the boats. But I knew about working with my hands." He flexed his fingers inside the gloves. "Wood and wire, mostly. Stone some—I was a mason in Kansas." He took a shuffle step toward Nyla and lowered his voice. "The brotherhood," he said quietly to her, scanning the room as if for suspicious ghosts. Then his face sobered and he shuffled on past her toward a battered Coke machine. "I worked in that house nearly sixty-five years. I knew Molly Ketcham, but not the older sister, the one who built the castle. She was gone when I came here. Lots of pictures of her in the house, though."

She was excited. "You mean a woman built that castle?"

Masters didn't answer. He cranked the handle on the machine and retrieved a bottle of pop. "They were in lumber, see, and I worked in their mill. With the wood."

She watched him laboriously place the pop bottle in the opener on the Coke machine door; his gloves made every move unwieldy.

"Wish I'd seen them haul in that stone." He looked at her and put his two gloved hands together around the Coke bottle. "Every stone up there's dove-tailed, see, just right for a tight fit. Just like this." He looked at his hands and kept muttering to himself.

"You got bags?" he repeated, his face going blank as he stared at her. Before she could answer he said, "Hard to believe what they do sometimes. Lots of blue-eyed Indians where I grew up in Kansas. And they were cattle rustlers too. Never knew where they came from, but they were the kind that

14

would bring a box of rattlesnakes from Oklahoma and plant them just like corn or wheat. That's the one thing I liked about the stone house. It kept out the blues."

He shuffled back toward Nyla, who stood staring, fascinated by his peculiar conversation. He picked up her suitcases. She followed him silently to the last room at the end of a musty hallway. The room was small but had windows on two sides; with those windows open awhile it would air out nicely.

Masters inspected the room from floor to ceiling; she could only guess he was checking for "waves." When she offered him a tip for carrying her bags, the money disappeared into his glove but he kept his eyes on hers. He took two quick shuffle steps toward her; her impulse was to back away but she held her ground.

"Not a blue," he said. He started back for the door, adding, "Us men they use for lights weren't made to smile much." Then he shuffled away in his sticky rubber-soled boots.

No tourists were visiting Burnton's Historical Society. When Nyla walked in, she wandered through the exhibits, stopping to read captions on the many photographs. She found a picture of Thaddeus Hamilton, the *Beckoner*'s first publisher. In another room all the photos focused on Burnton's maritime history and there was a model of the steam schooner Lizzie—the ship which had made over 700 runs from Burnton to San Francisco. In yet another room, early Burnton cranberry growers in sweat-stained hats smiled at her out of linotypes. She was amused by a pair of "bog shoes." In the logging room were photos of ten-ox bull teams pulling logs down skid roads and cold decks of logs ready to be hand-peeled and rolled into the river. The general history of Burnton was displayed in the main room; the town's first printing press was still operating in the museum. She noticed two chapbooks printed on this press. One discussed the two fires that had burned the town to the ground in 1914 and 1936. What ultimate irony in the town name: Burnton—Burned Town.

The fire booklet mentioned the lighthouse Nyla had seen on her quick drive through town. Recently restored, the Coquille River Light had blinked 28 seconds on and 2 seconds off during its operating days, and was the last of eight lighthouses built along the Oregon coast. Many ships had foundered in the wind and surf on the shifting sand bars of the river mouth, including the famous three-masted schooner *Advance,* which had gone down in 1906 loaded with gold bullion. So something is still gold on the Gold Coast, she thought; someone should notify the skeptical spirit of Robert Frost.

She hadn't noticed the man observing over her shoulder as she read about the lighthouse until he said, "I wish we still had our light."

She turned to look at him.

"There's something soothing about those lights; the one at Cape Blanco still beams on and off." He smiled at her. "Keeping the night from spinning too many secrets."

Standing before her was the most dapper man she'd ever seen. His pink shirt was crisp and perfectly tailored; cocoa-brown slacks matched a monogram stitched on his shirt pocket in the initials PDT; he wore soft suede loafers. His deep tan seemed odd in this clouded, greyer Oregon sunlight. His wide forehead, edged by receding soft brown hair, was a little shiny.

"Have you been to Burnton before?" He put out a cool, loose hand to shake hers.

"No, I've just moved here from Denver."

The man's green eyes shied from hers slightly. "I'm Perry Day Truman," he said. "Curator of Burnton's Historical Society." He smiled again, flashing dazzling white teeth. "Did you enjoy our exhibits?"

"Yes. Especially the model of Lizzie."

Perry Day Truman lifted a hand dramatically to one cheek. "Lordie, that took Steve Winderwood and I just months to put together, one tiny piece at a time."

Again the easy smile made his tanned face glow. "I'm really glad to meet you. We've had a slow day, though there'll be more people coming later this month closer to the Cranberry Festival."

"Quite a big event, I hear."

"Oh it is, it *is!* A full dress ball for the princesses, tiaras and gowns galore, and lots and lots of gorgeous red roses for the winner!"

16

Perry Day Truman chuckled, his eyes sparkling at Nyla. "You'll have to excuse me, but I always enjoy a dress-up event just overwhelmed by flowers. I considered opening my own floral shop, but books and history are my first love so . . . " He sighed and winked at her; she could guess he was a great success with Burnton visitors with his easy manner and enthusiasm for the museum.

"Would you like some tea, Nyla?"

"Tea would be wonderful."

"Oh good. I have Lemon Mint Mist brewing just this minute!"

The curator took her elbow gently and led her toward a table near the front window. "You know," he said confidentially, "the maritime room is my favorite. I am simply sea-obsessed."

She loved his twinkling eyes, his familiarity that somehow did not impose.

"Shells, driftwood, crab skeletons, *everything* on the beach, I just love it. Cora Corona—she owns Neptune's Nook—we have a running contest for capturing glass floats that come in."

"Floats?"

"Yes, glass markers that break out of fisherman's nets. Most are clear but some have a green or blue tint. The ones marked by glassblowers are the best. They can come from Japan and Germany. Cora keeps her telescope peeled on the beach all day, so she's ahead in the contest right now. I've found my best ones at night with a flashlight. The tide brings them in. And at night I can beat out that darned telescope!"

Over their tea, Nyla discovered she'd started out her first day in Burnton not only with a feature story idea but also meeting a near expert on the story subject.

Perry Day Truman had inherited the limestone castle at Land's End.

"I haven't actually inherited it yet. This litigation with the former owner's son and daughter has tied up the deed with the estate. Joan Ruddye willed the house to her close friend and companion, Valerie Prosper, in whose will *I* am heir to the castle. But Joan's children are contesting and the estate is in the hands of a court trustee. Really, it all boils down to that bunch of greedy Seascape capitalists."

17

Unlike Gruff Hamilton, Perry was more than willing to talk about Seascape. "It's a big tourist hotel project. The developers want the Land's End property for the view and beach access. In order to have both, they'll have to tear down the castle. What they really want is to get rid of every trace of the Ketcham women who built that house and the lumber empire that went with it."

So what Mitch Masters had told her was true—the castle on the bluff was a woman's fortress. Her gothic plot was thickening.

"Mitch Masters told me a woman built that castle, but I didn't know about the family empire."

"A very colorful family, the Ketchams, immigrated overland from Kansas in eighteen sixty-one. The two sisters built the first major mill here and bought range land near Klamath Falls just before the area developed into the state ranching center. The younger sister, Molly, was one of the first women to earn a forestry degree at the University of Oregon and she expanded their holdings with the purchase of timberlands. Their brother came back from Fort Stevens at the end of the Civil War and worked in Druscilla Ketcham's mill for a short time. Then he built his own." Perry winked at Nyla. "You might say there was strong sibling rivalry. He called Druscilla 'The Little Colonel.' "

"So why would Burnton townspeople allow the house to be razed? They have an excellent tourist attraction right here in the castle."

"I quite agree. It makes me furious. Seascape will be nothing more than a dressed-up Howard Johnsons, just so much glass and chrome—to replace Druscilla's queendom built in that castle with fifty railcars of sixty-pound limestone bricks cut and dressed at her father's quarry in Hays City, Kansas. That castle survived both Burnton fires." Perry sighed. "Ironically, in Druscilla's girlhood, she lived through two fires that melted the Ketcham's prairie soddies right to the ground. That's rich history, unique and irreplaceable." Perry sounded exasperated. "I keep suggesting they incorporate the castle into the Seascape plans, build their new hotel across the street, but the developers insist on that spot on the bluff. And Joan's

18

kids are no help. She was a gem, but her children are both cut-throats. Big bucks, that's all they care about. They can't wait to get their hands on the property to sell it to Seascape. But I'll fight them to the end."

"Isn't there anyone from the state or federal historical societies who can help? What about other Ketcham relatives? Sounds like you need more clout."

"More clout is exactly right, but now it's in the hands of a judge. As for government agencies . . ." Perry took a delicate sip of his tea. "They get very touchy about some things."

"Yeah," Nyla nodded, "especially litigation."

Perry looked at her, his tan flushing deep red at the neck. "Something else. Like the castle's *suggestive* history."

She looked quizzically at him. Perry hesitantly explained. "Druscilla Ketcham never married. Her sister Molly did marry, but strictly for convenience, to produce a daughter. Her only companion for most of her adult life was Mercy Hayworth, daughter of a wealthy state judge. After Mercy died, Molly shocked the entire town by befriending a free black evangelist, the Reverend Olympia Swan. They raised Molly's daughter, Vanessa, together and she then inherited the castle, willing it on to *her* daughter, Joan Ruddye. The castle has always passed to women, until, of course, Valerie willed it to me."

"Joan and Valerie," Nyla questioned, her voice soft for Perry's sensitivity, "were a little more than close friends, weren't they?"

He seemed relieved by her deduction. "Yes. We were all good friends, in a special little group that also included two others, the Randolphs—us against the world, if you know what I mean." He smiled sadly. "Joan was like me—always filling her pockets with sea stuff."

He looked at Nyla. "Though no one in this town will admit it, there's a consensus that tourists or history buffs will see the limestone castle as Oregon's Queer Territory, and avoid it like the plague." This time Perry's smile was sardonic. "Of course, they completely underestimate the number of gay tourists and historians."

With this remark, his eyes met hers, and at some level of special friendship, Nyla and Perry met as well.

"Twice this town burned at the crux of its destiny. Some city fathers still believe that destiny is possible but they also believe the castle must come down before that can happen. I'll keep on using every contact I have, though I don't hold any hope for help from the state. The National Gay Task Force is aware of what's happening, and there's a newly formed group in San Francisco—the Gay Historical Society. They're working on petitions now. I know Burnton city fathers are afraid I'll turn the castle into a freak retreat but all I want to do is keep it standing, to respect the rich history it symbolizes."

Perry kept his eyes on his teacup. "Last year I wrote a complete history of the castle which credits the positive lesbian influence of the Ketcham women, Mercy Hayworth, and Olympia Swan. Their contributions to this town were considerable. I wrote the history primarily for the gay community, but if I have to, I'll use it to block Seascape or any other attempt to tear down the castle."

"Do you think there's a good chance for the Seascape project succeeding?"

Although he smiled, Perry's eyes were unsmiling. "Only over my dead body."

The afternoon was waning into early evening; the shadowy museum moved a quiet mood in around the two of them.

Nyla patted Perry's hand. "I want to thank you for sharing so much about the castle and Burnton with me. I may be a new-comer here, but I think you see I am no stranger."

His eyes brightened. "Would you like to see the castle? I don't have the deed yet but I do have the keys. The housekeeper, who is the court trustee, gave them to me."

They made a date for the next afternoon.

At dusk Nyla found herself back in Old Town and on the wharf. Behind Sam's Fresh Fish were stacks of wooden fish boxes large enough to make kitchen tables. Fences along the jetty road were of twisted driftwood, creative coastal decor. In one direction, the lighthouse offered its blank eye to the ocean; in the other—below the houses on the loop—tidelands stretched out, nothing but beach, free sandy space out to the infinity of water and horizon. As she stood on the jetty, she breathed in the strong smell of green moss from the pilings and ruins of the boatworks.

Old Town was thronged with people at the dinner and cocktail hour. She noticed a wide shop window she hadn't seen before, a boutique from the look of it. No "tuxedo look" here as in Denver, no preppy polo shirts. The mannequins were still a bit on the affected side; one a svelte brunette beauty in a swank safari suit and flannel shirt ensemble, casting a fly rod. "Coastal Tourista," Nyla dubbed it.

In the window's reflection, she noticed another woman

also amused by the mannequin. Their reflections exchanged a glance, then a full-fledged curious gaze.

The other woman had wild, curly red hair, an exploded Afro—the windblown loose locks of Everywoman's dream—certainly Nyla Wade's. She couldn't take her eyes off that hair. Hair you wind your fingers into with a soft burrowing, stroking the scalp as you tunnel slight touches above the brain, knowing you are massaging the mind. Hair you tug a little with the first

21

rushes of desire, hair that holds the head back from you when you want to dominate, to take. Hair that smells of lilac and woodruff, like Sara's had, those scents you fall into when you bury your cheek in such hair, when it brushes your breasts as that mouth on that face purring with messages from that brain slips past your barriers and finds what makes you release, what makes you clutch the hair with frantic fingers.

Had they been in a crowd, Nyla would have touched that hair and the other woman would never have known it.

She felt as suspended in time as the fisherwoman tossing her line—she wondered if she could say something to the other woman. Before she could decide, her companion reflection gave her another look as she reached up to run her hands through that mass of red hair—not curious this time, but a dare.

A truck horn honked and the red-haired woman turned to respond. Still watching the reflection, Nyla saw her get into the truck and give a cheek kiss to the man driving. As their heads touched, they seemed to look alike, both wearing wild caps of red.

Reluctant to settle in for the evening in her small room at the Shady Stay, Nyla decided to see the ocean at night. She walked far out over the tidelands; it was not yet dark but the sun was slipping toward the ocean's embrace. Shore rocks beckoned irresistibly with a walk-through cave; Nyla giggled at all the little black crabs scaling the rock. She loved the mauve-on-mauve vulval colors of the tidepools.

Coming out the other side of the rocks, she saw someone standing perhaps fifteen feet away and turned slightly from her. She stepped back into the shadow of the cave and watched. A man, she thought at first; but when she saw the face, he was only a boy—an unusually big boy, with a vacant look. The same boy who had run at her car up on the loop. He was examining a star fish, and seemed perplexed that it was stiff. After turning it over and over several times, he placed it gently back on the sand and lumbered down the shore.

The bottom of the sun was drenched; Nyla looked out over the black sea. Someone else was coming up the beach—an older woman wearing a blue sun-visor cap, thongs dangling in one hand.

"Hello," she called and walked right up to Nyla. "You one of the new summer folks?"

"No, I just moved here. I'm going to work at the Burnton *Beckoner*."

The woman cackled. "Good luck lasting with the likes of Gruff Hamilton!" She scrutinized Nyla. "You're a looker, all right, but that won't faze him. Those old Navy boys chew up lookers and spit 'em right out. No use for the finer things in life. Not mean, exactly, just no flexibility to 'em, a little like a spined grouper."

Nyla smiled at the woman's assessment of Gruff Hamilton.

"Good luck anyway. If you need to know what comes in with the tide, stop in at Neptune's Nook. I'm Cora Corona."

"The float collector?"

"How'd you know?"

"Perry told me."

"Sweet boy, Perry, but not so smart. Walks the beach too late at night trying to find his floats. No sense about sneaker waves. Besides, it takes a lot to outdo Cora." She winked and did a little hop in the sand.

Nyla asked, "What's a sneaker wave?"

Cora seemed glad to offer information. "Waves come in in trains. If several collide, a huge unexpected wave can develop fast and sneak up on you. You never want to turn your back to the ocean. Perry, he trusts the water spirits too much."

"Perry was telling me about the limestone castle. I want to do my first feature story on it."

Cora abruptly dropped her thongs and rubbed one foot. "You do, huh?" She stared hard at the ocean and Nyla suddenly felt a wall go up between them.

"Perry says there's rich history in that house."

Cora rubbed the sole of the other foot and then picked up her thongs as abruptly as she had dropped them. She told Nyla in a tone as icy as the water, "Look here. Perry wasn't around the day I saw them bring out the bodies. Just like on TV, on one of those wheeled carts and all covered up in white sheets. I'll never forget that sight. No one will, and most of us don't want to be reminded."

"What are you talking about?"

23

"The widows—both of them murdered in that house. They got some local boozer for it, so it should be done with." Cora glanced out to sea again. "I'm not necessarily for tearing down the castle like some folks, but I am for getting on with life." She walked away from Nyla, saying over her shoulder in a slightly more congenial tone, "I watch the beach. I know what comes in with the tide. Come up to the shop and see me sometime."

When Cora was gone, Nyla stood rooted to her spot on the beach. Burnton could boast not only a castle on its bluffs, but murders in that castle as well. She shivered, and not from the cool breeze off the water.

Finally she walked further down the beach, watching the lights from town near the north shore shining just enough above the bluffs to create the illusion that everything was flat and on one plane: rocks, beach, sea and surf all blended as one surface. The huge humps of sand swam out of focus and she felt the waves threatening to roll up all at once over the yards of beach like a roaring runaway carpet. Despite Cora's advice about sneaker waves, she turned her back to the water to stare at the lights on the Loop. It was then that she realized how far she'd walked on the beach—to Land's End—and there, directly above her on the bluff, sat the limestone castle. Its sightless windows revealed no secrets but took her in, as if the house itself were observing the newcomer.

THREE

Ghosts Rattling the Soul

Oregon morning and sea breeze awakening. Nyla smelled sea salt as if right in her pillow. She breathed in the new scent and turned over on her back. Her dreams had been full of the eye-like windows of the castle staring at her. Two lesbian lovers had died in this town, in that old castle. Murdered by a local boozer, Cora had said. Why hadn't Gruff Hamilton told her, or Perry Day Truman? It felt personal to her—like the murder of Sara's hooker friend in Boston. She wanted to know about the house and the murder it held and why no one talked about it, why Cora had declared, "It should be done with."

Murder on your mind your second day in town, Nyla Wade. Audrey Louise would accuse you of sifting through skeletons that should stay buried.

Smiling as she thought of her friend, she got up and took a look out her windows. She could see the wharf; Burnton's summer blew in at a cool 65 degrees and the sun fell through a grey sea-fog screen. The Chamber of Commerce pamphlet reported that Burnton beaches were not for bikinied sun-bathers. "Great waves for body surfing," the pamphlet promised instead. Not without a well-insulated sea parka, Nyla decided. But how in the devil to swim in a sea parka? She had so many things to find out in her new town . . .

25

She reported fifteen minutes early to work. Gruff Hamilton had brewed a great pot of coffee and even poured her a cup. "Got anxious," she told him, taking the coffee, and he smiled quickly with one side of his mouth. Then just as quickly he frowned and went to his desk as if pulled on a tow line, dove unerringly into the piles of paper and pulled out one sheet.

"The school board's reviewing their budget tonight over at Burnton High School. Seven o'clock. Be there sharp with No Doz. The meeting'll be a grueler.

"Also today I want you to start interviewing merchants for a special Retailers Review section. Since the Cranberry Festival is a major event for tourists, we're running this in a special edition for hand-out. People visiting will have a map of the town and the entire Gold Coast. We include short features on Burnton history with photos from the museum. Perry usually supplies those." Hamilton lifted his glasses and peered under them at Nyla. "You did meet Perry?"

She did not know what reaction he expected; she simply smiled and said, "Yes, I did. A very nice man."

"Anyway," Hamilton continued, dropping the glasses back on his nose, "the review will hopefully boost their sales. We do this every year and I'm more than thrilled to turn it completely over to you."

He directed her to one of the desks behind the counter. "You can camp here. I've laid out the last couple of Retailer Reviews. Once you've looked them over just go out there and have at it." He checked off an item on his sheet of paper.

"Friday night the Lioness Club has old-time movies for the seniors at Oceanview Home. You might want to drop by, it's on the Loop near the hospital. And when the stringer columns come in you can play editor."

Gruff gave her a one-sided grin again and then swiveled in his chair, his back to Nyla. Instead of taking his cue she asked, "Why didn't you tell me about the widows' murder at the castle?"

Hamilton didn't turn around. "Still focused on that castle, Wade? I don't suggest you include mention of the murder in your feature." He swiveled to look at her. "Your *proposed* feature."

26

"Why not? Why doesn't anyone want to talk about it? Something amiss in the way it was handled?"

The editor yanked his glasses off and tossed them onto his desk. "Not that I know of, but for chrissakes don't go getting *investigative* on me." He said the word with contempt. "Do your damned feature on the castle—its romance, allure, architecture, its plumbing even, I don't care. But let the murder lay. It was tragic and messy and horrible, a town nightmare like every town has. What's more important—it isn't news anymore."

Nyla wasn't sure if Hamilton's attitude held a real warning or just the gruffness that had earned him his nickname—but she had plenty of time to find out.

The door to the pressroom opened. The clack of the Goss was loud. A tall brunette headed toward them. She was about thirty-five, wearing baggy trousers and a plain blue shirt, brown shoes with no design in the leather. There was something passé Amelia Earhart in her style—Nyla had the feeling the woman had just stepped out of a Rosie the Riveter poster.

"The dumb headliner's squeezing the letters again," she said, scrutinizing the newsprint with a frown. "Guess you'll have to take your special tool to it, Gruff." She leered at him around her sheet of newsprint, her grin accented by bright red lipstick, and then saw Nyla. "Whoops, sorry, just an inside joke. Gruff has a real touch with these cranky old machines and I always accuse him of having a magic screwdriver."

Gruff lifted his glasses and scowled at her.

"Oh dear, I'm just getting myself in deeper. Let me start over. Hi, I'm Jean Thomas."

"Glad to meet you. Nyla Wade here."

"Oh yes, in from Denver. How do you like the sea air? Nothing like that good ole mountain dew, is it?"

Hamilton squirmed in his chair, turning from them. He glared into his endless piles of paper. "When you two have finished the social amenities, see if you can't crank out some copy for this week's edition."

"Work, work, work!" Jean winked at Nyla and headed back to the pressroom.

By 4:30 Nyla had completed four interviews with Burnton

merchants. Sophie Longstead, owner of the Sea Galley Restaurant, boasted a special recipe for stuffed butter clams. Ed Noonan of Ed's Wrecking Service showed off his new noisy machine which bent metal. "Crushes a whole car in one bite," Ed boasted. The Coquille Medical–Dental director gave a friendly but hurried interview and provided a four-color brochure. "The Smile and Heart Doctors," the brochure advertised, making Nyla smile. She finished her final interview at Walker–Powers Insurance Agency. Everyone seemed willing to cooperate, all shared a penchant for sidetracking into the history of the town, its first cranberry crop and festival, its fires, its future. All the business owners had tourist season on their minds: Sophie for one didn't think they'd see the business they'd had last year. There was something else the merchants all had in common—a strong interest in Seascape and what it would mean to Burnton.

"More jobs, especially your domestics, maids, and such," Sophie said. "And more folks eating my butter clams!"

Seascape's chrome and glass held hope, hope for new money and better times. The merchants had more to say about the hotel that would be built than the castle presently standing. The limestone castle seemed an expendable part of the past, just an old house where old murders had occurred. No one brought up the murders except Ed Noonan. "Too bad about those ladies—even though some called it comeuppance. It taints a place. Seascape will be brand new."

"I don't like to talk about it," Perry said as he and Nyla drove to the castle. "It happened last summer. A local beach bum died in his cell over at Coos Bay. The shoes he had on matched prints taken at the scene and there was a scratch on his neck from the struggle with Val. My two friends murdered . . . I'm still not over it."

Nyla was surprised to see Perry's eyes moisten.

"They were brutalized, the nutso just walked in the open back door. Suddenly it was over—our talks for hours; we never got tired of each other's company. Val Prosper and I had backgammon wars, Joan Ruddye and I walked on the beach. My closest friends—closer to me than my own parents."

28

They reached the construction at Land's End turn-off; a portion of the street had been rock-drilled into pieces to expose drainage pipes. Perry said, his hands gripping the steering wheel, "I was at home with Joan and Val. My parents don't want to know me."

As she had with Sara and Nikki, Nyla felt instant loyalty to the two widows she'd never known and to Perry, whose loss was so painful.

Perry's eyes caught hers. "When I was with them, you know, no one looked at me with that question in their faces. We all accepted each other and joked about ourselves and loved our difference. We were at ease together." He pulled his powder-blue Saab into the castle driveway. "Well, here we are." Perry squeezed Nyla's hand as if trying to brighten his own mood.

As they approached the carriageway and front porch, Nyla admired aloud the detail of the stone carving. Perry explained that most of the bricks were pitch-faced, except around the sills and door headers, which were tooth chiseled. He patted the yellow stone. "Druscilla was ahead of her time—she built the outer wall of limestone two feet thick with an inner wall of Oregon sandstone. Then she filled the eight inches between with coal cinders, which kept the house warm and soundproof. She also inlaid the foundation with a slab of granite. That was her ultimate fire protection."

She was about to ask how the Ketcham timberlands had fared in the town's two fires when Perry said, "If two lesbians hadn't been murdered in this castle, I'm sure masons in Oregon and Kansas would fight tooth and nail to keep this place standing. Just for the stone work."

"Prejudice counts more than people, I guess." Nyla stepped up closer to him and touched his arm.

The short entryway was dark, the house cold, quiet enough to echo. Perry pulled back curtains in the inglenook, revealing a huge fireplace across from cushioned seats lining a bay window.

"How long did the actual construction take?" she asked.

"About eighteen months, including oxcarting the stone fifteen miles from the railhead at Coquille. Most of the

29

furniture is priceless."

"Joan's cutthroat kids haven't picked it over already?"

"I told them I had a guard on the place." Perry grinned. "I said I'd sic my friend Seth on them." His smile spread. "He's big, oh is he big!"

They headed toward the great hall dining room.

"It was a risk for Druscilla Ketcham to build in stone. Most lumber magnates built their homes as monuments to the durability and versatility of wood. This house is short on bedrooms and long on dining chairs. Druscilla wanted to be able to seat fifty for dinner, she wanted to offer hospitality as her mother had on the prairie."

The dining room was indeed a great hall, running three fourths of one side of the castle and lit by crystal eight-armed chandeliers.

"No guest stayed long in the house," Perry told Nyla. "It was Dru's sanctuary from everything, including the judgement of those who found her unfeminine, especially her brother."

A fireplace was centered in the wall that showcased the Ketcham portrait gallery. Built into the facing of the fireplace were the four original limestone bricks Druscilla Ketcham had brought overland from Kansas by covered wagon. Perry ran his fingers over the four bricks.

"These were cut smaller than those used for building, but were still no small freight to bring on the Overland Trail. Within the wagon party, the family came to be known as the 'four brick Ketchams.' "

Nyla stared at the portraits over the fireplace. Perry told her with a twinkle in his eye, "Dru wrote in her diary that brother David was a 'strapping boy not at all plain looking, with chestnut-colored hair curling to his shoulders.' Why was *she* the one to come across country with him?"

Their laughter resounded against the great hall walls. Perry indicated one of the portraits. "Molly Ketcham and Mercy Hayworth used to race around town in a cart with a pair of black horses. Molly had a fondness for scotch, sometimes she'd swig right from the bottle."

"A scotch drinker—a woman after my own heart." Nyla grinned at Perry. They left the great hall to the slow glow dimming of its crystal chandeliers and went to the other side of the castle.

"A Japanese contractor only the Ketcham sisters would do business with in those intolerant times gave Druscilla this desk," Perry told her as they stepped into the office occupying the front tower of the castle.

Hinged in three sections, the closed Wooten resembled an elegant steamer trunk; open, its center section had a drop-leaf writing surface with drawers underneath and vertical book shelves. On either side were countless lockable compartments. The Wooten was black laquered and decorated with white Japanese symbols; she could see some of the compartments had glass fronts and were filled with sea treasures: bits of shell and driftwood.

Perry chuckled. "It probably won't surprise you that this desk was viewed as masculine in its day, which made it all the more attractive to Druscilla."

"Desks can reveal power in many ways," Nyla mused, thinking of her own desk and all she'd been through to find it, and divine its special secrets. "I'll have to show you my roll-top when I get it out of storage."

Two sets of sliding doors revealed the entire expanse of castle from the Wooten desk to its mistress's bedroom. Perry walked the length of the three rooms to stand by the bed; he and Nyla looked at each other.

"Quite a view from the throne, isn't it?" Perry called.

"And quite a throne," Nyla answered staring at the bed as she walked toward him.

Standing nearly eight feet tall at the headboard and four feet at the footboard, the bed was built from rosewood—and in the shape of a sleigh. How magically protective, Nyla reflected—Druscilla could rule her castle from her bedcovers, snuggled into the sleigh bed and imagining herself drawn along over Catherine's Russian tundra or sailing down Cleopatra's romantic Nile. From the bed, her empire and her escape were entirely in view: the office that was the helm of Ketcham Enterprises, and the ocean's vast yawning just outside the window. *Up here, nothing will catch on fire.* Druscilla's voice fairly echoed out of the castle walls.

31

"Come on, I want to show you the blue window!" Perry took Nyla's hand and they bounded up the black walnut staircase and onto a floor of highly-polished redwood.

The tropical aura of a hot house greeted them inside the conservatory. They were surrounded by plants green and leafy, bathed in colored light.

"Dru often started her days here," Perry said, his voice hushed.

Muted light trailed into the room, a cobalt blue, melting every crisp edge with a unique softness. This blueness streamed from the huge stained-glass window which had made Nyla think of a cathedral.

"The wheat shocks on either side of the design symbolize Dru's parents and the four stalks indicate herself, Molly, David, and the youngest brother Daniel, who helped Jason run the limestone quarry."

Everything was shimmering blue. Nyla felt a peace within the conservatory as if life were suspended in the bloom of plants and the lustrous blue reflection. She realized Dru Ketcham had created a womb room within her queendom's stone citadel.

As Perry and Nyla spooned an early supper of chowder at the Sea Galley, he grinned. "I have suspected the man Molly Ketcham briefly married was a fellow of our persuasion. And before Molly became pregnant, many townspeople feared she might leave the castle to Olympia Swan. A North Bend newspaper article described Olympia as a tent-bender revivalist with enough stature to fill a church door frame and lift the rafters in invocation. After Mercy's death in a logging accident, Molly grieved for more than five years. But she found love again when she went to a prayer meeting and beheld the galvanic black lady preacher."

Nyla and Perry laughed together. Perry went on, "Apparently Olympia Swan lifted Molly's dormant white soul out of its malaise till it buzzed at every nerve ending. Immediately after the services, she invited Olympia to dinner at the castle, and Olympia never left! They raised Vanessa together. Vanessa waited until she was forty-three to have her first and

only child, Joan Barney Ruddye. Joan, of course, inherited
the castle and you know the rest of the story about her will
and Valerie's. Joan married a marine architect who pioneered
designs in luxury yachts—maybe you've heard of the Stanley
line—the Cadillac of the big boats."

"I'm a landlubber, remember. Not many yachts in Colorado."

Perry grinned. "I'll drive you over to Coos Bay next week
and show you some Stanleys."

"Great!" She watched him in fond amusement as he ate
his chowder. He fluttered a look at her as he lifted the spoon
and crooked his little finger. She asked, "Why are the kids
contesting? Strictly money?"

"That and family reputation. When she was alive they pre-
tended Joan wasn't lesbian. When she died they couldn't talk
about it enough, to draw on the worst prejudices of justice.
How could she in right mind will the family castle to her
female lover instead of her children? They're slavering to get
the money out of Seascape. Disgusting." Perry dropped his
spoon into the chowder bowl. "Valerie certainly didn't need
Joan's money. She inherited a fortune from her husband. The
castle was willed to her for sentiment's sake."

Leaning closer to Nyla, he narrowed his eyes; the soft-
edged, tanned cheeks hardened as he tensed his jaw. "I'm
not going to let them tear down that house, Nyla. No way.
If I have to stage a full-fledged picket line, I will. I'll organize
a coast-to-coast caravan of uppity queers that'll make people's
heads spin."

Perry's expression became a smirk. "Valerie always said
I looked fluffy as a kitty. Well, people shouldn't think I've
got no claws. Everyone tells me I should sell out to Seascape
or make a deal with the Ruddyes. Make a bundle, let the
castle go. I'm not after a fortune. I can't have my friends
back . . . I'm not letting their castle and the gay history of it
be taken away too."

He stared into the chowder bowl. Nyla told him, "This
is some crusade you've taken on single-handedly."

Without looking up, Perry replied, "Oh sure, I'm a regular
he-man." Then with devilment in his eyes, he said, "Actually,

33

I'd rather sleep with a he-man than be one."

"Oh Perry, you don't need a Steve Reeves, you need an Oscar Wilde."

Her new historian friend's tan blushed as pink as his shirt. "Hey, I meant—"

"I know what you meant." When he looked at her, his eyes were tearing. He took her hand. "I'm glad you're here, Nyla Wade. You may be the best newcomer this town's ever had."

Perry drove Nyla back to her car at the Historical Society building. She offered him a warm hug. "Thanks for the guided tour. I had a great time—not just for my story, either. For me too."

Perry looked at her shyly, then said, "Oh, I forgot. I brought you a copy of my manuscript on the castle." He gave her a manila envelope. "Another thing—I want you to meet my pals, the Randolphs. Will you come by the Oceanview Home on Friday? They're showing *The Big Sleep*."

"Sure. I need to cover it for the paper anyway."

"Mixing business with pleasure can be dangerous." He winked.

"I bet you'll protect me," she countered with a smile.

The yellow faces of the shore lights lacing the Loop showed a fuzzy misting. "Looks like fog rolling in," Perry said.

"My first fog."

She felt time pressing her to get to the school board meeting, but she didn't want to leave Perry. It seemed they could talk about anything, and there was much she wanted to say, to ask—about Burnton and gay life and Perry Day Truman himself. Perry stared for a moment out toward Bullards Island and the dark silhouette of the lighthouse.

"Sometimes I think it never happened. The murder, I mean. Sometimes I think I'll drive up to Land's End one day and the shutters will all be thrown open and I'll hear Valerie laughing. They'll be back from some long secret trip that scared the hell out of us, but now it's okay. They're safe. They're alive. My beloved friends are home to their castle again."

By eleven thirty, Nyla Wade realized she was irritated as hell at the Burnton school board members, the four men and

34

three women who were great at complaining and lousy at deciding. Finally, at midnight, the board achieved a vote on the new tax rate. As they were adjourning, one of the men said, "This'll have the taxpayers up in arms." A colleague was not so worried: "No one will notice once Seascape gets going."

All evening she had felt the tug of Perry's manuscript. But she had a nasty headache by the time she left the school to drive slowly through the damp fog back to Shady Stay.

As she passed through the lobby, Mitch Masters exchanged nods with her, his eyes on the bottle she carried in a brown paper sack.

Even though the sea air was cold, it tingled Nyla's skin and kept the stuffy room from closing in. She poured herself three fingers of scotch neat, snapped on the lamp by the bed. The gold glow through the fringed shade caught her attention—a warm reminder of Audrey Louise, of the fond and familiar. The room seemed a little more her own; some of her weariness faded. She appreciated the scotch as it soothed its way toward the pounding in her temples. Despite her headache and the lateness of the hour, she couldn't resist Perry's manuscript. She curled up on her bed and began to read.

Nyla fell asleep during her second reading of the manuscript. She was somewhere with Dru Ketcham on the Overland Trail along the endless winding Snake River. The same dream recurred: she was standing in front of Druscilla's portrait in the castle's great hall. Druscilla's upright stance, slender waist and shoulders were accented by a special dress with a bib of material folded back on either side of the bodice like the narrow lapels of a man's coat. Five bows ran up the front of the dress from the hem to the break in the lapels. Druscilla's chin was firm above the high white collar and her eyes met Nyla's—not like a painted image but a woman alive and with a message for Nyla. Druscilla's expression riveted her with a keen sense of portent.

Other restless dreams floated in with the fog, stirred by the scenes Perry had written. He had been able to draw fact almost to the realm of fiction, to offer up the flesh-and-blood Ketchams in their troubled prairie homestead, and the immediacy and impact of them reached right off the page, right into Nyla Wade's sleep.

Rose Ketcham felt an extra pull of faith when her daughter Druscilla was born. And as the child grew up to be a quiet girl who kept her heart away from words, that faith between them grew. They could in a look tell each other their silent souls.

For all his boisterous enthusiasm, Jason Ketcham made Rose a caring husband. Their oldest son, David, was a curious mixture of his parents: willing to run headlong after a whim but not simply gullible. The youngest child, Daniel, had a shy shuffle that marked him different from other children his age: not fearful but completely unaware of fear, so Rose had to protect him more than her other two.

Late in 1854, Jason told Rose of his new dream: the freedom of the plains was calling to him. He wanted to move the family from Indiana and homestead in Kansas. So it was when Druscilla was eight, David ten, and Daniel five, they left their frame house on the paved Indianapolis street to sway across the miles in a prairie schooner, always watching for the first sight Jason promised: a sea of grass from one edge of the horizon to the other. Grass indeed was what they found and very little else when they finally stopped in Kansas near Big Creek, in the area that was to become Hays City.

The sea of grass fed the oxen well but was no shelter from the searing heat of the day and rains pouring through the wagon canvas. Against the elements, Dru and Rose worked shoulder to shoulder, trying to cook bread in a skillet, trying to start a fire in the wind. They collected buffalo chips for fuel and hung out the bedding every day to dry. They felt each other's unseen tears when thunderstorms swept in upon them by surprise and soaked everything again, sending their best quilt wind-whipped and spiraling off into the dirt.

Rose gave incessant warning for snakes in the unceasing grass; Dru wished for magic snakes to turn into sticks, any stick of real wood: a walking stick, logs on the fire, fencing of new pine still oozing its sweet brown sap, "fake honey" as they called it back in Indiana.

Not enough trees to yield a house rooted on Big Creek banks, so the Ketchams built a sod house. It held little better

36

against the elements than the wagon had; Daniel awakened one night to find a copperhead slipped out of the rain through the chinks of sod blocks and curled at the foot of his bed. He watched it for half an hour and never screamed. It was Rose who screamed when she saw it. That snake was the prairie and you were surrounded by it and you couldn't keep it out of anything you built.

Slow and persistent, Jason held his private hopes, especially that he could pass on his dream to Rose, so she would eventually befriend the prairie as her homeland. Their first two years of wheat and corn came in, and two other families settled near them to partially end their initial isolation. Rose gained women friends to quilt with; Daniel got a pup. A girl about David's age kept him happily miserable. But Dru still kept to herself, sitting for hours at the oxen pen with "Babe" and "Samson."

In 1859, Molly Ketcham was born, the family's first "prairie child." Dru midwifed for Rose; when Molly was wrapped safe and sleeping, Dru envied her new sister having no longing for any other place, no regrets that the soddy wasn't a frame house on a paved road.

Summer of 1858 began a year-long drouth that burned over the plains, heat wavering like funny fog just above the tips of the tall grass. When most of the wheat and corn withered in the heat, Jason picked a half acre near the house to keep alive what grain he could, knowing it was their winter salvation. Hope was Jason's god; he fashioned a water wagon and drove to the river every day, filling every bucket, basin, pot, or container. Then he guided the oxen slowly around that half acre, with Daniel carefully tipping water into the furrows. Hope rewarded their hours of labor with some tenuous, green sproutings.

One August afternoon, the Lasky and Dover families came in their wagons for a Sunday picnic with the Ketchams. The food was a prairie banquet: dishes like rare rabbit stew, prairie berry pie, dried carrot coffee, and Rose's specialty, skillet bread. When the evening came, one of the Dover men pulled out a harmonica and all the adults got to clapping and dancing. They could have kicked up their heels right over the moon,

*they were so happy in their fellowship. They forgot the heat
and let the music cool their souls. Druscilla was watching the
moon, with the music floating around her, watching the
horizon . . . you'd have thought the sun left a layer of herself
at nightfall, but it ran clear across the prairie with the soddy
right in its path.*

"Fire, Papa! Fire on the horizon!"
*Harnesses jangled wildly and the oxen surged in their yokes;
everyone was shouting and grabbing at the children. A huge
orange tidal wave of fire rolled in toward them, roaring and
hissing like a steam engine, jumping hastily dug trenches and
igniting even the canvas the men were using to beat out the
flames. Eventually there was no hope and everyone fled to
the river. Jason drove the oxen still yoked right into the water.
Coughing from the smoke, everyone had to wet their shirt
sleeves and skirts and hold them to their faces for some relief.
In water up to his waist, Jason ripped off a sleeve to wet the
oxen's nostrils and stood with them all night to keep them
calm.*
*Druscilla would never forget what they saw when they
climbed up the creek bank in the morning. The soddy had
melted in upon itself and all their belongings. The wagon
boards of the doorway were just charcoal and the half acre of
hope had disappeared into spikey stubble bent over like ghost
joints. Smoke puffed up from ash piles, some still glowing.
The morning heat boiled the burnt smell until they were all
coughing again. The ground was black for as far as the eye
could see.*
*Jason and David set out with the Laskeys to check their
dugout. Then they would walk the two miles to the Dovers
to see how they had fared. Rose headed resolutely toward
what was left of the soddy; the sod blocks crumbled as she
kicked them aside to rescue a pot, a basin. Druscilla was immediately at her side, the two of them sifting through the
ruins.*
*The fire left them no choice but to build another soddy.
Rose refused to even consider a creek bank dugout. "That's*

like asking the snakes to dance in on their tails for dinner," she said.

When he set his fourth crop in 1860, Jason prayed to him-self every day as he walked behind the plow. He stood vigil half of most nights, with Rose watching the other half, for that treacherous wave of fire or any red flickerings in the darkness out beyond the borders of the homestead. Every day of late spring when he rubbed the wheat tassels between his fingers, he felt his heart take a kick in his chest. "One day at a time, Lord, let us live safe and harvest success." The closer harvest time approached, the more his eyes scanned nervously over their vulnerable little world.

Not man nor beast nor force of nature came to harm the fourth Kansas crop of Jason Ketcham's wheat and corn, and he had grain enough for their family and to trade for other supplies: butter and cream from the Dovers and wagon planks from new homesteaders which shored up the second soddy.

In their little community, the men talked about Indians, and abolition heating up pro-slavery forces in Missouri territory as well as Atchison. The Kansas men agreed they wanted a free state. It had been six years since the Osawatomie raid on John Brown's family but none of the border ruffians had bothered homesteaders in their area. "Too far inland," Claude Laskey was sure. "Bet they heard you were out here, Claude, and it scared 'em too much," John Dover joked.

Druscilla watched Rose patch a hole in the quilt with a flannel square from one of Daniel's worn-out shirts. The night fire crackled and Dru nudged the pile of buffalo chips with her shoe.

"What do you *think* of abolition?" she asked her mother. Rose's needle drew in and out; the smooth and soothing move-ment of her hands mesmerized Dru.

"I think every person should be free to follow their own dream."

"Did you follow yours when we came to Kansas?"

Rose's stitches turned the corner of the patch, careful to blend into the design. Dru smiled, figuring her mother could *probably plow a perfect five-pointed star out in the field.*

"I followed your father with our children. This family was and is my dream."

Staring into the fire, Dru searched her own future, finding no husband there, no difficult prairie births of her own children in that vision. But she could hear her heart, restless to own her dreams, drumming up and down like dancing flames. Rose glanced at the fire; instinctively, Dru threw another chip into the embers. The patch was disappearing into the quilt as if it had always belonged. Rose's voice fell proud and sad against the flickering shadows.

"I'll admit this prairie was never part of my dream, though it didn't fight us much this year and I'm grateful for that. But it's no friend to me. I'll never trust it."

When President Buchanon signed Kansas into the Union as a free state in 1861, David got drunk and Jason threw Claude Laskey's horse collar on him. A few months later the Civil War erupted and it nearly took the horse collar again to keep David from marching off. Kansas wasn't spared; Quantrill and his bushwhackers made night raids on the volunteer soldiers in Lawrence. No one knew if they'd come any farther inland.

Dru took to sleeping with a shovel by her bed and listened to her mother turn against the covers for many sleepless nights. Sometimes Rose would get up and stoke the fire and then watch again at the window. But this time Dru knew it was not nature her mother feared, but angry men.

A sound . . . one stone striking another . . . like the pebbles Daniel whizzed against the slate rock on the creek bank . . . the sound woke Druscilla. She strained to pinpoint its direction—east, over by the new family's soddy. Dru gripped the handle of her shovel. Daniel's dog was listening too, his ears pricked. Just a harmless night sound . . . but then it grew louder, ricochets against the air. The dog stood up with a small whine.

"Easy, pup." Jason's voice from the blackness by the window startled Dru. He was completely dressed and had a rifle in each hand. *"Wake your brother."*

Dru leaned over and shook David by the leg. He sat up sleepily in his bed and heard his father say, *"Get up quick and quiet, boy. The new settlers have been hit by bushwhackers."*

40

David pulled on his pants and boots; Jason tossed him one of the rifles. Rose came from her bed and sat next to Dru, smoothing her daughter's hair.

"Rifle shots over by the Simpson soddy," Jason told her.

"Looks like burning now too," David reported from his view at the window.

"You and Dru grab Daniel and Molly and get yourself to the creek bank. Take blankets and this . . ." The revolver looked huge in the dim light of the soddy. "Whatever happens up here at the house, Rose, don't let no one near you and stay in your hiding place until you're sure they're gone."

"You think it's Quantrill?"

"Don't know. It doesn't matter. What matters is they may mean to do us harm and we mean to see they don't."

The prairie was a sea of black grass against blacker sky when Rose and Dru went out the soddy door and headed for the creek bank. Rose had a sleepy Daniel riding piggy-back; Dru carried three-year old Molly over her shoulder and the shovel in one hand. With gunshots filling the distant night air, they hurried, against each other's hard breathing and the night, stumbling on uneven ground. Rose held the revolver; Dru had the blankets.

When they reached the creek bank, they looked back at the soddy, almost invisible in the night blackness. But flames burning the Simpson place were clear to see. Then a sound came to them, new and peculiar: a rumbling that Dru and Rose felt right up through their feet into their frightened hearts—horses' hooves and lots of them, pounding furiously toward the soddy.

"Mama, someone's coming!" Daniel cried and then they were all crashing down the creek bank's crumbly slope and into the underbrush. "The dugout ruins!" Dru called and Rose rasped back, "Yes, quickly!" It was hard to find bearings against the night and fear; the quilt snagged on stiff twigs and Dru tripped, tumbling forward and rolling on her side to keep her weight off Molly. She felt the brush claw her cheek.

"Over here!" Daniel called as Rose helped her daughters out of the prickly weeds. They burrowed into the hollow of the old dugout, which was collapsed on one side so the entrance was not easily visible. A thought panged in Rose's brain

41

*about snakes dancing on their tails. "Come on in tonight,
you're more welcome than snakes on horseback," she said
to herself.*

For Rose and her children, the new prairie torture was
being able to hear everything but see nothing. First there was
a queer silence after the thrumming of the horses' hooves, and
then sporadic gunshots. Finally a volley of guns, men crying
out and shouting, the horses neighing wildly. At one point,
someone came crashing down the creek bank near them, but
whoever fell did not get up again. Rose clutched her shivering
children to her under the blanket; the revolver rested on top
of their covers. The sounds of the fighting seemed to go on for
hours. The children fought sleep but finally their huddled
warmth made them drift off and even Rose, exhausted from
her vigilance, bent her head down over her brood and dozed.

It was near dawn when she jolted awake to a new sound;
at first she thought it was someone coming through the underbrush on the far side of the creek bank. Then she recognized
the crackling of flames. Her worst fears engulfed her; the rebs
had lit the underbrush on fire and would smoke them out.
David and Jason lay dead in the ruins of the soddy and she
alone must save the children. Quietly she roused them, until
their eyes were alert upon her.

"We've got to try and get to the Laskey's dugout," she
told them. "I don't know how close the bushwhackers are
but I think they're burning the underbrush so we can't stay
in here. I'll go out first and you all follow. If I shoot the
gun, don't look back. Just keep going and get to the Laskey's."

They all nodded; Dru had her shovel at the ready. Rose
poised near the dugout entrance and cocked the revolver.
She thought she heard the brush crackle just around the corner.
The last thing she felt before she jumped out of the dugout
with the revolver was Dru's touch upon her shoulder.

As soon as Rose stepped out from the blind side of the dugout, a man caught hold of her arm with one hand and pulled
her by the waist up against him. Inside the dugout, the children
recoiled from the sound of the revolver going off. Then Dru
heard her mother crying.

"Thank God you're alive, Jason. I almost shot you!"

There had been 12 men in the rebel raiding party, most
of them drunk. Jason and David picked off six of them and one
suffered a broken neck when his horse pitched over the creek
bank. The rest of them retreated. David took a bullet in the
arm but luckily, it went clear through; still the wound was

serious. And so was the condition of the soddy, badly burned when the bushwhackers torched the roof. Jason and David spent most of the night fighting back the flames and dragging out what belongings they could save.

The shovel Dru had saved to split a rebel's head instead enlarged the creek bank dugout and the family camped there for a few days. The Dovers were willing to take them in until another house could be built, but Rose wouldn't talk about it for a week. Finally Jason had John Dover bring over his wagon and he loaded everything into it, including the children. Standing at the entrance to the dugout, he called to Rose.

"Unless you plan to live in this dugout by yourself like a prairie witch, you better come on out now and go over to the Dovers with the rest of us."

Rose didn't answer. Jason called again.

"If there was a way to give you wings, I'd fly you back to Indiana. But there isn't, any more than there's a way to live in this hovel of a dugout. The next rain will bring Big Creek right into our laps."

Still Rose didn't respond.

"What can I do, woman!" Jason yelled impatiently. Rose walked out of the dugout, pulling her shawl close around her. Keeping her eyes set on the wagon and Druscilla, she said as she passed her husband, "Maybe stone is the only thing that keeps away fire. I feel like stone myself right now."

For the next few days, everyone gave Rose a wide berth for her mood. She wasn't sulky or unpleasant but it was clear the prairie had pushed her to her limit, and she needed time to heal. Healing was foremost on everyone's mind for David too, who went into a fever. Louise Dover thought maybe the bullet nicked bone as well as flesh.

At dinner one night several weeks after the raid, John Dover shared an idea from Whipper Jones, head of one of the new families. Whipper was a smithy by trade, but had worked some in stone. He'd had a look at the creek slate and said it was limestone, which could be cut into bricks by a process called sledging. "He knows about mortaring too," John said, with the bare flicker of a smile at his wife Louise.

"Stone, eh?" Jason said, catching Rose's eye. "For building."

Rose met her husband's gaze with a hint of response in her face.

"Well," Jason sighed, winking at John and Louise, "it's worth a try."

Later that evening, Rose and Jason stood in the crisp moonlit air outside the window where Druscilla slept on a floor pallet.

"How long will it take to build a stone house?" Rose asked her husband.

"Can't tell. I don't know anything about sledging or mortaring. Whipper will have to teach all of us. John is willing to start a house with me now, with his son and Daniel helping until David heals up."

Jason saw his wife's reflective expression and her pale cheek, softer and paler than the light of the moon. "Don't worry, Rose. With the families working together, we'll get a stone house built that no fire can ever touch. These old flatlands haven't beat us yet."

Rose leaned into her husband's arms and listened to his heart beating its strong, regular pace. Her own was not beating so strong, not nearly as sure as it had when they came from Indiana. She wondered if her soul-out-of-balance made her heart falter; as much as she loved Jason and their children, she hated the prairie that had not yet yielded them a home, the prairie that burned up their dreams time after time. She took Jason's face in both her hands. "Promise me you will build a house of stone."

"If there's any way possible to do it, I will."

Whipper Jones didn't promise that sledging limestone would be easy; all the men were soon well acquainted with the muscle power required and the inexact bricks that resulted. Creating building blocks from stone hidden under prairie grass was slow going. Wiping his forehead, Jason stared at the few feet of cream-colored stone he and John Dover had laboriously uncovered. He was reminded this land wasn't going to give up anything easily. But the men were persistent, feeling the *heat of past fires still licking at their destiny.*

After several weeks, the men got better at sledging. David's arm was healing; when he was overeager to help with the rock breaking, Dru threatened him with the horse collar again. He couldn't handle the sledge hammer right away, so he drove the wagon to and from Big Creek every day.

Within a month, the Dover wagon pulled up to their soddy and Jason announced as he stepped in the doorway, "I have a present for you. For both of you," he said, indicating Rose and Louise. "Bring it in, boys."

John and Daniel came into the door, carrying a square piece of limestone.

"The first of four cornerstone bricks for your new stone dream house," he said to Rose. "The gift for you, Louise, is that all of us eventually will be out from under your feet so you and your family can have some privacy again."

Louise clapped her hands and then gave Jason a hug. Rose walked over to the stone, looking at it like something magical, as if she was almost afraid to touch it. Druscilla came from the ox pen and David from the wagon to share in the moment.

"You are going to get it built, aren't you?" Rose asked Jason, her eyes glistening at him. He nodded. Rose looked at her good friends and each of her children and finally, as she reached one hand out to touch the cornerstone of a dream, with the other hand she reached for Druscilla.

On the verge of wresting a home from the prairie that would not burn nor crumble in a furious Kansas wind, the Ketcham family suffered a new shock that turned the entire tide of their pioneer history. Unknown to any of them, the faltering in Rose's heart was not spiritual alone. Once she had touched the cornerstone, her spirit indeed made some peace with the rigors of the prairie, but her body did not. Within eight weeks of the first sledging, when Whipper Jones had dug half the six feet of mortar kiln and the men and boys were developing into real stonemasons, Rose Ketcham died in her sleep.

Fate burned out the hope of the entire family with Rose's death, as surely as drunken strangers had torched their soddy.

46

They walked around dazed, as if looking for someone who had disappeared without a trace.

Dru stayed by the oxen pen, even after dark, singing in the moonlight or petting the animals' square heads. Something in their yellow eyes soothed her better than any human touch, though many a night Louise Dover thought her heart would break from wanting to comfort the girl. The only wisdom John Dover could offer for the Ketchams' mourning was to keep them traveling to Big Creek every day to break more bricks. Rose was gone but her dream was not; Jason's promise to her must be made good.

Returning on a July day from what was becoming a bona fide limestone quarry, a rare event awaited Jason: he had a letter from his brother in Oregon territory. He sat on the porch at sunset and read the letter over and over again, smoothing it against his leg each time he turned the pages. After a supper in silence, he addressed his family and friends.

"My brother Fenton writes of doing well in Oregon. He says there's trees growing on top of each other and so a good lumber business could be had."

Jason's words faltered slightly. He looked at his friend. "John, can you remember how long it's been since we saw trees enough to even think of lumber?"

John Dover smiled. "Too long to remember a date, that's for sure."

"Fenton lost his wife a year ago and has a girl Molly's age to take care of alone now. But he's about as far from the war and bushwhackers as you can get. He says his homestead is twenty paces from the ocean."

Jason's eyes settled on Druscilla's 15-year-old face, desperate for an escape from grief. With a sad smile, he said, "It isn't a homestead like this. Fenton lives in a real frame house."

The father and daughter looked at each other a moment.

"I'd sleep without fear if I knew my girls were safe at the ocean."

Jason told them his plan: to build the stone house of Rose's dream into an inn that would house new families and soldiers. Daniel had the best hand for stone in the bunch of them and he would help make the dream come true.

"As for you girls, I want you safe from this war and any more of the prairie's surprises. Dru, you'll find you a husband in Oregon and raise up Molly and Fenton's girl with your own children. David, you're seventeen and I know you want to go fight for the North. But first, I'm asking you to get the girls to the ocean—to Fenton in Oregon—on the Overland Trail."

Druscilla felt her mother's heart join her own in painful wonder that her father could give up even more of his family after all they'd been through. At the same time, she knew she wanted to go. Maybe in a new place she could hold dear the memory of her mother's life and let go the ache of her loss.

When the moon was "half a rockin' chair" and summer night air played a cool tease, Dru was thinking about her father's plan as she stood in the ox pen, stroking Babe's ears and the hair in between Samson's eyes. Her father whistled to her in the dark.

"Mind if I join you?"

"Come ahead."

He leaned up against the side of the pen. "In a week or so, I'll be sending you and David and Molly up to Ft. Kearney in Nebraska to get your supplies for the trip. You can take the oxen. If any animals alive can get you to Oregon, they will."

"Will it be dangerous? Are there bushwhackers?"

"I hear there are. But you'll have David and the wagon party. And you're no lousy shot yourself."

"I'm thankful you taught me to shoot, Papa, after the raiders burned the soddy."

Jason took a look at the moon; the breeze fluttered the memory to him of that night Rose had asked for his promise about the stone house. For a moment he was sure if he just put out his hand, he'd feel her warm, pale cheek again beneath his fingertips.

"I'm thankful you're taking to my plan, Druscilla. Don't think I don't want to hold all of you as tight to me as I can and never let you out of my sight so you won't slip away like your mother did. But that's no way for anyone to live, especially a man as headstrong as David or a girl as spirited as

48

you. You'll both have a better chance to go on with a hopeful life in Oregon. Fenton won't require much if you help him with his girl. Just be for her and Molly the way your mother was for you. And write me how Molly turns out."

"You think I'll ever see you again? Or Daniel or the Dovers?"

Jason was glad only the moon could see the kick of doubt in his heart.

"Of course you will. Roads are coming in all the time to make travel easier. And we'll get the railroad here eventually too, I'm sure of it."

The moon had no voice of comfort for them, for their choice of separation.

"I want a favor from you, Papa."

"Speak your mind."

"I want four limestone corner bricks to take with me to Oregon."

"That's a lot of weight to add to your wagon, Dru. I'm sure there's limestone in Oregon."

"Maybe so, but it won't be Kansas stone. And it won't be part of my mother's dream."

Dru felt the sting of tears, felt them drop heavy and warm on her cheeks. She thought of all those tears she'd held back in her life, a well full of them just for the prairie rainstorms and soaked quilts. She already knew about the ocean; she had that many tears inside her for the mother she'd lost. Darkness cloaked her aching heart, and her wet cheeks. She heard her father sigh and wondered if he felt her tears in his soul.

Jason took a friendly pull on Samson's ear. Then in the darkness, he put a gentle hand on his daughter's shoulder.

"You'll get your bricks—I'll cut 'em small and Daniel can smooth 'em out. It won't take long."

The window eyes of the limestone castle and the eyes of Druscilla Ketcham beckoned the psyche of Nyla Wade, made her toss and turn in her sleep, fling aside her covers. Near the foot of the bed, flames licked a soddy into ashes; gunfire echoed around the tight walls of the small room. Sounds in the surf were the turbulent rivers across which Dru rafted the

49

limestone bricks. And outside Nyla's window, Molly Ketcham stood hand-in-hand with Olympia Swan as fire again threatened the family livelihood. As if the fog held twenty hands that brushed her in her sleep, Nyla shook wide awake, sitting up with a jerk. Her eyes sighted back into the past, to that burning Kansas horizon, to Dru's eyes burning with an unknown message. The fog cloaked the ghosts of all of them, and like a sermon by Olympia Swan, rattled Nyla's every nerve ending with invocation.

FOUR

Someone Done Those Widows Wrong

Nothing short of hot black coffee could clear the cobwebs from Nyla's groggy brain. She rang the front desk; the ringing echoed at the other end of the hall. On the tenth ring, the receiver was picked up.

"Hello. This is Nyla Wade in room fourteen. Could I get some coffee?"

There was no reply.

"Hello, hello? Is anyone on this line?"

No answer. She sighed. *Just a cup of coffee, Lord, make life simple for once.* "Hello. Please answer me. Who is on this line?"

She heard someone clear his throat and then say very quietly, "Ricks, ricks."

"Mr. Masters, is that you? This is Nyla Wade, remember?"

Again the silence. She was about to hang up in frustration when Masters said, "I can bring you some coffee, I guess. Jefferson isn't around."

"Oh, I'd be *so* happy if you would. Bring the whole pot."

Abruptly the line went dead. She shook her head, then went to shower and dress.

Half an hour later, she was dressed but still minus her coffee. She yanked open her door to stomp down the hall

51

after Mitch Masters and almost ran into him. He was carrying a large tray which contained a coffee pot and cup, and also a plant wrapped in purple paper.

"I thought I'd lost you," she told him, recovering her balance.

Mitch clacked his dentures. "Coffee," he said. Then indicating the plant, "Someone sent this to you."

She peeled back the tissue up around it and hooted with glee at the leaves edged in black and lavender. "Hot damn, it's a gloxinia!" The flower had to be from Audrey Louise.

"Come on in." First she poured and took a sip of the coffee and sighed with relief, then opened the card with the flower.

Mitch did another inspection, apparently searching for the mysterious waves. After patting the top of Nyla's scotch bottle with one gloved finger, he said, "Queer looking plant if you ask me," and then shuffled out the door.

The coffee revived her. Touching the velvety gloxinia leaves, she phoned Audrey Louise to catch her up on life in Burnton. She could have predicted Audrey's friendly warning: "What are you doing snooping into old murders already?" Her friend's peal of laughter momentarily dissolved their distance.

Nyla's second phone call was a quick one to her parents. To them she emphasized life as a small-town reporter and not the details of a small-town murder. Her third call was to the *Beckoner* office to let Gruff know she'd conduct several interviews for the Retailer Review before she came in to type her school board story.

He chuckled. "How late they keep you up?"

"Late enough."

As she went down the hall, it occurred to her that Mitch might know something about the widows' murder. He was their plumber, after all, had lived in Burnton since Molly Ketcham's time.

He was not at the front desk, but the back door of the hall was standing open. Behind the Shady Stay a lean-to was built up under the kitchen window and attached to a narrow aluminum shed about fifteen feet long. In front of this structure

52

was a work bench covered by a vast assortment of rusted motors, pieces of metal, sawed lengths of two-by-fours with nails driven into them. Battered buckets and pans held more junk, each a particular collection. Three half-built bicycles were piled beside the bench and something that might pass for a doghouse huddled on the other side. There were numerous cans of dried silver paint everywhere, the bushes bristle-stiff and stuck forever in their glittery graves. On a barrel up over the work bench sat the frame of a large fan, its electric innards removed, its rotor turning in ocean breeze—protectively scattering any pesky waves.

She walked toward the lean-to and was startled by ferocious barking. Mitch popped his head out, saw her, and moved one gloved hand; the barking ceased.

"Quite a watchdog you've got there."

"Can't tell who might come around." Mitch looked down the slope toward the beach. "Hard to believe what they do sometimes."

"Who?"

Mitch's eyes narrowed. "I told you before. The brother-hood." He didn't look up at her. "They have a machine that sends out waves. They hook onto you and put you through your acts with a light."

She moved closer to him. The dog crept out of the lean-to and growled.

"Dobro," Mitch said quietly. The dog sniffed warily at her.

"How does the brotherhood hook onto you?" she asked the old man.

Mitch set down the glass insulator he'd retrieved from some downed telephone pole. He lowered his voice, his eyes darting around as he spoke. "They can only hook a wave onto an agent, who uses the light and hooks onto others. Each agent has a flower and a metal in their back. About here . . ."

He ran one gloved hand down Nyla's left shoulder blade. Then he scrunched his own shoulders and touched the front of his stained jacket. "I always wear a coat no matter how warm it gets. I have to keep my back covered and keep my hands working. They like a hand, see, but they'll take a finger. So I keep covered up. I keep working."

She remembered what he'd said about the blue-eyed Indians. "Are the blues agents?"

Mitch cocked his head. "You ever see a blue?"

"I'm not sure." Was there any sense in the old man? Or did he talk with space aliens who flew in at night and then whizzed away faster than an electronic beep?

"They aren't none of 'em agents. They're enemies. Kidnappers and rustlers. I only saw one out here. He jumped out and sent a thunderbolt up under Molly Ketcham's car to explode it. I shot a wave into him and he disappeared."

Mitch puttered with one of the bicycles, turning the foot pedal so that the wheels spun. He jerked the pedal back and the wheel braked with a whine. He squinted at Nyla. "You might have iron, like Lady Bull. But they don't use women much. Saps all your strength for birthing."

"Can you shoot waves on your own, without the brotherhood?"

Mitch cackled his squealy, edgy laugh. "The brotherhood is always in charge of the waves."

"Have you ever met the brotherhood?"

Mitch squealed so with laughter that he knocked a whole pan full of brown beer bottles off the work bench in a loud clatter. "No, you never see their faces," he giggled, shuffling toward Nyla. "They keep them covered. To keep the secrets better." He put out his gloved hands; she took a step backwards. The dog growled. Mitch kept shuffling but stopped within a foot of her.

"You know, they like a hand, but they'll take a finger. So I keep a glove on all the time. You don't want the brotherhood at close range hooking on a wave. The magnetics could kill you."

"What were the widows? Were they agents or blues?"

Suspicion stirred in Mitch's expression; his eyes glazed for a moment and he looked warily at her. "They weren't neither one." His voice was lifeless, hard-edged. The tone of his words clutched at Nyla's heart when he said, "Someone done those widows wrong."

Her own voice faltered as she asked, "Were you around when it happened? Did you—"

"Hey Mitch, you up there? Get ahold of the dog!" The man's voice came from the slope to the beach. Dobro started up again and Mitch pushed her into the lean-to but didn't shush her—as if he wanted her to fuss.

Coming up over the edge of the slope was a tall slender fellow in blue jogging pants and a windbreaker, a catch-bag over his shoulder. He smiled from behind large glasses as he approached them. His slightly bulgy eyes were curious and nervous. His smile featured front teeth that reminded Nyla of a cartoon muskrat. If he grew a mustache, the whiskers would be perfect.

The man came directly toward her, smiling as if they were old friends. For a moment she panicked: had they met before and she'd forgotten? He took her hand in both his—she recoiled from the clamminess of his touch. Anyone so willing to be friendly should have warm dry hands.

"I'm Father Jim Hammister." Now she understood his eager approach. "St. Mark's Episcopal on Copeland Avenue." He blinked behind his big lenses.

She introduced herself.

"Yes," he said, "you're the new *Beckoner* reporter." As she looked at him he added, "Ministers get the news pretty fast about newcomers."

She noticed Mitch eyeing the minister with something less than enthusiasm.

"Mitch, I brought you some copper wire." The Reverend indicated his burlap fishing bag. "Where shall I put it?"

Mitch dug around for an empty pan and without a word held it out. As Hammister dumped the bag he said over his shoulder to Nyla, "Mitch sells this to Ed over at the salvage yard. He tell you?"

She shook her head. She caught Mitch's eye and was surprised to see him put a finger to his lips.

Reverend Hammister looked at Mitch and then at Nyla. "You find Burnton interesting enough to spawn some good stories?"

"I think there's quite a lot of interest here." She smiled innocuously. "I'm going to do a feature on the limestone castle."

"Really?" Hammister brightened. "It's a grand old house. Too bad Seascape wants to tear it down. Of course, those terrible murders . . . perhaps the house has seen better days." The lanky minister stretched. "Well, guess I'll get on with my morning jog." He looked at Mitch again, who merely nodded. Then Hammister sprinted off down the slope toward the beach, burlap bag bouncing on his hip.

Mitch giggled and rolled his eyes. "Holy men are worse than blues. Never trust 'em." The old man pushed at some of his tacky bric-a-brac, staring after Reverend Hammister. He moved his lips as if in conversation with an invisible audience, occasionally clacking his teeth to mumble, "Ricks, ricks."

She wanted him to continue their conversation about the widows. Before she could ask anything further, he surprised her, almost reading her thoughts. "I was up there the day before. They had sand again in the bathroom pipes. I cleaned 'em right out. Next day I was on the beach and saw the police. I knew the wave that hooks the guilty was haunting that house." He nodded, muttering to his ghost friends again.

Impulsively, Nyla squeezed his arm. "Who did that wave hook onto, Mitch?"

The unpredictable old man shuffled away toward the door of the lean-to. He turned, regarded her with a puzzling half-smirk. He worked his hands in his gloves and looked down at them a moment. Then he said, "You know that as well as I do. And you know about the blues too."

She was completely perplexed. Yet Mitch seemed certain— sure of what he saw in her.

"Yes, you do."

She stared at him; he stared at his gloves.

"Someone done those widows wrong." He looked at the footprints in the sand.

She wondered what kind of expert could decipher his bizarre language, translate his meaning. Too bad the Reverend Olympia Swan wasn't around to interpret Mitch Masters and his own version of talking in tongues.

Mitch went into his lean-to. "Thanks for the coffee," she called to him.

56

The trusty Mustang purred good morning when she started the engine; she patted the dash. She was ready to back away from the Shady Stay when squeaking brakes caused her to check the rear-view mirror. A postal jeep was pulled up directly behind her car. A woman sorting letters jumped out and headed toward Shady Stay.

"Hey!" Nyla called to her. "I need to get to work. You're parked right behind me."

When the woman turned to look at her, Nyla was surprised and delighted—she was the store window reflection, the woman with the flaming shock of red hair.

"Excuse me, but I'm blocked in."

"Yes, I know."

There was no smile to wrinkle the postwoman's cheek freckles. Reverend Hammister could give this woman lessons on the over-grin, Nyla thought. She was already an expert at the non-grin. Nyla under-grinned, and asked again, "Please, I'm late already. Could you just pull your van up a couple of feet?"

The woman bunched up the letters she was sorting and whacked them against her hip as she walked to the Mustang. When she leaned down to look at Nyla, her green eyes were flashing. For the first time in her life Nyla felt the urge to say, "My, but you're beautiful when you're angry."

"Lady, if an ambulance, a police car, and a postal truck are all coming down the street, who do you think has the inviolate right of way?"

Nyla didn't answer. She only saw the dimples that created laughter in her, dimples that didn't fit the postwoman's early morning bad temper.

"If you didn't guess the postal truck, then you won't understand why I'm not moving my jeep one inch. We're the Feds, lady, we don't have to move."

The woman's retreating back was no more sociable than her non-smiling face, but this second set of cheeks was just as appealing. Nyla wondered if they were freckled, too. She sat patiently—and grinning—behind the steering wheel. Moments later the postwoman stalked back to her jeep and without looking at Nyla, slammed the door and roared off.

With the distractions of her restless dreams, Mitch Master's peculiar stories, and now the red-headed postwoman, Nyla's mind was not on the Retailer Review. She slogged through an interview with Copeland Avenue's laundromat owner, and Dixie Wiland of Dixie's conch shells from Australia and pink plastic flamingos for everyman's lawn.

At 10:30 she sat in the Mustang and took a deep breath. She knew she should go to the office where she belonged and type up the interviews and the school board story. But she also knew what she wanted to do was visit the police station for a look at the widows' case file. How could she just get down to business when the eyes of Druscilla Ketcham were haunting her dreams? She headed down Copeland to find City Hall.

Officer Ted Bales was typing two-finger catch-up on his paperwork when the attractive young woman walked into the squad room. If the Chief hadn't been in his office, Bales would have wolf-whistled. Over at the coffee pot, Officer Randy Petrowski forget the open spigot and let hot coffee run over his fingers. Who in the hell was that bombshell at the squad room door? Sergeant Phil Allen noticed the sudden silence in the room and looked up to behold his officers beholding Nyla Wade.

Clearing his throat, the Sergeant cast a reproachful glance at his men and greeted the visitor. "Can I help you, Miss?"

Allen was tall and splendid in his light blue police shirt; Nyla bet he had his uniforms custom tailored. She liked his greying mustache and the greeny-grey of his welcoming eyes.

"I'm Nyla Wade, reporter for the Burnton *Beckoner*. I'd like to have a look at one of your case files."

Reporters usually made Allen bristle. But she didn't seem to have that snooty press-has-sacred-access attitude. "Any case file in particular?" he asked. Bales snickered at his desk. Petrowski overstirred his coffee.

"The file on the widows' murder up at the limestone castle. I believe it was just about a year ago."

The police sergeant had been leaning down at her from his six-foot height; he straightened and his smile disappeared. "That case is closed, you know. May I ask your interest?"

Now it was her turn to try to smile. "Sure. Since I'm new in town, I'm introducing myself with a feature on the castle and its architecture. But I want full background—a good reporter does her homework. Same as a good cop."

Allen would have bet his paycheck that the lady usually got what she wanted with that smile, but he wasn't altogether sure he liked her calling him a cop. All the same, there was no reason she shouldn't see the file.

"Randy?" Allen motioned toward Petrowski. "Show Miss Wade to records and get her the file she wants."

Petrowski couldn't get his feet moving fast enough. Ted Bales stood up at his typewriter and nodded to Nyla. "Let me know if you need any further assistance," he volunteered.

Petrowski took her to another floor of the building and consulted the case file log in the records room. He told the records clerk, "Number 1478-H, M.S.P."

Nyla settled down at a small wooden table between a row of floor-to-ceiling case file shelves. At her back, the windows were inset with wire mesh. She looked down to the end of the row of files. Petrowski, habitual coffee cup in hand, leaned against the records desk, staring at her. She smiled and opened the file.

She reviewed the preliminary investigation notes, neighborhood canvass, Offense Report. She took down the names and addresses of Joan Ruddye's children. She studied the crime scene sketch initialed by S. Randall. The outline of the two bodies in the sketch chilled her.

The coroner's report was blunt and grim. Cause of death—stabbing, probably with a kitchen-variety steak carver. Joan Ruddye had expired in her sleep from three wounds in her chest, Valerie Prosper from multiple wounds as she struggled. Coroner William Prather remarked on the ferocity of the attack, indicating that many of the punctures in her hands and arms were defense wounds. He estimated both women had died within a period of fifteen minutes of each other and from body temperature upon discovery, he had assigned time of death at 11:00 P.M.

No evidence of sexual molestation. Moderate amounts of alcohol had been consumed. Trace evidence included fragments of white silk fiber on both victims, probably from their caftans, or a designer scarf as suggested by the housekeeper. Black silk filaments of unusual nature found only on Valerie Prosper. Appeared to be Japanese silk, from the particular reel of extremely fine filaments into a strand of thread; no items in the house matched these. Prather's suggestion: filaments came from attacker's clothing.

Valerie Prosper's fingernail scrapings revealed traces of blood type O, matching neither her own nor Joan Ruddye's. Nothing unidentifiable to the widows discovered in bedding or items strewn on floor or in floor sweepings—except sand, probably brought in when attacker entered. On the rug just outside the bedroom door, three footprints in blood. And one in the sand at the edge of the outside steps.

The crime scene was all too clear in Nyla's imagination. She looked up; the file folders swam into a murky blur. The room was suddenly too quiet and too cold. She forced herself to look at the file again.

Newspaper clippings from the Coos Bay paper related the

60

discovery of the murderer's shoes by North Bend Assistant D.A. Jim Strunk, and the resulting arrest of a local drifter, R. Eugene Williams, nicknamed "Tramp."

A photo of the rug footprints along with print tape from the scene were of considerable interest; she noted a footcast had also been made and hoped she could have a look at it. If only coroners wouldn't measure things in centimeters; she was reminded too much of her failed math class in high school. How the suspect could wear a size 10 man's shoe on his 23.77 centimeters foot was beyond her.

She noted the persons listed in the fingerprint elimination report: both victims, the Ruddye siblings, housekeeper Cohista Farrell, plumber Mitch Masters, neighbor Loamie Newsome, friend Seth Randolph, Ritchie Dennis, Sheriff Ben Wasser, and the Reverend Jim Hammister. They all made sense except those of Ritchie Dennis and the Reverend's. She could almost feel Hammister's clammy handshake again as she wondered when and why he'd been at the castle the day of the murder.

As she was recording the names for her own notes, she saw three capital letters and a question mark penciled in at the bottom of the preliminary investigation notes: DOG?

A detailed autopsy report was available at the North Bend crime lab, she read. An unpleasant prospect, but maybe she'd have a look at that when she sought out the footcast. She closed the file and sat back in her chair. Even without much crime beat experience, she judged the evidence circumstantial but convincing. All signs in the case pointed to Tramp Williams, who unfortunately had died before offering any alibi.

"Excuse me, Miss Wade?"

An officer she had not previously seen stood next to the table. His sandy blond hair had been razed in a buzz cut and his chin was strictly former fullback, but his eyes showed some sensitivity.

Steve Randall was surprised when Nyla Wade looked up from the file. She looked enough like Jacqueline that she might well have been the ghost of his high school sweetheart who had eloped with someone else.

"Excuse me, I'm Officer Steve Randall."

His grip on her hand was firm and warm.

"Oh yes—didn't you do the crime scene sketch on the widows' case? I got a good sense of the room from it—almost too good a sense."

They stood hand-in-hand, awkwardly. The deep well type, Nyla thought. Not bad looking. Likely he'll ask me out. Unlikely he'd ever guess I'm not interested in men.

Randall finally remembered his mission. "Chief Karp would like to speak with you. To fill you in and answer any questions you might have. Do you have a few minutes?"

"Okay by me." Nyla picked up the file. "Any chance I can get a copy of this? To study at home?"

"Sorry." Randall shook his head and smiled. "But you can come back and review it any time."

Police Chief Walter Karp tightened his tie when he saw Randall bring Nyla Wade into the squad room. He started to put on his suit coat and then thought, Hell, it's hot enough already in here.

"Welcome to City Hall, Ms. Wade. I trust you found our officers and records department cooperative?"

"To the letter, Chief Karp."

"Find out everything you wanted for your research?"

"I appreciated having a look at the case file, but I admit I found the details pretty grisly."

"The murders were grisly. Worst I've seen since I came to Burnton."

"And solved with circumstantial evidence?"

The Chief didn't hedge. "A great many cases are solved with circumstantial evidence. Sometimes it's that simple."

"Everyone had solid alibis?"

"Solid enough. And none of them had motive."

Nyla didn't comment but raised her eyebrows and then looked briefly at her notes. "Can you tell me about Ritchie Dennis?"

"One of the town unfortunates, a retarded boy. Size of Mean Joe Greene but harmless as Beaver Cleaver."

She remembered the boy on the road when she first came into town, the same boy on the beach with the stiff starfish.

"What's his alibi?"

"His print was only a latent, found on the window sill outside the widows' bedroom. He's somewhat of a window peeker anyway, but neighbors report he was just curious. His mother verified that he was at home with her from seven-thirty that night."

"What about Seth Randolph?"

"Long time friend of the widows. Had a glass of wine with them early that evening."

"And Reverend Hammister?"

"Stopped by to invite the widows to a church function. Later he and Randolph were at the Lighthouse Inn playing darts."

"Mrs. Farrell was the housekeeper, right?"

Karp was surprised for a moment to have his memory re-running those awful steps with Cohista back down that hallway to that room; her trembling next to him, her cheeks streaked with unending tears.

Nyla waited.

"Yes, she found the victims."

"What about Mitch Masters? Whoever committed this murder was crazy, and Masters seems to be off in his own world."

Karp chuckled. "You forget, Ms. Wade, this murder was charged to a particular individual. As for Mitch, he's maybe peculiar but too frail to hold his own in the struggle with Valerie Prosper. Besides, he was around town the next few days and no one observed that crucial mark on him—the scratch she gave her attacker."

"How could they? He wears a coat all the time."

Wade was no slow starter, this was clear. "Officer Bales checked it out personally."

"I see. It wasn't noted in the file."

"Possibly not," Karp said, unruffled. "Masters acts a little fearsome at times, like Dennis, but he's just as harmless."

"Does anything he says ever make sense?"

Wade wasn't out to accuse anyone of lax policing. Karp loosened his tie. "Maybe, to someone. Cora Corona thinks he's had shock treatments and that's what he means when he talks about the waves. Whether he makes sense or not, he hasn't caused anyone any trouble."

63

"Is Coroner Prather a certified medical examiner?"

This question sounded more like a challenge; Karp sat up in his chair.

"No, an elected coroner. But he's an M.D. with many years' experience."

"As doctor or coroner?" When Karp didn't answer, Nyla added, "This is mostly for my information. Every place you go has a slightly different policy. Did anyone else examine the evidence, any other agencies or experts?"

"Coroner Prather is enough of a local expert. Look, the shoes were matched to the prints within four days of the murder. Besides, if we'd sent any of the evidence on to Portland or Washington, we might still be waiting for a case number or worse—the evidence would have been lost in their backlog. The North Bend crime lab people didn't think it was necessary."

Nyla flipped several pages in her notepad. "What about the silk fibers—anything ever found to identify them?"

"The white ones, yes, from Mrs. Prosper's designer scarf. The black ones were never identified."

"Nothing on Williams to link that?"

"No."

If she expected him to explain or justify, he didn't. She knew from the crime file the Coos Bay police theory that Williams had dumped his clothing after the murder.

"I think I've taken up enough of your time, Chief Karp. I do thank you for being so cooperative about this file." As she turned to leave, she remembered the word penciled on the investigation notes. "One last question. Was there something about a dog in this investigation?"

He didn't respond immediately; Nyla could see him carefully choosing an answer.

"The widows had a watchdog they usually kept chained outside the house. The night of the murder, Tramp Williams would have had to come within a few feet of that dog to enter the back door. Yet none of the neighbors reported the dog barking."

Nyla Wade and Walter Karp looked at each other. He thought she would ask if any of his officers had since discovered why the dog did not sound the alert. Instead she just gave him an irresistible, heart-tugging smile, tapped her pad against her forehead, and left the squad room.

Karp pulled his tie even looser and leaned out the door of his office. "Quite a reporter the *Beckoner*'s got themselves," he said to no one in particular, staring at the squad room door still swinging from Nyla's exit.

Steve Randall looked at the Chief. "Seemed like a pretty gutsy lady to me. I wouldn't have wanted to dig in that file cold."

Petrowski turned to him. "Oh, I spared her the gross stuff. I ordered the file up M.S.P.—Minus Scene Photos."

When Nyla made it to the *Beckoner* office about noon, Jean Thomas and Gruff Hamilton were deadlocked over type style for an ad. Jean stuffed her hands in jacket pockets and told Nyla, "Gruff wants Bookman, as ever. Geez, it's boring. We do *everything* in Bookman."

Hamilton took a huge bite of a ham sandwich. "Jean wants something far out, like Univers," he mumbled, his mouth full.

"Sounds like computers," Nyla commented.

Gruff sounded irritated. "This is a floral ad, for chrissakes."

"Okay Gruff, how about Korinna?" Jean held up the type sheet.

He chewed violently. "Too Russian."

She shifted to another sheet. "Thunderbird?"

"Sounds like cheap wine."

"I know how it *sounds* but how does it *look?*" Jean snapped.

"Are you jack-of-all-trade types always so friendly to each other?" Nyla picked up a type sheet from the desk. "What's wrong with this one? Venus Bold—a regal sort of type, *flowery* almost. Perfect for a floral ad." She added, "Or don't you have the nerve to run an ad in Venus Bold, Gruff?"

Jean Thomas started a slow grin; Gruff narrowed his eyes and then gulped the last bit of bread and ham as if he'd like to gulp Nyla Wade in one bite too. "Enough nerve, my tush. Run the damned ad in Venus Bold."

Jean headed for the press room with the type sheet. Nyla rolled a sheet of paper into her typewriter to start on the school

65

board story. Hamilton asked, "You have a nice interview with Chief Karp?"

"Should I be impressed by the grapevine?" She didn't mean to sound flip, but her editor yanked his glasses onto his nose and said, "He gave me a call. Wanted to be sure you were legit. You didn't bother to show a press pass."

Hamilton opened his drawer, drew out a yellow card and flipped it onto Nyla's desk. "Just don't go overboard on this castle thing, Nyla. I never said I'd run the story, you know."

The *Beckoner* came out on Wednesday and she perused it in her room at Shady Stay. The floral ad in Venus Bold type looked great. Less promising were the FOR RENT ads, which clinched a decision she had been considering. The monthly rate for Shady Stay was more than reasonable; the ever-absent Mr. Jefferson would never make his fortune off the hotel's rentals. For now, she would keep her furniture in storage and stay at the hotel until she got the castle story finished and had more time to look for her own place in Burnton.

Humphrey Bogart in *The Big Sleep* was the fare for the seniors at Oceanview Home on Friday night. Nyla found her way to the rec room which was crowded with Lioness members arranging cookies on trays and filling pots with coffee and tea. Perry and his friends were nowhere in sight.

"Miss Wade, so nice to see you again." Reverend Hammister's clammy hand reached to her before she could jam her hands into her skirt pockets. She left him quickly to talk with the home director.

Mrs. Whatley was friendly and enthusiastic about all the Oceanview activities and Nyla knew more about programs for seniors within the next few minutes than she could ever possibly print. She glimpsed two men up at the front of the room setting up the movie screen.

"Perry!" she called. They hugged each other and then giggled. She was so glad to see his familiar face that she patted the lapel of his camel-colored leather blazer. "I lost sleep reading that manuscript of yours. Not once, but twice."

Perry beamed and then said to the other man, "Seth, this

is Nyla Wade. Remember? I was telling you about her."

The big man brightened. "Hey, I've had some good times in the Mile High City."

"I just bet you have," Perry teased.

"Seth Randolph, by any chance?" Nyla asked, remembering the police file.

Seth stood up to his full height and nodded his head of red hair, shaggy as thick carpet. Nyla recognized him also as the man in the pickup truck who'd stolen away her fantasy woman reflected in the store window, the woman who had turned out to be the postwoman. Before she could ask Seth where to find her fantasy in the flesh, that very red-haired dimpled-cheeked, under-smiling postwoman stood before her.

"My friend, meet my friends." Perry took Nyla's arm. "Seth and Lucy Randolph, the famous flame-haired siblings of Burnton, this is Nyla Wade, famous reporter from Denver, here to win a Pulitzer for the *Beckoner.*"

Seth did a little half-bow; Lucy stood unmoving. Nyla smiled and said, eyes on Lucy, "I'm glad to meet you, though Lucy and I have already crossed paths." Lucy did not smile.

"Members of our special clan," Perry whispered to Nyla.

"You a Bogart fan?" Seth asked.

"Not really. I'm covering this for the paper."

"I love Bogie," Perry interrupted. "Now that was a *man!*" He and Seth winked at each other.

"A smart man. He made a million bucks talking out the side of his mouth."

The three looked at Lucy.

"Isn't this movie based on a Raymond Chandler novel?" Nyla was over-grinning again at the red-haired sister who answered, "Yes. You a mystery buff?"

Nyla considered mentioning *The Red Headed League* as her favorite Holmesian caper, but thought better of it. "Yes, I do read mysteries."

"Read any of the Kate Fansler books?"

"I liked her *Theban Mysteries* best."

"Ever read any of the Girl Group mysteries?"

"Those were *my* favorites," Perry chimed in. "Everyone else was crazy over Biff and Joe Hardy, but I was literally *lost* in the Girl Group books."

"Keep your voice down, bright eyes." Seth nudged the slight historian.

"Don't ruffle me, big boy." Perry smoothed his hair.

"So what was your pleasure, Per? The Motor Girls, the Khaki Girls, the Airplane Girls?" Lucy showed an honest fondness for Perry.

He leaned in between the two women. "Must I admit my penchant for the back seats of cars? Of course it was the Motor Girls!" They all cackled with laughter.

Riveting a look on Lucy, Nyla said, "I didn't really appreciate other girls until I wasn't a girl anymore. But I think I'd have been a Khaki Girl. I always loved the pockets on khaki shorts. Do you ever wish you could put someone special in your pocket?"

Mrs. Whatley signaled lights out. In the darkness, Nyla considered her boldness, and by the flickering light from the screen, saw Lucy give her a sideways glance. Bogie kissed Lauren Bacall, who responded, "I like that. I'd like a lot more of that."

Perry invited his three friends for a nightcap after the movie. "See you later, schweetheart," he called to Nyla as they all headed for their cars to rendezvous.

Perry lived in a duplex just off the Beach Loop, about half a mile from the limestone castle. His apartment was as chic and clean as the man who lived in it. Agate wind chimes tinkled on his gabled front porch.

"I really like your apartment, Perry." Nyla was admiring the sofa and matching chairs—bamboo frames with beige seat covers accented by lavender irises. These were placed on a persian rug, basic beige with two wide border stripes in deep brown and lavender. A giant vase on one stereo speaker was a signed Lalique, uniquely shaped like a beehive. Over the mantel a painting in a clear acrylic frame covered the entire wall: a blue wave about to curl over the whole room.

"This place always reminds me of the Mary Tyler Moore set," Lucy teased Perry.

"I'm a big fan of Mary's." They went off giggling to the kitchen.

68

Seth picked up a record album and read the cover notes. Nyla watched him. Midway through the movie, she had begun to wonder if the police had considered him a suspect in the widows' murder just because he was so big. Everything about him was giant-sized, from his meaty calves to his solid shoulders and massive neck. He could be a stand-in for the bulkhead of a boat, she thought. But he moved lightly on his feet, and gentleness suffused his expressions.

Lucy and Perry returned with a tray of glasses and white wine.

"So what's the latest from Seascape, Seth?" Perry asked. "Are they still telling you to finish the drainage work?" He poured wine for his big red-headed friend.

"Do we have to talk about this?" Lucy moaned.

Perry ignored her and informed Nyla, "Seth has a small construction company and he's the big lug who's torn up the street at Land's End."

Seth added, "Townspeople thought Seascape would go in overnight so they had no protest about the street construction or inconvenience. When the Ruddye's lawsuit blocked the start of the building, everyone grumbled but figured the delay would be short. The Seascape people thought the same and told me to start digging. The lawsuit dragged on." Seth made a mock grimace at Perry. "Landowners started to squabble— they were receiving assessments from the City for drainage improvements. The City and Seascape had arranged to split the construction bill."

"With no ground broken on the hotel, people started to wonder if it would really be built," Perry continued. "They felt like they were being asked to pay for a pipe dream."

"But there's only a small portion of the street blocked off at Land's End," Nyla said, tasting her wine.

Seth chuckled. "Yes, *now*. Four months ago that street had a center lane opened up six feet wide and half a mile long so we could get at the drain pipes. People complained we'd dug a monstrous pothole."

"Seems to me the Seascape people jumped the gun."

Perry raised his glass at Nyla. "Confidence before contracts! Seascape didn't count on the perseverance of Perry

Day Truman to keep the limestone castle intact." He looked at Seth. "Strunk still stalling on your payment?"

Another name from the crime file perked Nyla's interest.

"I got a partial payment last week, only thirty days overdue this time instead of sixty."

"Or ninety." Lucy's tone was sharp. When Seth and Perry were telling Nyla about the Seascape construction snafu, Lucy had kept her eyes on the golden oval of wine in her glass and said nothing. But her expression showed she had strong feelings about the situation.

Perry went on. "I know it's tough on you, Seth, what I'm doing about the castle. Everyone resents me for keeping the dreams of this town from coming true. Why don't they hassle James and Joyce Ruddye? They're the real villains."

"When do you think the litigation will be settled?" Nyla asked.

"Depends when the judge makes a decision. We got a fairly quick preliminary hearing but were bollixed up when the judge ordered continuance to study the wills."

Lucy stood up, drained her white wine and set the glass loudly down on the mantel. "Burnton people are chomping at the bit. Seascape is to them what Disneyland is to Anaheim. They can see dollars dancing just out of reach."

"Strunk's the ringleader, keeping things stirred up," Seth said. "I think he's behind the premature order on the drainage work. Just so people will think some progress is being made."

"He's not as heroic about the progress of paying your bill, I notice."

Perry and Seth nodded at each other.

Lucy's second entreaty, "Do we have to talk about this now?" collided with a question from Nyla, "Did Perry tell you about my story on the castle?"

No one answered. Seth looked into his empty wine glass. Lucy turned toward the mantel, her posture taut and closed off from Nyla. Perry sighed loudly. Still neither of his friends would respond.

Nyla stood up. "I'm sorry if I've made everyone uncomfortable. I realize these women were your friends and maybe you feel my interest is an intrusion."

Perry wanted to help. "I told them both you were all right, Nyla, one of us. But it's still so difficult for us, even after a year . . . "

"I know—"

"No, you *don't* know." Lucy pushed abruptly away from the fireplace, turning a furious face upon Nyla. "I'll give you my interview short and sweet. Joan used to say we pay for our passion at no small cost. She and Val paid with their lives."

Before anyone could react, the whack of the screen door echoed Lucy's exit. Perry looked mortified. Nyla wished she'd never opened her mouth. Seth seemed riveted to his glass but finally looked up at both of them.

"If it's possible, *she* took the deaths hardest of any of us. In a way, she's alone now. Close as she and I are, she's never been able to talk to me about it. I so much as mention something—even talking about the road work—she flies off the handle. I think she sees Seascape as a final burial. When the castle is gone, the ground smoothed over like nothing was ever there, and then that damned hotel going up . . . she's hurting but anger is all she can show."

When Nyla started toward the door, Perry put a hand on her arm. "Good instinct, hon, but I'd give her a minute or two."

"Let's have another glass of wine," Seth suggested.

He and Perry tried to smooth over Lucy's outburst by reminiscing about the mistresses of the limestone castle.

"Val was boisterous and Joan had grace," Seth recounted.

"Val had grace too!" Perry disputed. "What about that gorgeous neck of hers?" He touched Nyla's hand. "I coveted her neck. Joan said it was scandalous how I indulged Val's penchant for scarves. She had the ultimate collection."

"Val used to tease that Joan was quite a love poet." Seth and Perry smiled at each other.

Nyla said what came into her mind. "Anyone know what happened to her poems?"

"I suppose they're still at the castle."

Nyla questioned further, "Her kids didn't take them?"

71

"Oh my God . . ." Perry put his head in his hands. "There's no telling how they would pervert Joan's innocent poems."

"Not to mention prejudice a judge." Seth's observation made Perry groan. "Don't get too upset, old buddy." He patted Perry's arm. "But have a look for them soon."

Nyla looked toward the front door; Perry caught her expression of concern. "Go ahead."

She half-expected Lucy to be gone, but she was on the porch, watching cars round the Loop. Nyla touched the wind chimes softly.

The fury was gone from Lucy's face. She took a deep breath. "Sorry I blew my gourd in there."

"Maybe you can't believe this since I didn't know the widows, but I take their deaths personally."

Lucy didn't turn toward her. A car passed them slowly. "Reverend Rat," Lucy said, the anger gone from her voice. "Patrolling for lost souls."

"You mean Jim Hammister?"

"Uh huh. He's a squirrel."

"I thought more like a muskrat."

Lucy allowed herself a chuckle.

Nyla looked at her watch. "Almost midnight. How early does a postwoman get up?"

"Five-thirty most days."

"Is that why you were so cranky yesterday? Didn't get enough sleep?" Nyla grinned; another car scanned them with its headlights.

"You like to walk the beach at night, Nyla?"

"I think I'd like it better if I had some company."

"Fine. How about Monday after work? Meet me near the South Jetty road about five-thirty."

FIVE

The Dog Didn't Bark

A policeman's holiday—he rarely took one. All he'd ever wanted to do was go to work, catch the first whiff of burned squad room coffee, and fill his spot. When he'd made detective those many years ago in Brooklyn, the top brass had said no one else could fill a spot like he did. But now he wanted a vacation, even a few days in San Francisco, and Cohista to go with him. They'd take a leasurely drive down the coast, have some high class meals, maybe go clear to Santa Barbara to soak up some sun. He could call the Miramar Resort and reserve the Grande Scale suite; he could see again how Cohista looked in the moonlight. She reminded him of an Indian princess. Her skin was incredibly soft and white in contrast to her dark hair and eyes. It had been one helluva long time since a woman stirred him like she did.

Smiling into the mirror, he took a swipe with the razor under his chin. How would they register at the hotel? Not as Mr. and Mrs. Walter Karp, for sure. A thought struck and he let the razor drop into the soapy water. He laughed. Strunk— they could register as the James Strunks and that would give the cocky-ass Assistant D.A. a gripe to stew about for days.

Karp scratched at a spot in the mass of black chest hair on his left pectoral. He smiled at the mirror again, thinking of Cohista stepping into his arms as they glided around the Miramar ballroom to *Scheherazade.*

Then a flash of memory made him squeeze his eyes shut and grab both sides of the sink—Mindy filling up the screen with her writhing, and those men doing every vile thing to her that flesh could withstand . . .

"Honey, you better hurry." Cohista patted his waist and then rubbed her chin against his back. "How come you always lose track of time when you stay at my house?"

Karp wrenched his eyes open to bring himself back to the ordinary bathroom. Before he could turn and take her into his arms, she kissed his shoulder and left the room.

Mindy's trouble and how he'd handled it had squelched any hope for him advancing in police work. He'd gone berserk, nearly beaten the pimp to death—so he'd copped a plea within ranks, within the police brotherhood. He wasn't proud of that, but cops were no different than doctors or lawyers. You could be marked by your own and still have someone do you a favor. That favor had saved his life—the transfer from Precinct Captain in Brooklyn to this job in tiny Burnton as Chief of Police.

The sink drain made a choking sound as Karp pulled the plug to watch the water swirl away. The career change had left him like some of the ghetto buildings in Brooklyn: a sagging shell with blank windows and no life inside. Slowly, over the past ten years, he'd started to rebuild himself. When he met Cohista, he felt a motor turn over that he'd thought was on the blocks for good, and he knew things would never be as bad as when he left Brooklyn. She knew about New York—not the details, but enough. And she hadn't cooled to him just because he'd made one stupid mistake.

He scratched that spot on his pec again and gave the mirror a lopsided grin. *In just a few days, babe, it'll be you and me, sun and surf, time to ourselves.* Wiping the last of the lather off his face with a towel, he ran the back of one hand down his cheek. Smooth as a baby's butt, the way he liked it, so he wouldn't rough up his Indian princess.

His smile dissolved as quickly as it came. He remembered a little over a year ago, another time when he and Cohista were planning a trip away. They didn't get to go because the call

74

came in, a Code One homicide from the limestone castle.

Karp threw the towel at a hamper in the corner. He wasn't in the mood to have his vacation fantasies interrupted. Why did that reporter have to show up asking questions about the widows' murder? The case was closed. Karp's reflection showed him a craggy frown. She could read that file over a dozen times and still not know how that day went down.

He'd driven the Beach Loop. Over-eager to have breakfast with Cohista at the castle, he was ready early, so he took in his town. No, it wasn't like Brooklyn, like working in explosives every day. Burnton was more like bunko: a lot of routine leg-work to bust the occasional scam. He ended up out on Three Bog Road just up from the gate to the Ketcham Mill where he could watch for overloaded trucks. He worried some of the county bridges might not hold them.

The dispatcher rattled traffic reports over the one stinking channel the county allowed. Karp ran over a vague plan in his mind, a way to patch in another radio channel only his city officers could use. That would be overriding county regulations but Coquille County with one damned radio channel for city cops, sheriff, and highway patrol was ridiculous and dangerous.

His stomach growled; he bit into a chocolate-covered cranberry candy. One day they were going to find a body in one of these bogs. Just like some damned mystery story: *The Body in the Bog.*

The radio squawked to life.

"Come in CP Karp. This is sheriff's dispatch. Your Number One is on the line."

"This is Karp. Patch me over."

A high-pitched squeal jangled Karp's eardrums. Damned outmoded county squawkbox... "Steve, that you? What's up?"

"Chief, we've got a Code One up here at the widows' house."

For a moment, Karp panicked. Could Randall possibly mean Cohista? She had gone to work within the last hour...

"Double homicide, Chief, both widows stabbed. I estimate sometime about eleven last night. Someone went on a terror up here."

"Cold search?"

"Yessir. Back door wide open, no tool marks. But we got a couple good footprints."

Even though he realized Cohista was safe, Karp's heart was pounding. He coughed as he said, "Anyone getting the plates?"

"Ted's on that now, sir, he'll do the neighborhood canvass. With your okay I'm securing the scene till the coroner gets here."

"Go to it, Steve, tell Ted to be damned careful. He smudged half our latents on the last one."

"Roger, CP, I'll tell him."

"When you called North Bend was the coroner home?"

Karp suspected Bill Prather was in his usual haunt, drinking and talking cheap strategy with Jim Strunk. They had big plans to end up Oregon politicos—Strunk as D.A. and even bigger game—maybe the House, depending on how much dough he could hustle. If Strunk was in, Coroner Prather would be in too.

"No sir." Karp heard his officer take a deep breath. "He was with Jim Strunk."

"Two of the county's short pissers," Karp hissed.

"Come again, CP? Didn't copy that last."

"Never mind. What else you got, Steve?"

"This might've been a disturbed robbery. Lots of stuff strewn around the bedroom. We haven't verified anything missing yet."

Karp realized who would have to help the officers with that duty.

"Is Cohista . . . Mrs. Farrell there?"

"Yessir. She found the bodies and put in the call. She's shook up pretty bad."

"Okay, Steve, I'm coming in from Three Bog Road. Get this clear—do *not* walk her through till I get there. I want all your work done and those bodies covered before she walks, you understand?"

"Yessir, CP. Anything else?"

"Yeah, one more thing. If Strunk or Sheriff Wasser show up before I do, remember it's *your* scene, *our* jurisdiction, *I* want

76

first look before anyone else except the coroner. Rope everyone else out and I mean *everyone*."

"Gotcha, Chief."

Karp slammed the magnetic cherry top up over the driver's side window, let the yowl out of its cage, and stepped on the gas.

The first rule in approaching the scene is to slow down— Karp knew that even as his car spun gravel around the road construction barriers at the turn up to Land's End. He couldn't help it. How awful Cohista must feel. It was one thing when you'd seen death before, knew how it looked and could psych yourself. But when it was two long-time friends and a knifing at that . . . he hoped it wasn't too . . . he slowed down and scanned the front yards and the flashes of beach between houses for anyone running too fast or lounging too loose. He knew what knifings were like. He knew to expect the worst.

After fifteen years of police work, he still wasn't blasé about death. It had its levels, from the feeling of running over an animal in the street to those few queer moments before he lifted the sheet over a victim and saw how clearly they had been alive and breathing people, laughing or belching their beer or dreaming how they'd spend a million bucks if they had it. Real people stabbed, shot, bludgeoned, strangled, or a combination thereof, right in the middle of *I Love Lucy* reruns or ironing a baby's T-shirt or boiling water for tea.

When he first started homicide, he took to sucking lemons on the job, biting hard into the peel just before he took his first look at the scene. He left that habit back in Brooklyn. It wasn't the gore that bothered him but the leaving of life and the arrival of death that he couldn't stand, that raised the hair on his neck and made him chew lemons. It wasn't the idea of lifting the cold arm of a raped and strangled woman or the possibility that some nutso was still near the body and might spring out of a closet to attack him that made him swallow more than usual when he walked onto a crime scene. No, it was that simultaneous metaphysical movement in the very molecules of the air: life leaving, death arriving. The transit of the two left him angry, depressed, frustrated. Death was that awesome setting in of irreversible finality, like a great gruesome black bird squatting over the remains. Nobody saw Karp's Bird of Death—probably no one else sensed it. He only wished he knew a way to predict where it might land next so he could blast it out of the air, firing all six rounds of his .38 into the hideous thing.

Sheriff Wasser's car was already parked in the driveway next to Bill Prather's when Karp arrived; Steve's black-and-white was angled next to them. In his rear view mirror, Karp saw Officer Ted Bales leaving Loamie Newsome's house. A dog chained up next to the castle barked incessantly, stretching its chain to the limit. Knotting up his tie, Karp wondered if the North Bend crime lab van was on its way. He was scratching his pec as he went up to the front door of the limestone castle, passing into the shadows of the carriageway. He touched the wheat carving in the front door jamb. This old house had made history again.

When Karp stepped into the front entryway, the house was quiet. Then he heard Steve Randall's calm, steady voice talking with Bill Prather. A flash of light from one of the back doorways told him Steve was taking crime scene photos. He wondered where Cohista was and wished Steve hadn't left her alone, to perhaps fall prey to Jim Strunk's prying questions.

As he started down the hallway, his attention was drawn into the front tower office on his right. A bay window facing the wharf flooded the room with light. The crackle of wood had attracted him; all of Sheriff Ben Wasser's considerable girth was squashed into an antique desk chair in front of a Wooten desk in mint condition. Wasser was frowning at the desk and poking into its contents.

"Morning, Ben."

Wasser jerked in the chair. "You damned detective types always have to creep up on a man?"

The sheriff grabbed for a handkerchief in his back pocket and took a liberal swipe at his perspiring face. He jerked his head at the Wooten. "All these damned little compartments. Damned fascinating."

Karp nodded, then headed down the hall. Echoes reached him from the agitated dog outside. He could see that the guest room had been ransacked, along with a hall closet. Blankets and towels had been thrown in heaps against the wall. The open closet door blocked his view into the main bedroom where he heard Steve Randall and Bill Prather. For a moment before he joined them, he wondered if the bodies were covered. His mouth twinged involuntarily, a pucker from the lemons of the past. He saw two wastebaskets set side by side on the carpet to keep anyone from the back doorway. At the entrance to the main bedroom, he saw the footprints.

The room was a shambles. All the drawers of one bureau hung off their tracks, clothes spilling out across the bed and onto the floor. Clothes from the closet had been yanked so hard off their hangers that the metal was bowed and twisted. Near the bed on the floor, what looked like a painting had been slashed and two sides of the frame broken. A jewelry box lay upside down, its contents scattered into the clothing. Pieces of some shattered knickknack glittered on the rug.

One woman had died right in the bed, the other just out of sight of the doorway. Her violent struggle was evident from the looks of the carpet and the wall. Bill Prather, his back to Karp, was holding up part of a sheet to examine the woman on the bed. Randall adjusted the police department camera on its tripod and nodded as Karp filled the doorway.

"This is the last picture, Chief. I'll do a sketch too—a simple baseline, you think?"

"Sure. Use the back wall for your marker." Randall took another flash. Karp saw spots for a few seconds. He gestured toward the wastebaskets. "What about the footprints?"

"Any reason I can't lift the whole section of carpet, Chief? I want the lab to look at the real thing. And wait, there's more."

Karp followed Randall; they side-stepped the footprints and went out the back door. The barking dog heard them and clanked the chain loudly; Karp wondered if the animal wouldn't dislodge its doghouse and drag it to them on the attack.

In the sand just at the edge of the last cement step, Randall showed him a deep shoe impression. "Nearly perfect."

Karp nodded. "The crime lab tech on his way?"

Randall stood up over the print, staring at it, and rubbing his lower back. "Nope, he's not. Coroner Prather says the tech has the flu. He asked me to make the cast."

"Yeah, I'll bet he did." Karp and his officer stared at each other, then down the beach at the retreating tide. "Any more prints out here?"

"No. I think the killer may have fallen down the incline there. Any further tracks would be erased by the tide."

"What time was it high?"

"Probably around midnight."

"Wasser been sniffing around anywhere he doesn't belong?"

"No sir. Took one look at the footprints and backed down the hall to the other end of the house."

"That figures. Where's Strunk?" It occurred to Karp to spit but he checked himself.

"I think upstairs, sir. Or maybe still on the beach. Took a short walk for some air, he said. While Prather examined the victims."

Karp could see half a mile in either direction down the beach, and Strunk was nowhere in sight. "Well, if our killer made his way past the far end of the castle, those two have tarnished any evidence by now." Karp did spit, in disgust. "Get someone to muzzle that dog, Steve."

"Yessir."

Finally the Police Chief could think of Cohista. His jaw muscle hardened as he asked, "Where's Mrs. Farrell?"

"In the kitchen. With Seth Randolph."

"Where'd he come from?"

"She called him after she called us. He was here when I drove up. Mrs. Farrell says he's a close friend of hers and the widows'. Actually I'm glad he was here with her—he's been a comfort."

They looked at each other for a moment in unspoken communication. Then Karp headed for the kitchen. Over his shoulder he said to Randall, "Get things cleaned up. I want her to take a quick scan and then go on home."

Bill Prather had left the bedroom. Karp stood in the doorway for only a few seconds. The two mounds of white sheet were surrounded by chaos, all of it frozen in time and silent.

The silence bristled, nested in blood spatters. Karp smelled feathers, the stench of an aviary, and that bird of his shifted itself near the white mound on the bed.

Cohista was sitting at the breakfast nook counter, staring out a back window. Her hands on either side of a cold cup of coffee were limp. Seth Randolph had squeezed himself into the nook with her; one of his huge arms was draped protectively around her. He made the brightly-painted yellow nook look almost like doll furniture.

"Oh Walt." Her voice wavered and she dabbed at her eyes. Seth slid out from under the counter, smoothing down the legs of his tight jeans as he stood up—a good six inches taller than the Police Chief.

Karp usually preferred to meet a man eye-to-eye, but he averted his eyes immediately to Cohista. "Have you given any-one a statement?" His voice was gentle; it was all he could do not to take Cohista into his arms. But he had to steel himself for the next difficult job.

"Yes," she said, "to Steve Randall."

"We may have to ask you some more questions later, but for now, there's just one more thing we need. I want you to walk with me back to the bedroom and see if anything is missing."

"Oh please, Walt, no. I can't go back in there." Her eyes implored him and then a barrage of tears shook her. Karp moved immediately to hold her.

"They're . . . everything is covered up now, Cohista. Just a quick look. I'm sorry . . . it's regulations. In case whoever did this took something. It might end up important evidence. Please."

She trembled against him; he held her closer. "Easy now . . ." Karp shot a glance at Seth, who was leaning against the sink.

"You need me for anything else?" Seth asked.

Karp rocked Cohista. "No, not now. You here yesterday by any chance? See the widows at all?"

"Yeah, about four-fifteen. I brought them clams for supper. We had a quick glass of wine and then I split."

"That the last you talked to them?"

The big man shifted his weight and cleared his throat. He looked the image of an ex-tackle for the San Francisco 49ers but his voice sounded weak. "Yes."

"Anyone around to corroborate that?"

Seth's voice broke as he answered, "I've been friends with Mrs. Ruddye and Mrs. Propser for nine years."

"Just procedure, Seth. I'll probably be asking everyone in town. Were you alone for the evening?"

"I had a date."

Finally Karp's eyes flickered onto Seth's.

"If you need his name, I'll get it for you."

"Later."

Ben Wasser scrambled noisily behind Karp, who had just sent Cohista home with Officer Bales. They were headed up the stairs to the second floor.

"You think the Big Boy did it?"

"What the hell're you talking about, Ben?"

"You know, the Dennis kid. He's always poking around here. Dispatch gets a call once a week easy. We've picked him up for window peeking too many times to count, so have your boys. Maybe this time he didn't just *peek* in, he *came* in."

"Dennis is a window peeker, not a killer."

They reached the top of the staircase. Wasser was persistent. "They said that about Ray Phillips too and he slaughtered eight people in Coos Bay without blinkin' an eye." The sheriff was red-faced. He hunted his pockets for his handkerchief.

Karp told him, "I'll look into it."

Across the room, Jim Strunk was looking at a leather-bound book. Bill Prather was seated in one of the plush library chairs, smoking a cigar, flicking his ashes into a sparkling clean crystal ashtray. Strunk remarked on the book in his hand, "This is a first edition *Frankenstein* by Mary Shelley. Must be worth a fortune." He ran his finger down the gilt binding.

Karp walked into their midst. "Lo, Strunk."

"Lo, Karp. Something messy down there?"

"Very messy, lots of blood and gore. They put up quite a fight."

"Worse than Haver Square?"

Strunk's question stung Karp like Prather's cigar smoke in his nostrils. Haver Square in Brooklyn—where every river rat hustler rented rooms for hookers at ten bucks a day, and made dirty movies with runaway girls, runaways like Mindy...

"Just about."

"Well, I know you'll get right to the bottom of things." Strunk dismissed the CP by turning his back and giving his attention to the books again. Mary Shelley in hand, he said, "These homeowners appear to have excellent taste, and the money to feed it."

Karp watched him apply his fingerprints to twenty more book spines on the shelf in front of him. Then Strunk wandered past him through the open conservatory doors. "Nice plants," he mumbled, opening the doors onto the terrace beneath the blue window. He took a long look at the whole of Burnton, the wharf, the ocean. He said to the three men at his back, "Those lesbos kept this view to themselves for a long time."

Prather blew out cigar smoke. "This place is gorgeous. God, I'd like to live here."

Strunk shot the coroner a look of disdain. Prather's face went ashen. Karp thought about spitting again, somewhere very near Strunk.

Apparently oblivious to the cold bodies in the bedroom below them, the Assistant D.A. was jovial. "Well gentlemen, I hate to say it, but these deaths are opportune. Now nothing stands in the way of Seascape."

"You sure the family will sell?" Prather asked.

"Hell yes, they'll make a mint. And this town'll finally have the history it deserves."

"You so sure the family inherits?" Karp wondered aloud. Both Strunk and Prather looked at him quizzically. "Just a thought," he said. Then with a half-smile, he asked, "Say, Jim, you get to see the battleground? Blood climbing the walls like leaves on a trellis. Want a look?"

He knew he'd paid the lawyer back for the Haver Square crack when he saw Strunk blanch.

"All done, Bill?" Strunk looked worried that Karp might try to drag him downstairs for a look at the massacre.

"Sure," Prather answered. "An ambulance'll be here any

83

minute—I'll take a close look at everything back at the lab."

They started for the stairs, Strunk still carrying the book from the library. Karp cleared his throat. Strunk looked back at him. The Chief's eyes traveled to the book.

"Ho, a monster story." Strunk laughed. "Can't resist 'em."

Karp extended a hand and Strunk gave him the book. "*Frankenstein*," Karp read the title aloud. "Fiction is so much neater than real life. Your real monster was in this house last night."

The castle and the horrible death it held had seemed stopped in time to Karp, but once he left the scene, events careened to a conclusion. Randall delivered all the evidence to the crime lab and called in Prather's autopsy date. The *Beckoner* editor called to prove that Burnton's grapevine was better than the street news in Haver Square. And a concerned Reverend Hammister rang up saying he'd heard from Mitch Masters that something was amiss at the castle.

"More than amiss, Reverend." Karp gave Hammister the whole story. The Reverend was more than sorry, more than willing to help with any arrangements he could. Karp was not consoled by Hammister's comment that even violent death took souls to eternal life. He was sure the widows wouldn't have been consoled either.

He met with his officers to review the preliminary investigation. He didn't think the killer had left prints for the finding, but results of routine investigation had more than once overridden his instincts.

"Did anyone hear the dog barking? It put up one helluva racket when I was there."

Randall looked at Bales. Bales swallowed hard. "Ah . . . no one mentioned it, Chief, not in particular."

"Did you *ask* them, Ted?"

"Ah, no sir."

Karp grimaced as if he'd just had a swig of squad room coffee. "Then call 'em all back and find out, Ted."

Bales skittered out the Chief's door, heading for a telephone. "Good work on the scene," Karp praised Randall. "The way you dust prints you could be a painter."

Steve Randall's grin was self-conscious. "Thank you, sir."

"You'll file the Offense Report?"

"Yes sir. It's already—"

"Think we ought to call up the FBI M.O. file or NCIC?"

"Don't think so. This is some kind of fluke—maybe it started out as a robbery. Someone saw that back door open and stepped in . . ."

"Probably someone local. That house's always meant money around here."

"Mrs. Farrell says the widows didn't keep much cash around. So the guy gets in there, finds nothing, Mrs. Prosper surprises him, then something snaps . . ."

"And a trespassing screwball who didn't plan a murder got more than he bargained for."

They were silent, reflecting. Finally Karp said, "Maybe."

Randall dropped an envelope of black and white photos on Karp's desk. "This is nightmare material if ever I saw it."

Karp forced himself to examine the crime scene photos.

"Wonder what it feels like," Randall said.

"What?"

"That snap inside a guy to make him kill that way."

Karp slid the photos back into the envelope and scanned Bales' notes, particularly the interview with the Lighthouse Inn bartender. Seth Randolph and Reverend Hammister had played darts there, Randolph from about six to midnight. Karp wondered what had happened to his date. He'd never thought about gays being stood up like anyone else. Jim Hammister had arrived about eight and left the bar at ten, mentioned he wasn't feeling well. The bartender observed that the minister had looked pale and kept excusing himself to the men's room.

"Anyone around to confirm Hammister back at the rectory?" Karp mused aloud.

Steve Randall's eyes widened. "The *minister*, Chief?"

"Just be thorough. Check on it. And anyone strange in town—check out the rest of the taverns, especially any carloads over from North Bend or Coquille."

"Yessir. It'd be pretty quiet though, on a Wednesday night."

"I know, I know, but check on it. Hell, maybe we'll get a break. I don't like the idea of this guy stalking around scot free."

Randall watched Karp scratch his chest. "Me either, sir."

"Anything on the footprints?"

"An expert's delight, an almost perfect impression in the sand except for a faintness at the toe. Men's Adidas Flyer, size ten, moderate wear marks. Suppose we could check county shoe sales within the past . . . what? Six months or so?"

Karp rolled his eyes; he could see the stacks of paper forming in front of him. "Let's wait on that. Just put out a county request to all Evidence Clerks—for immediate check on any shoewear that comes in. Keep it in effect a couple months."

"I'll get right on that, Chief. Anything else?"

"You think there's anything to this suspicion of Wasser's about the Dennis kid?"

Randall rubbed his eyebrows and worked his shoulders as if they were tight. "I doubt it, Chief. The guy looks like trouble 'cause he's so big, but I read him harmless and leashed pretty good by his mother. Besides, there's no way his foot would fit in a size ten shoe. His toes maybe, that's about all."

They smiled; Karp's own shoulders felt like two knotted fists. "One more thing, Steve. Disturbed robbery or not, this guy is crazy and I don't want him loose in my town."

As Walter Karp stood staring into his own reflection, reality and memory were inseparable. Within the same moment, he saw his expression in the mirror and his memories of that year ago during the murder investigation. He shook his head slowly but he was rooted in that spot in his mind, hooked in that time. He saw himself standing sock-footed in front of his TV, a beer in one hand, half a roast beef sandwich in the other. The six o'clock news of that year ago was changing his expression slow-motion from tired blasé into an unbelieving grimace of disgust.

A KOVD-Portland reporter was giving a live-action telecast from the Coos Bay jail. "Almost by accident today, Assistant

D.A. James Strunk uncovered a crucial clue to the murder of two Burnton women."

Karp turned up the volume, setting the beer down without taking his eyes from the television screen.

"In fact," the reporter continued, "within a matter of hours it will be verified if the shoes taken from a dead prisoner in the Coos Bay jail match a footprint made at the Burnton crime scene." The reporter gave the facts: Strunk had been at the jail for a client's routine overnight on a DWI charge. He noticed the Evidence Clerk packaging another prisoner's belongings, including a pair of tennis shoes, which he mentioned to the clerk in connection with the Burnton slaying.

The clerk was before the camera. He stammered out his story, blinking in the brilliant camera lights. "We found a drunk in Cell Seven dead from acute alcohol poisoning. The shoes were his. After Mr. Strunk brought them to my attention, I called the county crime lab."

That first TV report had been only the beginning. When the shoes matched the footcast practically to the ridge, Strunk was front page news around the state. Then more circumstantial evidence piled up on the drunk who'd died in Cell Seven: blood type O, fresh scratch on his neck, and a statement from a Coos Bay tavern owner who reported that two men had been with the drunk in his bar the night of the murder. They'd told the owner they picked up the man around midnight on Highway 107, just outside Burnton.

Signed, sealed, and delivered: the drunk was identified as Tramp Williams, no known address except General Delivery, Burnton. No relatives inquired about his body. Coos county police conjectured that Williams had had motive and intent: the motive money and the intent robbery. He was too drunk to worry he might encounter the widows but not too drunk to go on a murderous rampage once inside the castle.

Everyone was convinced and relieved. Strunk went on TV again, telling Oregonians, "My part was a minor one, really. Just a simple reminder to one of our excellent police clerks. Thoroughness—I learned it in the Air Force and see it now as the keystone for lawyers and policemen. It paid off for us in a big way this time. A terrible injustice befell those two fine Burnton ladies. But at least we've identified their murderer."

Karp snapped off the TV set in his recollection, but he couldn't snap off his unsettled feelings—even though they were now a year old. He moved to finish dressing and get himself to work, still reflecting. He'd bought closing the case, but the package wasn't perfect for him. Ted Bales found no one—especially Loamie Newsome, the nearest neighbor and a light sleeper—who had heard the widows' dog raise a ruckus the night of the murder. For Karp, something was off about that, some reason that dog didn't let everyone for blocks know someone was in her territory.

Karp questioned several people himself— a little field work kept him from feeling like he was stuffed behind a desk. Seth Randolph recounted that his date had simply dried up on him. Karp felt queasy as the big man told him somewhat plaintively, "I cooked clams and everything. When I knew he wasn't gonna show, I called Jim Hammister. He likes to play darts over a beer or two." Karp resisted assumptions about the Reverend; ministers dealt with all kinds of people in their work for the Lord.

He'd talked to Mrs. Dennis too, and she was adamant that Ritchie was home shortly after the Reverend saw him on Land's End Road, and that she'd kept the boy in for the rest of the evening. "He may be big, but I can control my boy," she told the CP. Mrs. Dennis also confirmed that Ritchie wore such a large shoe size that she had to special-order for him.

So the dog didn't bark, Karp thought after he kissed Cohista and got behind the wheel of his army-green Impala. He'd seen lots of oddball cases solved by circumstantial evidence, many of them weirder than this. The case was closed. And yet . . . Karp reached City Hall and jammed his plastic card into the slot box to raise the security door of the parking garage. The door yawned open like a huge venetian blind, the metal folds grinding. Nyla Wade's questions were direct enough but something in her bearing belied she was searching for mere

88

background information. Karp wasn't sure what made him the most uneasy—his own constant wondering during this past year, or Nyla Wade's new interest in an old murder.

SIX

Measure for Measure

Gruff Hamilton had his feet up on his desk. He was slow sipping his coffee, staring unseeingly at the clock on the bare wall. He often used this early morning time alone to think. Today he was thinking about complaining, was on the verge of it—but Wade hadn't missed a single assignment, so he was left with only his personal feelings about this limestone castle story. She was putting together one helluva good-looking Retailer Review, better than any he'd done, she and Jean had created a bang-up layout. But that didn't pinch his ego . . . so what was nagging him? Wade's alliance with Perry Day Truman? Truman came up with unique photos from the historical society for the Retailer Review and good ideas that might draw tourists to Burnton. Still, he was the town faggot and everyone knew it. Everyone also knew he was the roadblock to Seascape and he would simply egg Nyla on to do this castle story. Wade wouldn't make herself popular as Truman's ally. A reporter had to get in doors, ask unpopular questions—so why did she load the dice against herself by picking *him* for a bosom buddy? Divorcees—who could ever figure them out? Maybe she was still healing, and Truman was certainly no threat.

He liked Nyla Wade; she had pizazz, on and off the printed

page, could give the paper what it had needed for a long time . . . He'd even be inclined, down the road, to give her pretty free rein, if only . . . Sure, she was a little more women's lib than he preferred, but no harpy.

Gruff frowned at the clock. Should he talk to her about Truman or keep his trap shut? Journalists could be hard-headed . . . *She'll just accuse me of trying to play Big Daddy. So long as she meets her deadlines and keeps me free from school board meetings, let her run after this damned castle business. What the hell harm can it do?*

Nyla awakened full of nervous energy, restless to get the day over with so that she could walk on the beach tonight with Lucy. She couldn't help over-grinning and wasn't sur-prised when a brighter sun than usual broke through Burnton's chronic grey sky. Hospital and police reports awaited her on her desk at the *Beckoner* office. She should edit the stringers' columns too and there was the Toastmaster meeting and the bike-a-thon to cover. Instead, she was slipping in and out of two-lane traffic, the rusty Mustang shaking its trunk with the upside down T on it, over the twenty miles to North Bend and the county crime lab.

Van Davidson, Coroner Prather's right-hand lab tech, liked the looks of Nyla Wade immediately. He had plenty of time to talk with her; he'd finished autopsies on the two auto fatalities and accidental drowning the county had produced over the weekend, and his morgue slabs were empty.

Nyla introduced herself. She told Davidson of her interest in the autopsy on Eugene "Tramp" Williams and asked to see the footcast made at the limestone castle. She took notes as Davidson walked her through the facility. She showed her the lab's two spectrophotometers and briefly explained tests for mass and infrared. "These make do, but you should see the equipment in the state lab."

They reached the morgue. Van said with a grin, "The spare parts department." Nyla took a look at a silver gurney just inside the door, and balked. "Relax," Davidson assured her, his grin widening, "we're not making Frankensteins in here."

She pegged him for the type who'd conceal a rubber hand that came off when you shook it.

Davidson led her. "And now, the theatre! I've always wanted to do Shakespeare in here: *All's Well that End's Well.*"

The operating theatre was bright white all around a large center-stage table. A microphone perched over the table which was a heavy metal freak's chromium dream. But it was the sink built into the table that gave Nyla a queasy twinge.

She asked, "How does Coroner Prather run this lab? Shipshape, or more on the informal side?"

"Tight as a tissue," Davidson quipped.

"May I see the Williams' autopsy report?"

As Nyla examined the file, Davidson tried to focus his attention on a tissue sample under his microscope, but his real attention was on the V-neck of Nyla Wade's shirt front. When he lifted his eyes to stare at her, she was closing the autopsy file.

"All that make sense? Probably a new slice of life for you, eh?"

She thought venomously of scalpels. "It makes sense. Anything unusual about the Williams autopsy that you recall?"

"No, just that the guy had a liver Kuners would be proud of."

"Kuners?"

"You know, the pickle company. Pickled liver, as in acute alcoholism."

"Right." She looked at her notes. "Williams was average height, weight?"

"Actually, on the small side. Pretty emaciated. Drunks have this tendency to forget eating."

"May I see the footcast now?"

Davidson decided that Nyla Wade was hot-looking but a cold fish. He retrieved the footcast Steve Randall had constructed. "This guy's technique isn't bad. Almost as good as my own."

Only professionally, Nyla thought. "What did you conclude from examining the footcast?"

"Williams came out of the house on the run so the full

imprint of the foot registered into the sand, except for this minor vagueness at the toe. Probably caused from the looseness of the surface, so the foot turned within the shoe at a slight angle and the toe lifted, changing the weight of the impression in that particular area." Davidson pointed into the piece of plaster with a pencil. "You can see the Adidas trademark perfectly, and the wear ridges. We estimate the shoe was worn less than a year."

Nyla flipped back in her notebook, then consulted the autopsy report. Even someone poor in math could spot the discrepancy.

"How many inches is a centimeter?"

"Thirty-nine hundredths of an inch."

"I assume a size ten shoe does not indicate a ten-inch foot?"

"No, a size ten's about average for a man's shoe but the foot could be longer, twelve or thirteen inches. Width is also a factor."

"Thirteen inches—would be how many centimeters?"

He reached for a calculator on his desk top. "About thirty-three centimeters."

Again Nyla checked her two sources. Then she looked Van Davidson right in the eye. "Can you explain to me how the autopsy report shows Eugene Williams with a thirty-three point seventy-seven centimeter foot length and the coroner's report to Police Chief Karp registered it at twenty-three point seventy-seven centimeters?"

Davidson blinked, recalling that week over a year ago and the murder that had made every paper in Oregon and kept him busy round the clock—first autopsies on the two widows and then on the drunk. He'd had the flu and Coroner Prather was occupied with election meetings and strategy sessions, rubbing shoulders with important politicos. "Hold down the fort, Van," Prather had told the tech, who preferred to do autopsies alone anyway, even when he was sick. Prather was a nervous cutter. He was also a borderline botcher though only Davidson had been witness to that. But Prather had had the dollars to buy a medical degree and Davidson was forever stuck as Mr. Clean-Up behind that diploma.

"Probably just a clerical error. I had the flu when those

autopsies were done and everything looked a little blurry at times."

"You did say Williams was on the smallish side. How many inches is twenty-three point seventy-seven centimeters?"

With a sigh, Davidson did the calculation. "Something a little over nine inches."

"Certainly smaller for a man's foot, yes?"

"Yes."

"Did you do the body measurements, or Coroner Prather?"

Again blinking rapidly, Davidson felt a raw spear of panic in his gut.

"Isn't it procedure, Mr. Davidson, for Coroner Prather to conduct autopsies in a murder case, with you assisting?"

Don't let me sweat, for godssakes. The thought echoed in his head. "Yeah, right, that's procedure."

Still looking at her notes, Nyla asked, "And on the Eugene Williams case, procedure was followed, wasn't it?"

The lab tech set the calculator resolutely on his desk. He inhaled slowly. "Coroner Prather double-checked all the body measurements before he signed the autopsy report."

"So which measurement is correct?"

"The smaller number. That much wasn't blurry. Williams was a little guy."

A two instead of a three, no big deal, Davidson thought. But there was a deep freeze going on around his heart. He tried to comfort himself with the unassailable fact that Williams had had on the shoes—and that irrevocably pegged him to the murder scene.

Nyla Wade smiled and said mercifully, "I guess it could be pretty easy to write down a wrong number. Flu can make you feel like your head belongs to someone else. Besides, the other three numbers in the measurement are the same."

"Yeah. I'm no crack typist healthy, much less sick."

"Me either," Nyla's generosity continued. "Was that a pretty full week?"

"I'll say—first the two women and that was grueling. Eight hours apiece easy. They were pretty messed up, I had another couple days on tests, including their clothing. Then a couple of stiffs from the Coast Guard came in, so I did the military a favor. On top of all that, Coos Bay runs in Williams and says they want him stat. Gurneys were flashing around the halls like go-carts."

"Doesn't the Coast Guard have their own medical staff?"

"Oh, sure." Davidson relaxed a bit; he enjoyed talking shop. "These two soldiers hooked onto some bootleg booze that made chop suey of their stomach lining. They were on leave and rather than ship them back to base, the C.O. got the okay for us to take a look. And we'd already reported several other deaths by alcohol poisoning in the previous two months. Probably someone had a bad still and didn't know it, or didn't care."

"Anything come of that? Didn't Williams die of the same thing?"

"Sure, but how could you tell if he bought it on bad hooch or all the years of hard drinking? Coulda been the last bottle just took him over the edge."

Davidson looked at his cuticles; if he ever got booted out of the autopsy business he could give one helluva manicure with a scalpel.

"You have any other bodies in since the Coast Guard boys on that bad booze?"

"Other stiffs with the same signs? Not that I know of."

Nyla patted the footcast, thinking of Mitch Masters and his fond pat of her scotch bottle. Then she offered Van Davidson a warm handshake.

This is why reporters do their homework, like good cops, she told herself on the return drive to Burnton. Tramp Williams' shorter foot length inside that size ten Adidas should have shown up in the footprint and the footcast—and not just with a shallow impression at the toe.

She didn't need to be an expert to know that.

Or to know if there was any way an expert could prove it, then Tramp Williams did not kill the widows.

Ben Wasser racked the frame of a canvas chair on the deck behind Jim Strunk's office. He slurped his coffee, grinning at Strunk over the cup. "Hell of a hard life you got here, Jimbo."

The Assistant D.A. glowered at the sheriff.

"What do you hear from Seascape? Anything moving?" Strunk didn't answer.

"You make a dent in that judge who's studying the wills?" Strunk set his coffee cup slowly onto its saucer. "No thanks to you. You haven't scared up anything I could use for leverage."

"I hear he's on an extended vacation in the Bahamas."

"Terrific."

"I also hear a few things around town you might like to know." Wasser's eyes sparkled. He took another slurp of coffee.

"What've you got, Ben?"

"Seems the town sissy's got himself a new pal."

"Jesus, is that all? Just gossip about that fag's latest trick? I don't know why I ever expect—"

"Hold on there, Jimbo, hold on." Wasser hauled himself out of the deck chair. Coffee cup in hand, he strolled to the end rail and leaned on it, taking in the view of the wharf.

"Well?"

"This pal is *female.*"

"Oh so what—maybe Truman's had a change of heart."

Wasser chuckled. He turned, deliberately, to face Strunk. "This female happens to be a reporter. And she's planning a big spread in the *Beckoner* about the castle."

For a moment, Strunk seemed to stop breathing, felt the color drain from his face. Then his mouth twitched up in both corners in a quirky smile. He took a hard swallow of his drink— vodka, which he drank at all hours of the day. "So . . ." he said quietly, staring into the water sloshing against the deck posts.

"Nothing but trouble, a big splash of publicity. Showing that not inch-one of ground has been broken in the Seascape construction—"

"All right, all right, I get the picture!" Strunk jerked himself up out of his chair, which clattered back and almost tipped over. His fingers gripped the vodka glass hard. He said through gritted teeth, "This town has one damned sissy too many."

Wasser grinned. "I'll agree with you there. You know he's getting other queers to sign petitions?"

Strunk drained the vodka and bit into the ice. "Maybe we ought to get a better handle on what Truman is up to."

"Interrogation?" Wasser had the look of a hound on a bone.

"Hell no, I meant a phone tap."

"Ah, the perfect job for our little friend Al."

The vodka glass banged on the aluminum deck table. "Our little friend Al is only a runt I knew in the Air Force. He was a lousy mechanic and lousier at the brothels. He's all blow, a petty burglar, three-fourths bum and one-fourth stupid. And he keeps rotten company."

"You mean Max? He's okay, he just doesn't talk much."

"That's because he's too busy guzzling beer. No, Ben, keep them out of this."

Wasser put up one hand. "Okay, okay. Relax, Jimbo." Strunk was staring out at the water again. Wasser noisily drained the last of his coffee. "How can we stop this story?"

"I don't know yet. I'll think of something."

"Maybe this reporter needs a good scare. You know dames, just something to—"

"Don't do *anything* till I give the word. We've got a sweet deal working here, but it's got a hair trigger and you know it. If we can just get that judge back, just hang on . . ."

The sheriff reached for his handkerchief. He was already wet at the back of his shirt. Strunk kept his eyes on the water and did not see the sheriff's expression, which held no respect.

"Just don't go off on your own, Ben, I'm warning you. And be damned careful setting up that phone tap."

Wasser loudly blew his nose into the handkerchief and without another word, walked off the deck.

Kay Gardner's lyrical flute drew *Mooncircles* music as Lucy Randolph dried from her shower. She hummed, swayed a little with an invisible dance partner. One hand patted lotion down a taut, well-muscled thigh. "Does her inner thigh feel just like this?" she wondered aloud. Then she closed her eyes, floating on the music, imagining touching Nyla Wade's thigh in a smooth move, her palm sliding down that leg, fingers feeling the skin's heat. *Is there a scent of powder at her neck, a spot of blush just above her collarbone?* Gardner's flute made Lucy's heart flutter; its poetry reached inside her fantasies of Nyla Wade. She took a look at herself in the mirror, ran a casual hand through her red hair. First date and every date, she always wanted to be cool. Where did other dykes *get* all that cool?

She pulled on grey Calvin Kleins pressed so crisp they snapped, and a white puff-ball jersey that fairly ached with touchability. Cool did not necessarily mean confident—but confident she at least was. *When you're not born with cool, then you fake it. Most everyone who's cool probably does that anyway* . . . "Sure they do," she said aloud, and poked at her hair one last time. "Nyla Wade," she told the mirror, "I'm gonna fake you out but good."

Nyla parked her car in front of the Old Town shop where the fashionable fisherwoman was still casting her line. At the corner by the Wharf Restaurant, she caught sight of Lucy Randolph leaning on the driftwood fence fronting South Jetty Road. She was staring out to sea, down the rough water channel of the river mouth guarded by the now blind lighthouse, as if to divine her future.

As she looked at Lucy's body leaning slack and relaxed on that fence, involuntarily Nyla drew in her breath and held it. Like surf over shore, the events of her new life were beginning to break.

Walking toward Lucy, the last traces of Gruff Hamilton's voice echoed in Nyla's thoughts. "Damned good Retailer Review you and Jean put together." And then more loudly, his bifocals perched up in his bristly hair like spyglasses on a thorn bush, "You've still got lots of stories yet to write. Be sure you keep on your toes." All huff and puff but basically a marshmallow. Just so she never let Gruff know how well she glimpsed the marshmallow, they'd be friends for a long time.

"Are you expecting a grey whale to surface?"

Lucy turned around at Nyla's comment; she barely concealed the light of welcome that burned within her. "It isn't their season yet. Not even a loner would be in these waters now."

"What about a loner on shore?"

Like a fist balling up, so did Lucy's inner defenses, but she forced herself to remember that everyone makes overtures in their own way. Indicating a bucket she'd set by the fence, she said, "I brought some champagne on ice."

"I guess I should've brought hors d'oeuvres. I thought this was just a walk on the beach."

Lucy felt a moment's panic. Was her radar off? Had she been reading Nyla Wade wrong? *Be cool, be confident . . .* "Well, I thought we could build a fire after we walk a ways."

"Good idea. Anyplace we can get hors d'oeuvres to go? I want to do my part."

You will, you will. Lucy's reawakened confident voice calmed her heart, and she smiled. "I get more thirsty than hungry when I walk."

They looked at each other. Sundown was turning the horizon the same color as Lucy's hair and Nyla Wade felt the rush of an urge to grab a handful. Lucy's eyes traveled toward the tidelands. "Shall we?"

They rolled up their pant legs and carried their shoes; the water flirted with their ankles. The beach without strangers felt like an intimate place. The waning sun made light and cloud-etched designs like the eye of an agate.

For the first time since her arrival, Nyla could enjoy the beach at her leisure. She loved the rock formations, some sitting like giant stalagmites near shore. Farther out, rock jutting from the frothy water reminded her of a giant monster dipping its neck into the waves; four other smaller rocks close together had the triangular shapes of sails.

"Val used to swim out to that one big rock." Lucy's voice was soft as the grey clouds over the sea. "Made Joan nervous, but Val was stubborn. So she swam and Joan did needlepoint. Joan claimed to fear undertow; Val said what Joan really feared was her having a sexy mermaid stashed out at that rock."

Near a huge log, Lucy piled driftwood and started a fire. Wind blew in off the water and gusted in bursts that shadowed around the back of their log and stretched out the flame like a torch, a long orange finger of fire on the beach.

The firelight eased awkwardness; Nyla told Lucy about her

100

Minneapolis girlhood and her Denver wifehood. Lucy told about her father deserting the family when she was an infant, her mother dying when she was six, she and Seth being raised by an aunt in New Jersey. "This is no sob story, though," Lucy assured her. "My Aunt Lyde was cast in the same mold as Druscilla Ketcham, with enough moxy to be mother and father. You know how big Seth is—Aunt Lyde can make him quake in his boots."

They stared into the fire. Nyla asked, "What do you notice about a person first?" She had already given Lucy the answer to her own question: eyes were what she noticed in people. Now she probed Lucy's with her own.

Lucy felt the night closing around them and she wanted to take Nyla Wade into her arms before she knew the risk of such a move. "As for people generic, I notice their overall impression first, what kind of energy comes from them. With women, I admit the first shot of them I want is from behind. I'm a tush lover."

Nyla felt herself blush and hoped Lucy couldn't see that in the firelight. Finally someone to appreciate her own supple cheeks . . .

"All that roundness is irresistible to me. I can sit in airports or shopping centers for hours, just to watch those soft, sensuous seats going by."

Nyla's breath deserted her. Lucy smiled and took a slow drink of champagne. "They're so beautiful, especially by candlelight."

Nyla took a deep breath and nervously changed the subject, not wanting to admit her own lustful response to Lucy's rear view. "I've been thinking about the Girl Group mysteries ever since you mentioned them. I wish we had a contemporary version."

"Oh, we do. The Motor Girls and the Flying Girls grew up to be *Charlie's Angels*. TV simply gave the Girl Group T and A."

Nyla couldn't help laughing at Lucy's comment. Once she dropped her hostile veneer, the redhead had a good sense of humor, even a welcoming personality.

"Lucy, I know I upset you by mentioning my limestone

castle story, but I need to talk about it, and not just about the story—about the whole situation."

When Lucy didn't respond, Nyla put a hand on her arm. "I've read the case file and been to the crime lab. I'm no cop but things don't add up. There's no one else I can talk to except Perry." She had drawn Lucy's eyes to her own. "I'd like to have your help, too."

Lucy pitched a smooth stone into the darkness. "Well, I guess I can listen."

Nyla told her about the preliminary investigation notes, the fingerprint elimination report which included Seth's name, the question about the dog. And then her discovery of the error in measurement of Tramp Williams' foot. When she finished, they were both quiet. The fire crackled between them as their eyes held.

Lucy asked thoughtfully, "How did Tramp Williams get those shoes? And if he didn't make that footprint . . ." Nyla watched Lucy come to her own conclusion. "Then he didn't kill the widows."

"We'll need proof, an expert to examine the footcast. And we've got to find out more about Tramp Williams."

Lucy stood up and walked to the edge of the firelight shadows where she stared out at the black water. "You know, it amazes me how this world works. Imagine Karp and his cops suspecting Seth. Just because he's big and gay. It's all so typical and so maddening." She turned back to Nyla. "At the memorial services Jim Hammister organized, Seth and I were the only ones grieving for Joan and Val. For everyone else, it was a sensational circus. The only thing missing were the two caskets side by side.

"I got there late and couldn't find Seth. I stood at the back of the church. People were whispering but I heard enough, all their little homophobic lies about my two friends. It was like . . ." Her voice held tears. "Like everyone was *relieved*. The lesbians were gone and with them so were everyone's fears."

Lucy shook her head. "I found Seth out by his truck, just sagging up against it and staring into space. Neither of us could believe what was happening. What's *still* happening—this whole town wants to level that ground, build over that memory, forget it all.''

Nyla stood up and came close to Lucy. ''I don't want to forget those women. And I don't want this town to forget, especially if part of what they want buried are unanswered questions about this murder.''

Lucy took Nyla's hand. ''Oh, Nyla, don't you see? First we have to find the answers. Then convince anyone to listen. Then go up against the whole Seascape project. If this town didn't listen when two lesbians were brutally murdered, why would they listen now?''

''Because *these* lesbians are *alive*.'' Nyla gripped Lucy's hands with both her own. ''We'll find the answers and won't give up until someone does listen. Perry and Seth will help us. Four against the world, remember? And we *can* beat the odds.''

Lucy moved away to throw another piece of driftwood onto the fire. Studying the flames, her back to Nyla, she said, ''Straights wouldn't believe how wide a net we have to catch each other. Gays in every walk of life.'' The new wood ignited, popping sparks. ''Too bad our net didn't help ole Tramp.''

Nyla thought again of the black-haired sonnet writer and her poem about casting out a net. ''Think there's a gay footwear specialist in that wide net?''

Lucy grinned and Nyla was glad to see it. ''Seth knows this gay beat cop—''

''We've got to do it on the sly, though.''

''Seth will know what to do.'' She warned, ''You're going to open old wounds if you're right about Tramp Williams. You won't win any friends this way.''

''What if a murderer is still walking around this town?''

''How are you going to find out more about Tramp?''

It was Nyla's turn to smile. ''I think I've got an idea.''

Lucy brushed off her grey slacks; again she stared at the sea, as if it could wash up answers in silver-green strands of kelp. Nyla felt a need like wave action, the need to be held, to have arms around her and right now—Lucy's. Without hesitation, she walked closer to Lucy, so that their shoulders touched.

Lucy's profile glowed warm in the firelight. "You're a muckraker, Wade, face it. You've got a Mickey Spillane heart underneath a Doris Day facade."

In the next moment that sizzled like the heat of the fire, whether or not she knew it, Lucy Randolph was coolness-plus. Her eyes locked with Nyla's; one hand slipped around Nyla's waist and with a gentle jerk, she pulled the breathless Nyla to her. Her lips moved over Nyla's face toward her lips without hurry, testing, teasing. Lucy heard Nyla's small sound when their lips finally touched, when she flicked a hint of her tongue into that willing openness.

Spirals of plaster in the ceiling of her room at Shady Stay wound like a nautilus. Nyla's thoughts wound the same path. She lay unable to dress, unable to sleep. The spirals multiplied, tonight a million miles from her first kiss with Sara when they had chased down the mystery of Mrs. Porter's letters together, and farther still from the sonnet writer fantasies. A million miles in only two steps across the sand to close the gap between them—she could still smell Lucy's cologne. She traced her lips with her fingertip and remembered that urgent tug of Lucy's arms, the whole hot feeling of their two bodies touching.

The jangle of the phone was so unexpected that Nyla's heart pounded into panic and memories returned of phone calls in Denver, from strangers probing her life, calls meant to scare her.

"Nyla, this is Perry." The sound of a friend's voice slowed her racing pulse. "Sorry if I woke you, but I had to talk to you. I've been thinking about Joan's poems. I wanted to go look for them but . . . I'm just too nervous about it, it doesn't feel right to be pawing about in their privacy. I've been walking the beach all night worrying about it. Will you go with me, Nyla? Will you help me look?"

"Of course, Perry. Of course I will."

After the phone call, Nyla's thoughts wound in reverse direction within the ceiling spirals, Perry in them now—visions of him frantically chasing after fluttering pieces of paper, white squares of lesbian love poetry born away on a tidal wave. Echoing behind his frenzied chase was Cora Corona's warning—*He trusts the water spirits too much. He should watch out for sneaker waves.*

SEVEN

Casting Out the Net

As she drove to the castle, Nyla relished the muted yellow of the morning's cold sun. Perry was already there waiting for her on the porch, doing what everyone in this town seemed to do with their silent time—staring out to sea.

"Sure you don't mind helping me with this?" he asked, opening her car door.

"Of course not, but listen, time is short this morning. I've got to talk to Gruff before he's too wide awake." As they went into the castle, she told him about her visit to the crime lab and her idea for an article on Tramp Williams that had come to her when she was with Lucy.

Why so many people coming to the house? The brain behind Ritchie Dennis's blank face burned, working overtime on simplicity. *Weren't they all dead that lived there? Who would come to live there now?* He watched from his concealed place, his eyes focused on the doghouse. *No more dog—too bad.* The dog was better than the people even though she barked at him. He had watched her all his life he could remember, her voice was music.

Again his brain struggled, stumbled into a span of vacant memory, that night when he got so close, finally close to the doghouse. *No barking, was she sleeping?* He could reach out and touch her silky fur and never wake her, but forever feel against his fingers those silky ears. And then she wasn't there, so he looked into the window to see if she was inside the house. Only sleeping there were the two women. And then the person dressed like darkness had scared him by walking so softly up from the beach. Ritchie had plastered himself up against the side of the house so the person wouldn't see him; he almost cried, he was so scared. He sweated himself wet through his shirt until he could run away without falling, without slipping in the gravel on the road. *Maybe the person has the dog. Or Hide Hans.* Ritchie never went where Hide Hans lived because he was too scared.

Why so many people come to the house now? Will they bring another dog? There was no light in his eyes above the smile on his face that watched, faithfully.

Loamie Newsome watched too, from behind her screen door, as the cars drove into the castle driveway: first Cohista Farrell, then Perry Day Truman, and finally a young woman she didn't recognize. She felt entitled to keep watch on the castle, even though Cohista had been appointed by the court as trustee. Now with the house vacant, some of those high school kids might get funny ideas, might vandalize the place. And of course the Seascape folks were coming and going with no one to tell them anything. Loamie knew where she was needed.

She strolled out to her front fence and leaned in between the pickets. Staring at the castle, she remembered her dear friend, Joan Ruddye—a sweeter soul she'd never known. But even though Joan called the castle home, it was still ole Dru Ketcham's house. Dru Ketcham may have been rich, but she was an old maid. The blue window was something to see but Loamie would never choose to surround herself with stone—it held the creeping damp. She shook her head at the huge house. "A dry woman in a damp house," she said aloud.

As she looked the other direction down the road, she halfway expected to see what she'd seen so many times: Joan and Val returning after Val's swim and walking close together

108

as if they'd been holding hands. Sometimes they did; Loamie knew this and other things about them. A close neighbor sees things, hears things. I'm no snoop, she told herself, I was their neighbor and friend—well, *Joan's* at least.

Joan always led, her head of coarse grey hair appearing first above the line of the road. Loamie had heard Valerie tease Joan about her hair, call her "sweet bush" in that quieter tone of hers, when she would call softly to Joan on the porch in the evenings. They were a Mutt and Jeff, with Joan only reaching to Valerie's shoulder. Joan was compact, fleshy in the arms and hips. Valerie was lean and athletic, with small flat hips and long in the torso, fading into arms on the thin side and almost no bust. Her hair was the color of sand, swept back over her ears with tendril curls down her neck. Neither had showed her age or worried about too much sun and sea. At fifty-two, Joan had been Loamie's daily delight. At forty-eight, Valerie was a tolerable presence. She had come with Joan like a package deal and so you had to put up with her.

Loamie blinked rapidly, remembering that last day. She'd been at the fence as usual, waiting to greet them and balancing a plate of freshly-baked oatmeal cookies. They came up the road. Valerie was carrying her flippers; Joan had her basket of needlepoint. They were laughing.

"Baked some cookies," Loamie had called out to them. To this day she could remember their surprise that the cookies were for Val, offered without any sarcasm. Loamie had known it was a special day for them and to please Joan, she'd baked Valerie the cookies.

Someone else was coming up Land's End Road now, and not the widows' ghosts. Cora Corona was carrying her thongs as usual. "Waiting for the mailman to bring you your fortune?" Cora grinned.

Loamie answered irritably. "Phooey. Those contests are all rigged." She stared over at the castle.

Cora noticed the blue Saab. "Life back in that place again?"

"Something going on," Loamie answered. "First Cohista, then Perry, then some woman I don't know."

From Loamie's description, Cora concluded that the woman was the reporter she'd met on the beach.

109

"She sound like anyone you know?" Loamie squinted one eye at Cora.

"No one I know," Cora answered, staring at the blue car again.

Cohista had pulled the shutters back to bring light to the hallway. When Perry called to her, she answered from the dining hall. He and Nyla found her dusting the huge table. Perry explained their visit. It was obvious to Nyla that he was still struggling with a sense of trespass.

"We want to look for . . . for some poems Joan wrote to Val. They were very private and . . . well, not the sort of thing her children should get hold of."

"Do you know what they took after the funeral?" Nyla asked.

Cohista kept rubbing her dust rag against the shiny wood of the table as she reflected. Perry gave a heavy sigh.

"This looks like all one table, doesn't it?" he said nervously to Nyla. "Actually, it's five interlocking pieces, called a butterfly cut." His eyes darted to Nyla and then Cohista. "All the hardware ingeniously hidden on the underside." With another sigh, he said directly to Cohista, "Would I be right in assuming they grabbed whatever they could convert to cash? Furs, small antiques, silver, crystal?"

Cohista nodded. "They didn't bother her desk much. There was a family safety deposit box they had their own keys to. Joan didn't have a box for just herself."

"Or with Val?"

"No."

Cohista had always liked Perry. He was polite whenever he came to the castle, always asked about her as if he were really interested. He was being polite now too, considerate of her feelings even though she knew about Joan's poetry and the kind of love it reflected. It pained her to see him so distressed. "Where should we look? I'll help in any way I can."

Perry rubbed his eyes. "Nyla can only stay a short time so we'll make it quick. I guess we can check the office, upstairs—skip the guest room, you think?"

"Cohista . . ." Nyla put a hand on Perry's shoulder. "Will

110

you be around later this afternoon? I could come by after work and then we could really give the place a going-over."

Cohista smiled, passing the dust rag from hand to hand. "Surely. I could arrange that."

Perry took a deep breath and then sighed loudly, his gratitude obvious. "Thanks, both of you."

As the three searched the office, Nyla had the constant feeling that someone was watching—maybe just the lingering strong spirit of Dru Ketcham. She was certain the poems were not among the folders of correspondence, the bank account statements, the corporate reports of Ketcham Enterprises. She knelt between the sections of the Wooten and slid back one glass compartment to reveal a small white shell. Perry came over to her, touching the shell as if it were a sacred relic, a discovered bone. "This room is full of poetry," he said, "just not what we're looking for."

Upstairs they separated. Perry made a quick check of the library shelves while Cohista went to the music room. In the conservatory, Nyla was immediately surrounded again by the peculiar wooing of the green plants and the blue window. There was only one closet in this room where anything might be secreted, but before she opened it, she couldn't resist stepping through the terrace doors to see morning from this exalted view.

Morning rarely burst in Burnton; the sea kept a grey cap of clouds over the town. Nyla drew in the moist air, felt revived by the chill on her skin. She noticed two huge chairs on the terrace. One was formed of a massive ebonized frame with a gold-patterned seat cover. Nyla leaned closer—the arm rests were carved into gilt winged sphinxes with round pointing breasts and flared wings nubby in sculpted wood. The other chair was even more dramatically unique—busts of Cleopatra were carved into the curve of each arm rest with ormulu mounts. A sensual artist had rendered the Egyptian queen in cherry wood, from her golden layered crown to her full inviting lips. For the first time, as Nyla stood before the regal chairs and saw the complete panorama of Burnton from the terrace, she knew the full extent of Druscilla Ketcham's realm.

"Molly sat with the sphinxes, but for Dru, it was Cleopatra."

Nyla whirled at Lucy's voice; the postwoman stood at the terrace doors.

"But then, you figured that about Dru Ketcham yourself," Lucy added.

They looked at each other, last night's firelight tryst lingering between them. Nyla could feel Lucy kissing her again. Lucy walked to the stone railing, ran one hand through her red hair as she passed Nyla. "More fog tonight, I bet."

Nyla wasn't breathing. She imagined Lucy with a cascade of red hair falling across her face, and her hands ached to reach up and part that curtain, find the face, find that mouth . . .

"You like fog, Nyla?"

Nyla's answer came only within herself. *Only if it is not just another barrier I have to peel back to find you.*

When Lucy looked over her shoulder at Nyla, she realized that her new friend was staring at her without seeing. She liked Nyla's small waist, the shoulders slightly angled. She touched the tip of her tongue to her lips, the same way she wanted to trace Nyla's jawline, her neck . . .

"You find anything in the closet?" Perry's question to them was accompanied by a wide grin.

"I haven't looked yet." Nyla wondered if she was blushing.

"I caught her sightseeing." Lucy noticed Nyla blushing, and stuffed her hands self-consciously into her blue postwoman's pants.

If Perry had intended to tease them, he changed his mind. "Well then, let's look."

They followed him back into the conservatory and watched over his shoulder as he opened the closet door. The four shelves were stuffed with completed needlepoint designs still in their frames. Lucy ran her hand down one stack of frames, picking up a small round canvas embroidered with a seagull.

"Every stitch done in love, Joan always said."

Folks still feel safe in Burnton. Ben Wasser had seen Perry Day Truman leave, and he easily tripped the lock on his back door. *You'd think this type would go for deadbolts considering what goes on behind their closed doors.* Wasser walked through the living room to the telephone. *All this pink, a damned sissy color.* He unscrewed the mouthpiece, then jingled the coins in one pocket to retrieve a disk microphone about the size of a quarter which he dropped into the receiver. After he wiped the phone with his handkerchief, he wandered cautiously to the bedroom but stopped just within the doorway. *Damned waterbeds, no way to get any leverage. Wallow around like a bad boat ride.* He blew his nose. He squatted down trying to see the bottom of the bed frame. *Probably got some torture stuff stashed somewhere.*

As he let himself out again, the lock clicked back into place. He took a sloppy swipe at the door handle with the handkerchief. "Slick," he said aloud, grinning. "People are too damned trusting."

It was seven-thirty. Nyla hoped no one would be in the *Beckoner* office this early so that she could muster strategy to approach Gruff. What worried her was offering a reward for information about Tramp Williams. All she had in the bank was a hundred bucks, which seemed hardly enough. Where could she get more dough? Could she pay a reward in installments? She didn't think so, and when she saw Gruff already pacing up and down in front of the coffee pot, she didn't think she had a chance with her idea, either.

He was growling before she had her coat off. "You lose track of your calendar, Wade? We got a deadline today and you haven't touched the stringer columns yet. Jean's got an aunt sick so I need you on layout." He glared at her and then at the clock.

She took a deep breath, hoped Walter Peistermeister wasn't wrong about her, hoped that though Gruff Hamilton might try he would certainly fail to munch her up in one angry bite. "I'll get to the stringer columns in a sec. Let me tell you what I found out at the North Bend crime lab."

"The what?" Hamilton snapped.

Nyla ignored his snarl and gave him the facts about the foot measurement error. Before he could offer any resistance, she went on to explain her idea about an article on Tramp Williams. He was yanking his glasses off when she added that a reward might help collect information.

"You amaze me," he said, inspecting her from head to toe. "You find nothin' more than a typo on a report and you're ready to reopen a murder case. You're a reporter, Nyla Wade, not a detective, and no matter what they taught you in school, those *aren't* one and the same." He combed his bristly hair with nervous hands. "Have you been to the police?"

She shook her head. "I wanted to talk to you first."

He paced and frowned. He didn't like her idea, he told her. It hadn't been researched, was based on a guess. She was obsessed with this castle business and needed to get over it pronto. She should take her suspicions to the police who would no doubt decide she had nothing new except criticism for Van Davidson's clerical ability.

"Suppose I can get an expert to look at the footcast. Williams' foot was too small to make that kind of a footprint, Gruff, I know it. I have a gut feeling."

The editor's pause affirmed to Nyla that he might not trust guesses, but he respected gut feelings.

"Get me something concrete and we'll see."

"But why can't we find out something about Williams while I find an expert? All I want is information—where he came from, how long he lived here, who he saw that night. What about the two guys the tavern owner said he was with? Where are they and why didn't they talk to anyone?"

"The police may be thick but they aren't stupid, Nyla. You've already been snooping in their crime file and asking everyone in town about the castle. You run this reward thing and they'll start a file on *you.*"

Nyla squared her shoulders. "Let them. We have a right to get some information about a man who may have been falsely accused of murder. We don't have to say we think that in this article. We just say we want information and we'll pay a hundred bucks for it. We can use a blind p.o. box."

Gruff moved closer to her, too short to tower over her but intense enough to make her uncomfortable. "I'll tell you what we'll get for that article. A lot of damned complaints for our lousy timing. It's tourist season, you know. No one wants to be reminded of murder."

"Bury it on page sixteen. Put it with the cartoons. Better yet, the classifieds."

Hamilton smiled with his mouth, but his eyes held warning. "Too late. Deadline's noon."

She persevered. "I'll meet it *and* get the stringers ready *and* help you with layout. It's just information, Gruff, not an accusation that anyone screwed up."

He had half an inclination to chew her out but good—harangue her about his years of newspaper savvy stacked up against her inexperience concluded by his strong personal opinion that academia didn't prepare real writers. He didn't say any of it because Nyla Wade was a reporter of much promise who just might prove him wrong. Slowly he lowered his glasses onto his nose.

"I don't think you can find out enough to get a decent piece together in four hours."

Nyla knew he was weakening. "But if I *do*, you'll run it, right? With a picture?"

Gruff nodded. She went on, "What about the reward?" He just shook his head, checked the wall clock, and said, "Three hours, fifty-seven minutes and counting." He started shifting the piles of paper burying his desk as Nyla got her coat on. As she went to the door, he said from behind his stacks, "You need a bigger reward. Five hundred bucks at least."

"Where am I gonna get it?"

"Whatsamatter, Wade? You never heard of petty cash?"

"If you want to know what comes in with the tide . . ." Nyla remembered Cora Corona as she drove toward Neptune's Nook. Tramp Williams was as much a part of the beach as driftwood and floats—Cora Corona would know something about him. Nyla took the curve in the Loop and a truck honked at her. They both slowed and she coasted to the side of the road. The truck pulled a three-point turn; Seth Randolph rolled down his window as he came alongside her car.

116

"Lucy told me you want to cast out our net."

"Snare us a footwear expert. You think there's one out there?"

Seth worked his hands on the steering wheel. "Sure."

"We'll have to be coy, though. Soon enough I'll agitate someone by looking into the castle and the murder. We'll soon see who."

"You really think Tramp Williams might be innocent? Just from that error in the autopsy report?"

"I think we better be damn sure he was guilty. That little typo meant his foot was too small to make the print and our expert will help prove that. If Tramp Williams didn't kill the widows, someone else who did is walking free."

Seth stared down the road a moment, revved the truck. "Should be a helluva story."

His expression as he looked back at her was not accusing; Nyla saw that he wanted reassurance.

"Yeah, it may turn into one fantastic story. And even better, we'll lock up the maniac who killed your friends. I didn't have to know them as well as you did to want justice for them."

He looked directly at her, his ruddy face serious but accepting. Then he nodded, scooted up in the seat of the truck, gave a thumbs-up sign. "I'll put out the word."

As she drove on, she was excited about getting the story on Tramp Williams, and she hoped working on the layout wouldn't make her late for her search with Cohista. She wondered about Joan Ruddye's poems. Suddenly, one of her mother's warnings from childhood echoed in her thoughts: *Never put anything on paper you wouldn't want the world to see.* It seemed a shame that reveries written to a beloved could become a weapon—like Billy Jean King's letters to Marilyn Barnett. How different the public outcry about that relationship, compared to the public's indifference and denial of the love letters shared between Eleanor Roosevelt and Lorena Hickok. Whatever the jeopardy, it seemed there were always those few who took the risk to write each other their hearts. But that was another story. As was Nyla Wade's philosophy that hiding few secrets from the world was the best defense.

A row boat full of driftwood was land-locked forever near the front door of Neptune's Nook. Inside the shop was a house-sized version of Mitch Masters' work bench. Every possible type and color of shell was displayed, along with Cora's burgeoning float collection. The owner was not in sight when Nyla came through the door, and so she stood at the counter casually sifting through pieces of pink and yellow coral collected in an oyster shell. She remembered that Saturday would be Tony's birthday, and she scanned the jumble of the shop, wondering what sea collectible Audrey Louise's youngest son might like.

"I'm back at the scope," Cora Corona called from another room. Nyla found her standing on a crate, aiming her telescope toward the south jetty and slowly panning the tidelands with the long cylinder. She looked up at Nyla. "Wanna have a look?"

"I was admiring your float collection."

"I'm running out of room in my net. Still, they don't come in but maybe two or three a year. You have to keep alert or you'll miss 'em. Lotsa other beach pickers got scopes too."

They both heard the sound of the door opening in the other room and a hoarse voice call, "Cora? You got any hot coffee?" Loamie Newsome quickly found the two of them at the scope.

Although she was somewhat dismayed to have her time with Cora interrupted, Nyla decided to plunge ahead. She introduced herself to Loamie. "I'm writing a feature on the limestone castle before Seascape tears it down."

"*If* they tear it down," Loamie grumped.

"You think there's a chance they won't?"

"Depends who's more stubborn—Perry Day Truman or the Ruddyes and Seascape and Jim Strunk. I'd bet on Strunk. He's a dark horse but a steady runner." Loamie slurped her coffee resolutely.

"I know about the terrible murder at the castle."

Neither of the women would look at Nyla. She went on, "Still, I'm not convinced the best way to bury everything is to destroy such beauty." She persevered in the silence. "Cora's of the opinion I shouldn't dredge up the murder. I won't if I don't have to. What do you think, Loamie?"

"I know vengeance is the Lord's, but I'm glad Tramp Williams died. He robbed me of a dear friend."

"Did you know Tramp Williams?"

"We all knew him," Cora answered for Loamie. "Beach brine he was, lived out of garbage cans and whatever castoffs he could beg from the churches."

"They fed him down at the fish market sometimes but booze was what he wanted. He'd bother folks in the street for money."

"Was he a Burnton native? Did he have other family here?"

"Not that I know of," Loamie was firm. "And I know just about everyone in this town."

Cora didn't add anything further about Williams. Nyla was disappointed. "Did the police interview you?" she asked the two women.

Loamie answered quickly. "Oh sure, all about who I saw come to the house that evening and about the dog. She just didn't make a peep all night or I'd have heard. I sleep like the princess on the pea—every little thing brings me right to. I didn't live next to the widows for nine years without a sense developing. Whenever I heard or saw anything unusual, I went to check."

Unable to learn anything further about Tramp Williams, Nyla decided to explore what Loamie and Cora knew about the murder.

"Did anything unusual happen that night?"

Loamie told her, "Seth came by early in the evening, the Reverend came by later. Then Ritchie Dennis was on the road bothering the dog. We all shooed him off."

"Was Ritchie around a lot?"

"He was a damned nuisance." Loamie's eyes flared. "Always trying to pet the dog no matter how many times Joan reasoned with him. She let that boy way too close to her. He's not right, you know. I keep a broom handy on the porch in case I have to whack him."

Cora shook her head at Nyla; her eyes danced with amusement.

119

"But did Ritchie actually get into the house? Or too near the dog? Or anything?"

"Naw. Maybe once in a while when no one was home, he'd peek in the windows. I never trusted him. He could fall on you by accident and crush your bones."

Cora chuckled; Loamie squinted at her. "What're you laughing at? You never get close enough to anything to know what I say's the truth. Always glued to that damned scope of yours."

"You can still see what goes on in the world whether you're close in or not. You saw who was around the *night* of the murder. I saw who was around the next day."

Cora's remark caught Nyla's interest. "With the telescope? Who did you see?"

Cora gave Loamie a so-there look. "The cops had a couple of kibbitzers. Mitch Masters was hunched up in his niche down in the rocks. Then the Reverend came up the beach on his morning trek."

"The Hamster, Val called him." Loamie offered her information proudly.

"Don't gossip, Loamie," Cora reprimanded her.

"Don't tell me what to do, Cora."

"The minister kept close to the surf," Cora continued, ignoring Loamie. "Watching it come in and stopping every now and then to look out to sea. His arthritis musta been acting up cuz he was limping. As for Mitch, he was probably holding court with some sea ghosts."

"Crazy old buzzard," Loamie said. "You know he's a cheesafrantic?"

Nyla looked at her, puzzled. Loamie touched the side of her head. "Cracked, an incurable." She continued eagerly, "There was a spooky moon the night of the murder, too. Maybe we all shoulda known something bad would happen. Cloud moon, Valerie called it. Her husband was some kinda speed boat racer and he said cloud moon was bad luck. Sure was right."

"Do you know why the Reverend came by the house that night?" Nyla asked.

Cora shrugged. Loamie said, "He was always trying to get them into church. He'd of had better luck if he was the Fuller

Brush man, if you ask me. But Joan was polite. She didn't call him any names like Val did."

Nyla checked her watch. She had to get back to the office and do the stringer columns. She'd have to fudge the article about Williams unless someone at one of the churches who'd donated clothes to him could tell her more. "I certainly appreciate you ladies talking with me."

The three moved from the telescope room back into the front shop.

"What do you think a nine-year old boy would like for his birthday?" Nyla asked Cora.

The older woman brightened. With a finger to her lips, she sorted through her own chaos and selected a spined blowfish, varnished and mounted on a gold rod. The fish made Nyla want to laugh—it looked like a water cactus with eyes.

"Great. I'll take it." She turned to Loamie who was watching the two of them. "Say, Loamie, what about you and Seascape? Your house is closest to the castle. Have they made you an offer too?"

Loamie straightened her back, smoothed her dress.

"I don't mean to pry," Nyla cajoled. "I just wondered if you're as upset as everyone else in town about the castle preventing Seascape development. Seems like everyone stands to make some good money if the thing goes in."

"Maybe." Loamie said slowly, "I'll sell if the castle comes down. And I'll sell if Perry Day Truman moves into it or turns it into something . . ." She was eye-to-eye with Nyla. "Into something *peculiar*. Otherwise, I'll stay put."

"The castle comes down, you'll be smack dab in the middle of the Seascape tract," Cora said. "You stand to have them make you an offer good enough for a new house in Hawayah, a trip around the world, and then some. Do you good to travel, Loamie." There was a wicked smile on Cora Corona's face.

"Don't tell me what would do me good!"

"Interesting phone calls I'm getting this morning," Chief Karp told Steve Randall. They both stared at the dregs of their first cup of squad room coffee.

121

"Trouble?"

Randall was too serious, Karp often thought. He needed a girlfriend. "I don't think so. Just curiosity. And mighty quick communications around town. Say Steve, what about Nyla Wade? She reminded me a lot of the girl in that picture on your desk."

"She does look a lot like Jacqueline."

"Seemed pretty nice to me. Sharp too. Maybe you should see if there's anything you can assist her with, see if she needs to check records again. You know, do your policeman's civic service."

Randall grinned and nodded, keeping his eyes on the grey caffeine sludge that fueled him all day.

When Steve left his office, the Chief dropped the venetian blinds for a little privacy. He leaned back in his chair, and propped his feet on his desk. First Bill Prather had called, all chuckles and nonchalance about a typo in the report on Eugene Williams' autopsy. The report should have read the measurement of Williams' foot at 33.77 centimeters; the tech was a lousy typist and he'd had the flu, and if folks remembered last year and all the autopsies scheduled then, they knew things had been hectic. It seemed a pretty innocent, honest mistake. A corrected copy would be in the mail this very day. Then, before the Chief even had time to alert records, the mayor had called wanting to know why Nyla Wade was so damned interested in a case-closed murder. The Chief had assured the mayor that Ms. Wade was strictly on a homework assignment. Did that warrant her snooping in police files and bothering county crime lab employees? Karp was most intrigued that he had heard from the mayor, not Coroner Prather, about Nyla Wade's visit to Van Davidson. Karp rocked slightly in his chair; though the bird of death had eventually flown the castle, there were still feathers being ruffled over what had happened in that house.

As he dialed Jim Strunk's office, Bill Prather rubbed his stomach. The other line was ringing. His stomach pain seemed to keep rhythm. "Jim? Bill Prather here."

"What's up, Bill? Don't tell me you want me to ride out on

another call with you. Those things are getting a little hairy, even for an old war vet like me."

"Naw, Jim, no corpse call today." Prather took a deep breath and let it out silently. The pain thrummed just below his belt line. "Uh, Jim, I just wanted to let you know about something." Again he paused, licking his lips. "We had a visitor over at the crime lab."

"Who was it? Someone mistake you boys for the Parts Department?"

Prather grimaced and pushed one hand against his gut as he heard Strunk's harsh laugh.

"It was a reporter from the *Beckoner.*" The coroner glanced at the note Van Davidson had given him. "Her name is Nyla Wade."

Strunk was silent. Prather held his breath. Finally the Assistant D.A. asked, "There isn't anything for her to find over there, is there, Bill? I mean, the case is wrapped, isn't it?"

Prather's mind reeled back to a conversation he'd had with Strunk at a cocktail party over a year ago. The party was a celebration for Jim Strunk's future with the Democratic powers of Coquille County. Amidst the revelry, Bill Prather took the man of the hour aside.

"Something's a little off," he told Strunk.

The party-goers were loud and rambunctious so Strunk steered Prather into his darkened den. "What do you mean, Bill?"

"On the autopsy report. Something's a little off."

Strunk balled up the lapel of Prather's blazer in his fist. "Off? What do you mean, off? This is our trip to the Capitol, Bill. Nothing can be off, even a little."

Prather remembered Strunk breathing hard whisky and harder warning into his face. Now over the telephone, Strunk's silence made him feel that same sense of warning.

"Yeah, the case is wrapped, Jim," Prather said, feeling the defeat of his own lie. "Hell, I never shoulda bothered you."

As the coroner hung up, his stomach burned and he wasn't sure what he needed—an antacid or a stiff drink. *Something* to convince him Nyla Wade didn't know all his secrets.

123

EIGHT

The Warning

Nyla struck paydirt with the receptionist at the Methodist church. Tramp Williams had been a regular recipient of the church's clothing drives and at least once a week he'd eaten free at fellowship suppers. There was a brother in Portland, she thought, but he'd passed away. Maybe there was more family there. She guessed Tramp had lived in Burnton as long as she had, about twenty years.

Nyla didn't have time to track down possible relatives of Williams in Portland, and she was worried Gruff would renege on their agreement. But she was heartened to find he'd dug out the *Beckoner* file of previous stories on the murder, including Tramp's picture and the little information gleaned at the time of his death: he'd worked sporadically around Burnton as a cook, janitor, and finally at the fish market.

Though the owner of the market was out of town, Nyla got his assistant on the phone. The man told her Williams had swept the store out occasionally but had often used the broom as much to steady himself as for sweeping.

Nyla examined the picture, the booking photo taken when Williams was jailed in Coos Bay. The years of drinking showed in his haggard face. Though his age was estimated at only forty-three, he looked much older.

Hamilton's opinion of her article showed in his expression. But the story was short, and with the cropped photo of Williams, fit perfectly at the bottom of the classifieds.

"This layout saved your butt," Gruff told her.

They finished around five o'clock and Nyla raced to the castle to meet Cohista.

Loose pebbles scattered and fell over the bluff at Ritchie's back when he shifted his feet. His legs were a little stiff from sitting in his special spot where he could see the castle but no one could see him. He'd gone home for lunch and then come back with a pocket full of fritos and two apples. As he ate the snacks, he forgot to worry that his mother would yell about the road dust on his new pants. He could only remember one thing at a time and now he was watching the castle.

He knew the housekeeper, but not her visitor. The woman who opened her car door just now was familiar but he couldn't remember where he'd seen her. He stared hard, leaning forward, his hip sliding against gravel. Frowning, he tried to remember, and felt that nagging buzz inside his head. Who was she? Why did she walk so fast into the house before he could get a good look at her? The low glow of an idea cleared away his frown.

Silky ears, close enough to touch those silky ears . . . He could try to get that close again and see who the visitor was.

Nyla and Cohista Farrell searched the castle thoroughly. Sundown was coming quickly and they turned on every light in the place. Nyla tried to think where she herself would hide the poems—even reaching down inside huge vases and knocking at bookcases for a hollow spot. Cohista squeezed into the special pantries off the dining hall in case Joan Ruddye had reasoned no one would think to look for love poetry among the table cloths. Room by room they searched, snapping off the lights one by one behind them.

"Guess there's only one room left," Nyla finally said.

Cohista went quite pale. Then she wiped her eyes and took a deep breath. "All day I've been remembering that morning. Just like always, I took my walk from home, Loamie was out by her fence and Dobro was waiting for me, wagging her tail

126

and shaking her chain. She was a good watchdog and not everyone's best friend. Being with the widows, of course, I was one of her few buddies. Oddly enough, so was Mitch Masters." Cohista smiled. "It irked Loamie that Dobro barked at her."

Nyla smiled back, encouraging Cohista's reminiscence.

"We talked about the spooky moon—right out of a ghost story. Loamie told me that moon always brought out the crazies. Ritchie Dennis in particular, bothering the dog again. She bet he could break the back on a cow, and I teased her, told her she ought to call the sheriff for some protection." Cohista looked anxiously down the hall. "We thought the widows must be sleeping late because they were usually out early when it was warm enough for Val to swim. We both knew the evening before had been special for them." Cohista let a direct but swift look pass to Nyla. "I let Dobro in. I went to the kitchen, saw they'd boiled clams."

Cohista paused, then gestured as she spoke. "I remember pulling back the kitchen window curtain and being surprised by the calm surf. I was sure that spooky moon was forecast of a freak storm. All of a sudden . . ." Cohista's eyes widened as she relived her memory. "I felt this warm hairy weight spread up against the back of my legs. The sensation was so queer that I dropped the clam pot with a loud clatter into the sink. Of course it was Dobro up against me. She whined. She was staring at the door to the dining hall and . . ." Cohista hesitated. "I knew something must be wrong because she'd left a trail of urine on the tile."

Nyla was startled when Cohista began to walk slowly down the darkening hallway.

"I had this terrible lurch in my stomach, maybe there'd been a prowler or something. Then I remembered one time the Bodey's tomcat got in the back door and planted himself right in the middle of Joan and Val's bed . . . I told myself that was it. I tried to get her to come with me to check, but she wouldn't budge. It was all I could do to push her away from my legs. Everything looked fine in the dining room and down this hallway until I got . . ."

Cohista stopped at the linen closet and opened the door.

Nyla could see that the view into the bedroom was blocked by the open door.

"I got to this closet and there were blankets and pillow cases pulled out of it onto the floor. I felt how cold it was at this end of the house and realized the back door was wide open. It was then I got really scared."

Cohista's eyes filled with tears. She wiped them away. "I called out to the widows. I prayed there was an explanation for the closet. I prayed that damned tomcat was all that had the dog upset. Then . . ."

As if re-enacting the moment of discovery nearly a year ago, Cohista slowly pushed the closet door shut.

"A pool of sunlight fell over the carpet there." She pointed. "And then I saw them. My heart stopped. Those footprints in blood."

Cohista stood rooted in the spot just steps away from the bedroom doorway, even though now there was only grey, quiet air in that shuttered room.

"Shall I search by myself?" Nyla asked. "I could do that."

"No, I'll help," she said quietly. She and Nyla walked slowly into the room Joan and Val had shared.

Nyla looked around the room, tidy and placid, the unique sleigh bed part of absolute order—the blue bedspread with matching bed ruffle, the blue-on-white vase, the blue-capped Hummel boy sitting on a lace doily. There was no hint of the chaos described in the police file, no hint that death and ghosts held court in this place.

Gingerly, Cohista patted down cashmere sweaters in one drawer, lingerie in another. When she opened the drawer that held Val's collection of scarves, she lingered, picked up several. Meanwhile Nyla scoured every box in the closet, finding only shoes, hats, purses. When she pushed back the hangers in the closet, she found the broken picture frame with its carefully folded flaps of slashed canvas. She pulled the entire bundle out of the closet and unrolled it across the sleigh bed. She took an involuntary step backward. So unexpected was this confrontation with the portrait of a nude, so poignant the subject's expression that Nyla felt the color drain from her face. "Who is this?"

"Oh my," Cohista gasped.

Both women stared. Finally Cohista touched the bouquet of flowers painted in the nude's hand. "Rhodies," she mumbled, and then told Nyla, "This is Valerie Prosper."

Nyla noticed the scarf Cohista held. "The one who collected scarves? Perry mentioned that."

"Yes." Cohista didn't take her eyes off the portrait. "She'd worn one that day. The police asked me about it since no scarf was found in the bedclothes but there were some fibers present. She had two of a particular white scarf, but one had some tiny holes in it, moth damage. She often forgot which was which— Joan reminded her more than once to discard it. She must have, because I only found one in her drawer."

They both looked at the white scarf again, Nyla realizing that Valerie Prosper must have put it neatly away only a short time before she died.

"This is such a glorious painting," Nyla said, running her finger down the edge of one flap of canvas. She muttered to herself, "I wonder if it can be repaired?"

"Guess we came up empty-handed." Cohista helped roll the canvas back up and shut the closet's sliding doors. "Perry will be disappointed."

"Do you think Joan's kids have the poems?"

"No, I don't. If they did, they'd have spilled the beans by now. Who knows—maybe Joan destroyed them to avoid just this problem." Cohista looked at her watch. "Oh my, I'm late. I'm cooking dinner for a special friend." She smiled as she walked from Nyla. "Just pull the front door closed when you go. And one last thing—be sure to close the window in the office. Sometimes gulls get curious—one might come right in to join you."

Nyla went up to the conservatory to sit in the Cleopatra chair on the terrace. With the blue window at her back she watched the sun die its ritual death in the sea. As if she could hear the last sizzle of orange edge sliding underwater, she sighed in sadness that the widows no longer shared their precious view, that someone had so viciously slashed Val's portrait, that poor Cohista had had to find her friends murdered. She thought about Lucy and Seth at the memorial service, their grief interrupted by gossip; and Perry, having lost his own parents because of his gayness and then losing these close friends . . .

The rising moon was no cloud moon, no spooky-faced oval that could hide the secrets of murders-to-be. But it was not a bright moon either, more like a pale sigh. Darkness rolled in from all sides, over the town, over the ocean. Even the cobalt blue of the window blinked out with nightfall. She had not turned on a light in the library, and only a thread of moonlight helped her find her way back. The entire second floor of the castle stretched out before her in darkness. The vision of a knife flashing, brutally slicing the portrait, made her breath falter. Ghosts pushed against her as she found a switch and the relief of illumination.

She realized she'd left no lights on downstairs either. She remembered that the office door was directly catty-corner to the stairs, so she took a deep breath and pushed through the blackness down the staircase, a hand outstretched toward the office doorway. She cracked her knuckles against wood.

"Ouch!" Her voice echoed eerily down the hallway. She fumbled to the Wooten and found a desk lamp near the open window; it brought a small glow of light into the room. Something flapped outside the window, and she jumped heart-still at the croaky caw of a seagull. "Damn!" she yelled, banging into one of the rattan chairs and nearly toppling over it. "It's only a damned seagull, Nyla Wade. Get yourself together."

Before she could pull the window shut to keep the gull out of the house, a barrage of loud thumps banged against the windows across the hall. When she stepped back into the hallway near the front door, another pummeling thundered against the driveway side of the house. Her heart pounded in terror, her mind begged her legs to run right out the front door. Images from Cohista's walk to horrible discovery down the hallway haunted her. Then her mind argued that there were no ghosts, and there was an explanation for the strange sounds. Though she was panting like a fullback, she forced herself toward Joan and Val's bedroom.

When the first rock had hit and banged against window glass, he was hunched down near the back window and the doghouse. Ritchie couldn't believe it. It had happened to him again. Just like before, when he'd wanted to touch the dog's silky ears. This time he'd just wanted to see the woman's face. The rocks continued to fly. He scrambled onto the back porch on his hands and knees, tearing his flesh through his pants. Stones ricocheted in the pitch black night, and he was once again plastered up against the coldness of the castle. His eyes were wide with terror; his breath squeaked out of him.

Nyla inched across the darkened room. A stone cracked against the window pane and she jerked as if it had hit her. Another volley of rocks clattered off the limestone bricks; someone was throwing them in a fury. Nyla pushed closer to the pane, lifting the edge of a translucent curtain. The darkness revealed nothing. Rocks rained against the house. A stone hit the window again, the pane cracked. Nyla's hand flew up to cover her face and she felt a sprinkle of slivered glass.

Pounding from the front door resounded like a cannon. Muffled yelling echoed from the other end of the house.

"Nyla, let me in!" someone was shouting.

The pounding stopped, the barrage of rocks ceased. Running footsteps crunched in the gravel driveway but still she could not move from her spot. Part of her was melting into the wall, in this bedroom where murder had occurred. She wanted to call out, "Help! Before I disappear into these limestone bricks, before I faint forever into this stone!" But she could not. Nor could she tell that her own hand was bleeding.

Cursing the dead batteries in her flashlight and slipping on the gravel, Lucy ran past Nyla's car in the driveway. The footsteps ahead were quick, then gone. Whoever had been stoning the castle had made it to the beach steps and sprinted off before she could catch up. Lucy turned, breathing hard in the inky night. Suddenly someone else was breathing hard near her. She swung the flashlight in a circle, crashing it against flesh.

"No hurt! Not throw! Broham nishmon dogma, not me!"

Arms slashed out wildly, flinging first the flashlight far out

131

over the slope to the beach and then in one bear-like swipe, Lucy, who slid backwards into the gravel, her skin peeling against the stones. Gritting her teeth against the pain, she heard her attacker grunt away into the tunnel of blackness.

Nyla crept down the hall, her steps leaden, dragging herself in the silence toward the front of the house, toward the glow of the desk lamp . . . only to have her stomach twist in fear again when she realized that the lamp was no longer switched on, the front office and the entire first floor of the castle were dark.

The front door shook again with urgent pounding. Nyla recognized Lucy's voice, felt her knees go weak. Only a few steps to fling open that door and fall into Lucy's arms. Then she heard a sound—like someone shifting around against the office furniture.

She was drowning in the darkness and fear. Lucy was inches away. She rushed past the office doorway, a hand reaching out for the front door lock. Something surrounded her head with soft beating. She smelled salt and brine and the stench of wet feathers. The bird cawed and flapped away against one of the walls.

"Oh God, oh God," she kept repeating, her fingers almost too stiff to free the front door lock. Lucy immediately wrapped Nyla in her arms.

"Easy, babe, it's okay now. Easy."

"What the hell's going on in here?" A flashlight beam blinded them. Nyla and Lucy squinted at Sheriff Wasser. "I saw a light up here. You girls having trouble?"

A noise near them made Wasser shift his light—the dazed gull was flapping feebly against the fireplace.

Nyla shouted, "How did that bird get in here? Nearly scared me to death! Who was throwing those rocks? And how did you . . ."

"Hold it, hold it," Lucy tried to calm her. "Sheriff, shine your beam over here."

Wasser obliged with his flashlight. An arm still around Nyla, Lucy walked her to the office and found the wall switch, Sheriff Wasser's huge frame behind them. Nyla gasped. They all stared. On the desk top just under the open window was a mound of chopped fish, oozing a crimson trail down over the white Chinese letters in the open Wooten.

"I just can't believe it," Nyla said as Lucy drove the Mustang back toward Shady Stay.

Before they had left the castle Lucy had told Sheriff Wasser someone had decked her in the driveway and he'd had a look all around the house. "Guess you oughta get those fish cleared away." He'd wrinkled his nose and given them an odd, quick smile. Lucy had dispensed with the odorous fish and set the gull free.

"Did you see anyone?" The Mustang's lights cut through the night.

"No, but that wall of a person I ran into was not the same one throwing the rocks. 'Broham nishmon dogma,' he said. Then I went flying."

"Maybe that wall of a person was the one who dumped the fish in the window. It's a cinch the rock thrower couldn't have done both at the same time."

They drove around the curve of the Loop. The Mustang headlights scanned the front of Shady Stay.

"Whoever dumped the fish just wanted to lure the gull into the house to scare you, Nyla. It was a warning."

"It worked. I'm plenty scared."

She would have held Nyla against her to dissipate some of the fear if only the damned car didn't have bucket seats. "Are you plenty warned?" Lucy asked.

Nyla shivered at the thought of that moment in the cold castle hallway when she couldn't see the office lamp light. "I'm warned." Her voice was filled with resentment at whoever had decided Nyla Wade *needed* a warning.

"Yeah, but I'm betting you're not warned *enough*. You're onto something, Nyla, and besides that shamus heart of yours, there's a bulldog inside you too."

Nyla didn't reply.

"Tell me I'm wrong," Lucy persisted as she parked at the motel.

"Tell me you want to come to my room for a drink."

133

Nyla slammed the car door and headed inside.

"What can I fix you?" She had only scotch but couldn't think about hostessing now. The room that had seemed too small and cramped before felt cozy and safe compared to the castle.

"Gimme a double smash of loudmouth."

She had meant to make Nyla laugh. "Smash of loudmouth," she explained. "Bogie used to say it. Never mind—it means scotch and water."

Nyla ran the tap for a splash of cold water—Lucy could smell the drink halfway across the room. Nyla's hand shook when she gave Lucy the glass; she downed her own. Lucy rubbed one hip; she was beginning to feel her own scraped spots. Nyla finally noticed the dried blood on her own hand from two sharp scratches made by the broken glass.

"Oh hell." Nyla's tears swelled and spilled. She put her head down; Lucy took her into her arms.

"Take it easy. It's okay now. Let it all out. You're safe but you've had one helluva night."

Gently Lucy commandeered them to the bed. Nyla held onto her urgently, sobbing quietly against her neck.

A flame flicked in Lucy's stomach. *Keep your mind on comfort here, Randolph.* Nyla's breath against her made her heart hammer. Their lips brushed when she shifted her shoulder and Nyla held on tighter. Lucy wiped away the tears.

"I was so scared, until I heard you on the other side of the door . . ."

"All I could think of was breaking it down to get to you . . ."

Nyla hung onto Lucy so tightly she could barely breathe. She rocked her and after awhile, the scotch and Lucy's warmth let Nyla sleep, still in Lucy's arms.

Four a.m. The clock on the bureau showed its red eye of time when Nyla wakened. Not out of nightmares but from a familiar sense—another body shifting with her own, their warm profiles spooning. She rolled over to find Lucy awake too.

"I couldn't . . ." she started to say.

"Sleep," Lucy answered.

As Nyla touched Lucy's face and her lips, she noticed a new bandage.

"You bandaged my hand."

"It was the least I could do."

"How did you happen to show up at the castle? Just in time to—"

"After last night at the beach, I couldn't stay away. Didn't find your car here or Perry's so naturally I tooled by the castle and . . ."

They were quiet a moment. Nyla could feel the softness of Lucy's bare leg against her own.

"You undressed me."

"You were cooperative."

They smiled, their faces close. Nyla scooted even closer, kissed Lucy's hair. Lucy whispered into her ear, the breath tingling Nyla's neck: "Was I presumptuous?"

"Am I?" Nyla asked, her eager fingertips touching, her fervent lips seeking. With the same energy that had flared into fear hours before, Nyla pulled Lucy to her. Breath panted no longer from chasing footsteps in the night but from the chase of comfort into passion. They shared hungry urgent reaches for each other, moaned as loud as the pounding surf, took the gentle wild slide of loving across sheets and karma, fingers grasping at whispers and handfuls of hair and nipples and dreams.

NINE

A Reticent Reverend

Less than an hour after the new lovers fell asleep in each other's arms, Lucy had to rouse herself from their warmth for her postal delivery. Nyla didn't waken completely but turned to offer a sleepy kiss and hold onto Lucy's hand insistently. Lucy grinned and shook her head. In sleep and love as well as fear that bulldog spirit inside Nyla Wade prevailed. And Lucy didn't want to let go either—so she dressed clumsily in the cold air of the room, all the while keeping their connection. She kissed each of Nyla's fingers gently as she finally uncurled the soft holding of their two hands so that she could go. She left a quickly scrawled note on the dash of the Mustang before she jogged off into the foggy dawn.

When Nyla did awaken well past the time she was expected at work, she barely remembered Lucy's parting and felt a little grumpy that her bed now held only a ghost. Then she smiled, rolled into the covers and breathed in the fragrance of their loving, hugged her knees up around a pillow just like it was Lucy. *Tonight again I want her with me, want to fill myself with her secrets.* Nyla followed the ceiling spirals a moment and then found herself grinning. *I'm going to count her freckles, each and every one.* As she headed for the shower, she took with her sumptuous visions of Lucy Randolph's freckled flanks parading just for her.

Mitch Masters ran his hand through Dobro's black hair. The dog's eyes were shut, her body slack and content. Mitch stared at the newspaper and couldn't believe it. Muttering to himself, he held the newspaper closer. Yes, that was him all right—he'd seen this picture before when they'd claimed Tramp was a killer, said he had on shoes that had tracked blood from the widows' house. The old man narrowed his eyes, kept petting the dog. He stared around his shack as if he were sorting the layers of the air, the waves sent from the brotherhood. "Ricks," he said to himself, frowning and tapping one leg. "Ricks."

The danger and excitement of the previous evening so pre-occupied Nyla that she didn't even ring Mitch for her coffee fix. Would Gruff get wind of the warning to her and nix any further efforts on the castle story? Even though she was late today, they had this week's issue wrapped, so maybe he'd keep his lectures to himself. Still she rushed as she headed down the hallway toward her car, and her injured hand throbbed. Out the open back door she glimpsed the peculiar sight of Mitch Masters stirring a huge, boiling cauldron like one of MacBeth's witches.

He stirred placidly, then shuffled over to his workbench as he talked to himself, nodding.

"Good morning," she said, walking near the pot to get a look at his brew. Masters' protective dog started a ruckus from inside the lean-to but was quickly silenced. The old man looked at Nyla as if they were meeting for the first time; he stared hard into her eyes.

No, I'm not a blue, I'm an agent, she almost said. She gestured toward the pot boiling over the fire and resisted an urge to ask when it would be soup.

"You want some coffee?" He went so far as to motion an invitation inside the lean-to. Nyla looked at her watch. "Just take a minute," he added. He was not the social type— she wondered if he might have something to tell her. She

followed him, bending down so as not to hit the top of the askew door frame.

Mitch shushed the irritable dog under a cot full of rumpled blankets where a pan of grey socks was soaking in a murky puddle. On a three-drawer bureau a clock was stopped at 2:00; a fan, its innards swathed in black electrical tape, the blades facing the wall, was running with a purr.

Mitch brought Nyla her steaming coffee. He looked at the fan a moment. "Fans break up a wave, see, keep a room clear. You can't believe how full they can get of old waves." Slowly he sank into a chair; instantly the dog was at his knee, pushing gently with her black nose. The old man petted her as he spoke. "My wife's been dead more'n thirty-five years. Got two daughters back in Kansas. I had a boy but I hardly seen him since birth. I hear he drinks."

Mitch sipped his coffee with noisy enjoyment, then reached into a pocket of his battered sweater and peeled two crumbling cookies out of a wad of kleenex. As he handed one to Nyla, he said, "The blues switched baskets on me when my boy was born so the one I got isn't really my son. He's what you call a double, a trick of the brotherhood."

Nyla was surprised at how good the cookie tasted. She smiled at Mitch and let the coffee revive her.

"Them girls of mine are all right. They send me a little money every month." Mitch leaned closer to Nyla, cupping his gloved hands around the coffee mug. "This hasn't been a good year for water. I kept back off the shore, didn't fish ner nothin'. Didn't get into a bathtub either—you don't know when they'll hook onto you and drown you—right there, naked, in your own home."

He nodded resolutely. "A month ago they shot a wave on me that made me pour out two pails of blue water from my left ankle. The men down at the hardware store read that water just like writing. Whatever they saw was clear as words to them." The old man giggled and rubbed his ankle. "Left me sore a few days, though."

"Did you go to a doctor?"

"Doctors don't know nuthin', especially about the tricks of the brotherhood. Might as well find me a witch as a doctor."

140

He nodded again, and rocked slightly in his chair. "This week the wave hooked on me and sounded like a twenty-two caliber rifle shot when it hit. Made me act out what they call the Rose Canyon. I had two black lights in my back. They used one here and one in Phoenix. It burned both my hands and up one side of my neck. When it left me, it went out with a flash like a comet, right out my thumb in what they call the Iron Worm. I work my hands every day. Have to, to keep everything loose." He scanned the lean-to, eyes searching for the invisible waves. He looked at his fan. "I don't walk on any electrical wires. But I do work with motors. To run interference with the waves."

Nyla wondered how much of his stories made any sense. If only she could translate.

Masters stood up and rummaged in his bureau. She could see clothes mashed into one small drawer and the two others filled with wrenches, motor parts, pieces of wire, sawed-off hammer handles. He retrieved a small box of Tide and shuffled toward the door. Nyla followed him to discover he was not cooking anything edible—the cauldron was a rudimentary washing machine. He added the soap, stirred, and spoke again. "Back in Kansas, my friend Barry Flick and I played baseball. He was pitcher and I was catcher. We made quite a team. Coulda gone into it for money, us two. But I got the whooping cough. Stripped one side of my throat and left me deaf in this ear." Masters touched his left ear and kept on stirring his clothes. "Barry and me always liked a little schnapps after a game. Him and Tramp was alike that way."

Nyla's attention stirred. "Tramp? You mean Tramp Williams?"

Mitch nodded. "We had a little schnapps now and again."

Nyla almost spilled her coffee in her excitement. "Did you happen to see Tramp the night the widows were murdered?"

The old man's eyes glazed. He stirred his clothes in the boiling water and said softly, "He was with me."

Nyla wanted to grab hold of him but resisted. "Where? Where were the two of you?"

"Down on the beach. Just after sundown."

"Drinking schnapps? How long did you drink together?

141

Did he leave you? Or were the two of you together most of the night? Do you know what time it was when he left? Did he say where he was going?"

Mitch frowned at her, ignoring her questions. "When I worked on the plumbing that day, I looked up and saw something, now. She was there, see, at the window and she pointed her finger just like this." The old man moved his finger in a row making six stabs in the air. "The magician's touch, they call it. In just a minute, the magic room appeared." Masters giggled, bobbing his head in jerky movements.

Nyla could see that he was gone, back into that peculiar perception all his own.

"It's a door coming out of a sparkler, see, just like the Fourth of July. Lights dance all around, some with magician's blood in it. That was a door I never tried to open. I kept as far from it as I could and I never told anyone that I'd seen the one put the touch on. I just kept my lips tight shut."

He clamped down on his dentures to demonstrate his vow of silence. She was exasperated; what would it take to get him to talk more about Tramp and the night of the murder?

"Which widow was it?" She took a stab at his own story line. "You know, which one put on the magician's touch?"

Masters answered immediately, "The light haired one, Mrs. Prosper." He seemed uninterested in talking more about Tramp Williams. Time pressed Nyla; she stood up to go and Mitch said, "The minister don't believe a word I say. But he never saw the magic room. I might have shown him that morning except for the wave that hooks the guilty."

Nyla thought about Cora Corona telling her she'd seen Masters and Hammister on the beach that morning . . . Mitch giggled, talking to himself again. Nyla desperately wished she could see into his memory of that morning.

"Did you see the minister? Was Tramp still with you?"

Masters' eyes roamed visions of another world. Then he settled a look upon Nyla's bandaged hand. "I was in my spot early. Tramp and me tried to have a fire that night but the wind was blowing. The minister was tossing pebbles. I seen the spray of sand and stood up." Mitch's giggle bubbled out and his eyes glowed. "Surprised him good, I did." He shook his head and kicked at one of the driftwood logs under his cauldron. "He knew me but that smile of his was fake. He said I'm out for my morning walk, there's usually no one else around. I told him today there is." Mitch's head bobbed—he might well have been reading the surface of the water covering his laundry as if there were words on it, the story of that day a year ago. "I pointed to the castle. He walked around the rocks and saw the police up there. I told him I thought someone was dead. He didn't act surprised. I told him about the wave. He gave me that fake smile." Mitch looked directly at Nyla. "He didn't believe me but he didn't want to go up to that house either. He went off down the beach in the other direction."

Mitch gave his attention back to the boiling laundry, using his stir stick to pull up a mottled pair of long johns. He inspected them, then plopped them back into the water. "Ricks," he mumbled.

Nyla, closer still to the old man, looked into the pot. "But what about Tramp Williams? Was he still with you the next morning when you saw the minister?"

Mitch didn't answer. He just stirred his big kettle. Nyla wanted to shake him but she was sure he'd fracture into a million brittle shards and the dog would surely tear her to pieces if she touched him. Masters surprised her.

"He was gone by then."

Nyla couldn't hold back her excitement. "Do you remember when he left, what time it was? Was he planning to meet anyone?"

Masters leaned on the stir stick and squinted his eyes. He looked Nyla up and down, finally focusing on her bandaged hand again. "Does that hurt much?" She shook her head. Then the old man told her, "He left when the moon was coming down." He looked up into the sky. "Sometimes you can see it in daylight. Or maybe that's a trick too. Mirrors. The brotherhood," he giggled.

Nyla knew she must leave but as she turned to go, Dobro stood up immediately and let out a barrage of fierce barks. Even when Mitch yelled at her, she wouldn't be silenced. He had to leave his laundry and get hold of her collar before

Nyla could be on her way. At the door she looked back but Masters wasn't watching her; he was staring toward the incline to the beach. He said, "The Reverend went the other direction that day."

Nyla found Lucy's note on her car:
"At daybreak I'm stricken with a strange malady—
Five digit Fever for sorting zip codes. Hated to
leave you, doll face. Please keep all your digits
warm for me. Lunch at Amelia's? Noon."

As Nyla came into the office, Gruff was chewing with a vengeance on the eraser of his blue pencil. He didn't say a word, just slowly pushed his glasses up into his hair and watched her every move. She took off her coat and fussed with papers on her desk to avoid his eyes. The phone rang continuously but he didn't touch it, the ringing echoing back into the press room until Jean threw open the door and yelled, "Someone get the damn phone!"

"*You* get it!" he yelled back. "We're in conference!"

She slammed the door. Nyla heard the press whine down to a stop. The telephone went silent.

"Folks're not so happy this morning about my blurb on Tramp Williams," Gruff told her.

Nyla was afraid to eye the coffee pot. She asked tenuously, "Complaints?"

"By the bushel. I've talked to people this morning I didn't even know still lived here. You'd think I ran a damned nudie centerfold."

"What were they saying?"

"Just what I predicted. We have bad timing. We're threatening tourist trade. No one wants to think about murder just weeks from cranberry harvest. Williams is buried and should stay that way."

Nyla shrugged, knowing not to quote any righteous spiel about the right of the press to ferret out the truth.

"It gets better, Hot Shot," he went on. "Three people called to cancel their subs. The mayor was the least polite."

"The mayor? What's his beef?"

"Tourists fill city coffers, city coffers pay Adam Hall's salary, fund his programs. You might say he has a vested interest. He suggested I'd lost my touch for choosing what to print."

Gruff's sarcasm bruised her. She knew the mayor's remarks, even the mayor of a three-hick town, must have stung this three-generation newspaperman. But she still believed the article was for a good cause, no matter who flapped about it. "I'm sorry you're taking the rap for this, Gruff—"

"No risks taken, no results netted. It'll blow over. Besides, I want to see if this cockamamie idea of yours comes to anything."

"What if it doesn't?"

"I'll hang you out to dry."

"And if it does?"

Gruff and Nyla looked at each other. The editor's frown faded and the hint of a smile flickered across his lips. "Then I'll still probably . . ." They finished the sentence together, ". . . hang you out to dry." Nyla was smiling and Gruff was shaking his head. "In the meantime, there's work for you to do. Go talk to Reverend Hammister about his missionary tour to the Holy Land. And football practice at Burnton High School has started. I want your best coverage on both."

Gruff scribbled off the particulars for Nyla, who sank back into her chair. She wanted to relate what Mitch had told her about Tramp Williams, but he was upset enough. Evidence from town crazies might convince him she was crazy too. Soon her thoughts weren't anywhere near Tramp Williams, the Wailing Wall, or the chunky bun parade of adolescent halfbacks. Her mind looked ahead instead to the evening with Lucy, and she almost hummed aloud the song in her brain, about what the mailman can't deliver except personally, personally . . .

As Nyla was leaving the office to head to the Episcopal Church, Perry jerked the brakes on his blue Saab and pulled up next to the Mustang. He was all atwitter. "Lucy told me about last night at the castle. Dead fish and someone stoning the house? I couldn't believe my ears! How's your hand?"

"It throbs a little."

His cheeks were flushed. "Maybe this idea of yours about Tramp Williams isn't something you should pursue alone." He dabbed at his scalp with a pink handkerchief. Nyla patted his arm.

"I'm fine, really. I'm just mad someone would scare me like that."

"Lucy told me." He frowned.

"She told you I'm part bulldog—right?"

He smiled and touched Nyla's arm. "It's a very classy bulldog, all silver gleaming fur with teeth sharp and gnashy!"

She gave him a kiss on that irresistible tanned cheek. "It's an honor to be worried about by you, sir. I only wish I'd come up with our booty. Cohista thinks maybe Joan destroyed those poems."

Perry reacted with a look of horror. "Oh no, she *couldn't* do that! She told me how difficult it was to express her feelings on paper, such a great risk. Besides, Val would never allow her to destroy them."

"Maybe she didn't tell Val."

"They had no secrets from each other."

Nyla felt a stirring in her heart; some day she hoped to be that close to a lover. "Any nooks in the attic or loose stones in the cellar? Storage places? Trusted friends she might give them to?"

"I've wracked my brain. My lawyer's putting in a call to the Ruddye's lawyer, get some hint if they have the poems or not. I hope . . . oh God, they could make something decent and private into such a sordid mess." Perry brushed his hand across his eyes and Nyla felt a clear rush of emotion for him, a wish to hold him till all his troubles melted away.

"We'll be with you through it all." Nyla gripped Perry's hands for a moment in hers. "Whatever happens, you know Lucy and Seth and I are behind you all the way."

Perry's green eyes misted. Then he took a deep breath and told her, "Well, we may get some help. I've been on the phone all morning with Howard Penn of the Gay Historical Society. Oh Nyla, it's so exciting! Howard helped me get my petitions signed. We have about fifteen thousand signatures now. *Any way . . .*" He mopped his moistened brow again.

146

"The National Gay Task Force has a meeting at the White House with a liaison to the President and they've offered to bring up the castle and show our petitions. Isn't that fantastic!"

Nyla nodded eagerly. Despite the litigation and the threat to the castle and the lost poems, something was going right.

"I have the petitions now, but Howard's going to pick them up on his way to Portland. Then before we know it, they'll be in Washington. Who knows? Burnton might find itself on the six o'clock national news!"

"Perry, this is great, just great!" Nyla grabbed him for a hug.

"Oh, I forgot." He reached into his car and handed Nyla a book. "Since you liked my manuscript so much, I thought you might like this too. Out of Joan's private library." The book was *Pioneer Women.* "I think the author autographed it."

"Some day you'll be autographing a book too, Perry, all about the four-brick Ketchams. It'll be a best seller."

Nyla found Reverend Jim Hammister helping several volunteers in the basement cafeteria of the church. On a white cloth banner about fifteen feet long they were painting CHRISTIANS ACROSS THE SEAS: BURNTON, OREGON EPISCOPALIANS.

"Shall we dot the i's or make them capitals?" one of the volunteers asked.

"Whatever you like best," Reverend Hammister answered. "Nyla, what do you think of our banner?" He smiled with obvious pride.

"I think they'll be able to spot you rolling into Jerusalem."

The minister blinked from behind his big glasses and grinned, his muskrat face full of faith.

"I'd like to get some information about your trip—for the *Beckoner*, of course." Nyla thought Hammister always seemed to have the zealous glint of conversion whenever he looked at her.

Like floodgates opened to dry land, Jim Hammister talked about his missionary tour to Israel, pushing maps and brochures into Nyla's hands. "These missions are incredible. I organized one at my previous parish—a trip to Japan. The spirit of Christ was so strong—yellow hands joining white hands in a holy circle. Oh, it was nothing short of a transfusion of faith." The muskrat smile turned into muskrat bliss.

"Where was your previous parish?"

The Reverend blinked but didn't answer. His expression went blank and then he frowned. "These tours . . ." he said hesitantly, "have been like . . . lifelines for many." He shifted a paperweight and writing pad on his desk, averting his eyes from Nyla's. He kept frowning. "For myself as well . . . the tours, and my youth groups, especially in . . ." The Reverend fidgeted. Nyla watched him, wondering at his sudden nervousness. Finally he sighed, "In Georgia. Rome."

"Prophetic." Nyla smiled but Hammister didn't look at her.

He said intently, as if reciting, "In Genesis, children are named as God's precious flock. 'If driven too hard, they die,' Jacob tells Esau. The youth of today are driven in so many directions, pushed and pulled and pressured. The most important work the church does is with its young souls. My youth groups have always been important to me. 'Lo, children are a heritage of the Lord.' Psalms."

Hammister abruptly stood up. "I'd like to talk more about my mission to Japan, but I wonder how my volunteers are doing dotting the i's?"

Nyla stood up also, slightly perplexed by Hammister's change in mood. "Even in the days of Olympia Swan, volunteers probably raised the tent for her everywhere she went. Too bad modern-day politicos haven't come up with a formula for faith."

"Now *there* was a minister!" Hammister brightened. "Full-figured and faith-filled, she was described. Reverend Swan earned one of the richest chapters in Oregon's religious history."

"She lived in the limestone castle for a time, Perry Truman tells me. With Molly Ketcham, the lumber heiress."

"Yes . . . with Molly." Hammister's voice faded. Then his face filled with eagerness. "She used to preach in the Baptist church and do tent services all over the state. She was still saving souls when she passed on at the age of eighty-three.

Just keeled right over on her makeshift altar. Bet that shook up the sinners." Hammister smirked, his muskrat expression becoming more pronounced.

"I guess this town was pretty shook up when the widows were murdered in that castle where Olympia Swan once lived."

Hammister didn't respond at once. Nyla looked at him; he blinked at her. Finally he said, "Yes, the whole town was in shock for a long time."

"Did you know the widows?"

"Not well, though I dropped by to see them occasionally. I kept trying to interest them in our singles activities. As a matter of fact, I visited them early in the evening of the very night they were killed."

"When did you learn of their deaths?"

"Early the next morning. Chief Karp told me what happened. An absolute tragedy. They were both gracious ladies. Private but congenial people." Hammister turned one of his long white palms up, as if he were checking his own life line. "I have to tell you, Nyla, when things like that murder happen, I wonder about the way God moves." He turned the palm down on his desk. "In a way, it seems that I passed Death coming and going around those two women. I wish I could have known some way to protect them. I drove by the castle twice again that night when I went to the Lighthouse Inn and then returned home. I wasn't feeling well so I left Seth Randolph early." Hammister grinned. "You know Seth?" Nyla nodded. The minister continued, "We were having a few beers. I'm afraid I'm not much of a drinker."

Nyla smiled. "Did you see Ritchie Dennis that night?"

Again Hammister blinked at her, as if he were not quite sure of her interest, yet willing to talk about his knowledge of those events. "As I went up to the Inn about seven-thirty, he seemed to be on his way home. Poor Ritchie." Hammister sighed. "One of the weaker lambs in the flock. He used to be in the special school with the Brothers of Mercy outside Portland, seemed to thrive and improve there. But his mother wanted him home. I get a little worried about him playing up in the bluffs. He's just not aware of the traffic on that road. Never seems to notice the cars whizzing around the curve.

149

Especially in the dark."

"Seven-thirty's still pretty light."

"Depends on the season, of course, but I often see him out later than that. Did that night, now that I think of it."

"So you saw him *twice*?" This information was not recorded in the crime file.

"Yes, I guess I did. Offered him a ride home. But as I said, I'd had those beers and wasn't in the best of moods for persuading anyone."

"What time was that?"

"Oh, I guess around ten p.m. or so."

Nyla jotted the time down in her notebook, then asked to borrow one of Hammister's Holy Land brochures. As they headed back into the cafeteria, the Reverend asked, "Say, how do you like living at Shady Stay? Guess you see a lot of Mitch Masters."

"He's fascinating, despite his strangeness."

"He's an odd bird, all right, guess every town has them. But I'm convinced he's completely good hearted. Has he ever mentioned the blues to you?"

Nyla answered with a smile. "Yes, he's very vocal about the blues."

"Funny thing is, that makes some sense. He grew up in an area of Kansas where intermarriages with Germans produced some unusual Indian children—ruddy but blue-eyed—called the Goshuns, or in Mitch's language, the blues. There's another strange story he tells that has some truth to it. Molly Ketcham once took him for a ride in her new bullnosed Morris M.G. near an area of considerable geothermal activity. As Molly's new car passed a settlement of Elks Indians, Mitch caught sight of an Indian by the road and just then a geyser spurted up under the Morris. Nearly lifted the machine into the air. Just a simple geyser, but to Mitch, the blues and the waves were working their mystery again."

"Waves sent from the brotherhood, he tells me. And something about a finger and a hand. His latest story has to do with the Iron Worm. Maybe he and Ritchie could trade stories about the brothers."

Nyla and Hammister chuckled and shook hands. Nyla

noticed Hammister's clammy grip less than the twinge of pain in her wrist. "Ow, I can feel my arthritis kicking up. I thought you weren't supposed to feel that until your golden years. You ever have those twinges, Reverend?"

"Not me, I'm one of the lucky ones. Arthritis is not my malady."

As Nyla drove toward Old Town for her luncheon date with Lucy, a vociferous monologue raced through her mind. *Why was the Reverend more willing to talk about the widows' murder than his previous parish? Why didn't he mention seeing Mitch Masters on the beach? What had Mitch seen him doing as he came up the beach? Something—or wouldn't he have said he'd seen the old man? Why didn't the crime file reflect that he'd seen Ritchie twice that night? Had he really seen the boy again—or said so to help establish his own alibi? And if he didn't have arthritis, why was he limping that morning? For that matter, what was his shoe-size and what kind of jogging shoes did he wear? Number ten Addidas perhaps—and was that limp from a fall down the beach incline after he dashed out of the castle? But what was his motive? Could it have something to do with his previous parish, and what exactly was it about Rome, Georgia, that made the minister so nervous?*

Nyla sighed loudly. The part of journalism she never liked was having more questions than answers and no easy way to bridge the gap. She couldn't indict Hammister just for being defensive about his previous parish or emphatic about his youth groups. She knew she needed to fall back on her old standby, ever the journalist's salvation: *Dig deeper, do more homework, and the answers will come to you.*

She had barely parked her car when Lucy came running out of Amelia's with a sack and grabbed her hand. "I've gotta show you something!" They went running out of Old Town up the dirt road to the beach, and ended up at Lucy's favorite place, a walk-through cave in the rocks.

"At high tide, the cave's opening is flooded," Lucy told her as they walked hand-in-hand into the darkened space inside the rock. They crouched down a short passageway and came out the back end of a tunnel to surf-splashed rocks that

151

could not be seen from the beach.

"Total privacy," Lucy grinned. "And sea pussies."

"What!" Nyla was shocked.

Lucy laughed. "That's what everyone calls them. Anemones. Come here." She led Nyla to a niche in the rocks where a tide-pool had formed. Covering the bottom of the pool were numerous green and purple creatures, round and flat and soft-looking.

"They look like jelly doughnuts," Nyla said. Lucy pulled her hand into the icy water and when she touched an anemone, it closed softly around her finger, stroking her skin with fine filaments and soft sucking. "I get it, I get it," she said, blushing.

They spread out the deli picnic from Amelia's—fat sandwiches and tempting pickles—then laughed when neither of them could eat.

"Geez," Lucy said, "What a day—I gave the Simpsons the Cook's mail and the Cooks, I skipped their box entirely."

They sat close together, holding hands and watching the waves crash up between the rocks. "Seth had a cheshire cat smile this morning." Lucy cradled Nyla's bandaged hand in her lap. They kissed and held each other, scooted back on the rocks when a stray wave splashed them. Before they were ready, lunch time was over. "Bye, pussies," Nyla called softly. They stood in the dim cave for one last embrace, a kiss softer than the ocean's wooing, wetter than the water dripping all around them.

Darkness and sea fog just about had Burnton socked in. Jim Strunk, standing on the steps of the lighthouse, couldn't see a foot in front of him. He pulled his coat closer around his neck. The fog horn blared at the end of the old jetty and the waves were close and loud. For a moment, the water sounds made him think the tide had broken the sea wall surrounding him. *Just the fog making me jumpy. Never liked fog. Never liked flying in it, but we always did.* He remembered fog in Tokyo too, more like smoke—hot and full of stench, burning the eyes, opening to ghoulish slant-eyed faces.

There was more of Tokyo he remembered—that had been some R&R at the end of his hitch. He and his crew buddies staggering into morning after too much saki and so many nameless prostitutes . . . and then there were the memories his buddies didn't share, the outings back to the brothels that he usually took alone, except for a few times with Al . . .

He'd kept those particular tastes of his under tight rein since then. Maybe, once the Seascape deal came through, he'd indulge himself again, go to San Francisco where you could pay for any kind of pastime you wanted. In the meantime, he didn't want Wasser getting any hint of what Al knew about their service days together.

"Ow! Dammit!"

Strunk heard a thunk in the darkness and recognized Ben Wasser's voice. The sheriff came within a few steps of Strunk and stopped when the lawyer lit a cigarette lighter. The larger man was rubbing one leg. "City oughta clean up this damned driftwood." Neither man seemed at ease in the press of fog around them.

"You see the paper?"

Strunk nodded. He stared at Wasser over the small flame.

"That's not the worst part of it. You won't believe it. Truman was on the phone all morning with that guy in San Francisco. Those fairies set up a White House meeting, Jim, for chrissakes. And this guy is going to take Truman's petitions

153

with him. Jesus, faggots in the White House."

Wasser could see the flicker from the lighter reflected in Strunk's eyes. He didn't want to look at those eyes. They reminded him of a wolf's. "That girl still snooping is what gets me. After my little scare tactic at the castle, I was sure she'd back off."

"You were too late."

"So it seems." Wasser wished for a cigar. The wind wobbled the flame between them. "There's something else, too. Truman didn't say exactly. But he told this guy Penn, 'I've got the papers here. It's all set up. I just came from my lawyer's.' "

Strunk's eyes smouldered like sparking embers. "Does Truman have the petitions right now?"

"I think so."

Strunk snuffed the flame with a metallic click.

TEN

A Missing Friend

Nyla Wade wasn't about to begin a new romance without sharing it with Audrey Louise. Best friendship has its privilege, even long distance friendship. As she dialed, she guessed Audrey Louise would cluck approvingly, "Girl, are you *finally* in the throes again?" She also expected to be scolded for not writing safe stories that would make folks smile over their apple pie. What she didn't expect was Audrey Louise asking how soon Nyla intended to set up housekeeping with Lucy, nor to laugh so hard at Nyla's description of the sensual affect on the human finger made by an innocent sea anemone. "If only they'd called them sea pussies in the first place. Tony once had nightmares about them, he'd wake up screaming 'sea meanies, sea meanies!' Come to find out he thought anemones grew into the Loch Ness monster, a huge sea meanie indeed. Guess you just have to learn to translate them." As Audrey Louise chortled, Nyla could hear the three Landry boys warwhooping in the background. And as they hung up, Audrey Louise was mothering: "Better hold onto this Lucy gal. No one ever wanted to batter down a door for *me*!"

With a song in her heart and sweet hope on her lips, Lucy Randolph knew she was cool as Bogie at his coolest as she

155

tripped the light fantastic into the Shady Stay lobby. Mitch greeted her from the front desk with his silence, eyeing the wine bottle in her hand. She reached up to tip an imaginary fedora and curled her lip to ask, "How's tricks?" He nodded soberly as she headed for Nyla's door.

"How's my Khaki Girl?" Lucy soon asked.

"Absolutely enthralled," Nyla answered as they fell into each other's arms to kiss and laugh. They immediately snuggled up on Nyla's bed to talk, making love and friendship with their closeness.

Nyla couldn't resist winding her fingers in Lucy's red hair. "I avoided trauma by sheer will this morning, Lucy Randolph. Next time you better awaken me for a proper farewell."

Lucy chuckled, then kissed the tempting flesh between Nyla's breasts. "Will is your strong suit, all right."

"Speaking of trauma, I think I caused Reverend Hammister a minor one this afternoon." Nyla told Lucy about her interview with the minister and the myriad questions which occurred to her about him in relation to the murder.

"Sounds like he may have some secrets, but I don't peg him for the murder."

"Then how come he didn't tell the cops he saw Ritchie twice or mention seeing Mitch on the beach that morning?"

"He told you he'd had too many beers. And as for Mitch Masters, he probably just forgot."

"Okay, so explain the limping."

"Too much kneeling to pray. Come on, I'm no detective. But I might have a friend who can check up on Hammister. She's a minister for MCC in Atlanta. You want me to call her?"

"MCC?"

"The international organization of gay churches. Sometimes referred to by homophobic straights as Prayer with Perverts."

The two rolled on the bed with laughter. When they settled down again, Lucy touched Nyla's chin. "Really, though, my friend might be able to tell us something."

Nyla's eyes told her gratitude.

"Hey, Nyla, speaking of our net across the waters, Seth

156

found someone to look at the footcast and other evidence. We should know something soon." Then she added, "Maybe gypsies killed the widows. That's what Nancy Drew always said." They laughed again, joked about reviving the Nancy Drew and Girl Group mysteries with all lesbian characters.

Lucy told Nyla to run a bath; they would soak in hot water, sip cold wine, savor the tray of delicacies she'd brought. "Fruit for fruits!"

Succulence dripped in the juice from slices of melon and kiwi, grapes, a small mound of ripe strawberries. They fed each other, passed an orange slice mouth-to-mouth until it was warm and supple as their lips against each other. The strawberries burst with their bites, the passionfruit bursting rushes inside them. The bathroom steamed up like a sauna. Water dripped from their chins, salting their kisses. Like sea babies, they touched each other through a film of water, slid up next to each other blanketed by wetness in the big old-fashioned tub.

"I felt like such a pilgrim . . ." Nyla said and Lucy silenced her doubts with warm fingers against her lips. "You weren't." They held each other. "I wanted to be so cool," Lucy admitted and Nyla slid her hand down the wetness of Lucy's thigh. "You were."

The one blanket of wetness was exchanged for another, Nyla's worn-thin comforter soon kicked to the floor as the lovers wound themselves together, diving into each other's desire.

"Come to me, Nyla," Lucy whispered into a feverish kiss. "Take me with you," was Nyla's reply.

There had been nothing of these feelings in Nyla's past—the involuntary sigh when she touched Lucy's wetness, her own sweet flow, their breasts caressing. The build from light stroking to urgent forceful kisses, quick breath, similar sounds—so sweet to hear Lucy echo her. And then the amazing descent, Lucy's chin blazing a trail of goosebumps, her lips claiming Nyla for-ever with new full pleasure. She didn't want to rest then, and pushed Lucy back against the pillows and dove for passion again. And she talked to Lucy as she touched her, surprising herself with the way she could make Lucy moan. "I know what you want. I'll give it to you. But not just yet, in a minute, when

157

I'm ready, in a minute. Wait for me, you can't come without me . . ." The power of Lucy against her fingers, against her mouth, their pulses beginning to pound together until she couldn't hear anything but her own voice coaxing and Lucy responding.

As Joan and Val had rested after loving in the thud of the surf on their last night, so Nyla and Lucy lay together in the moonlight. They dropped in and out of dozing, rousing from the soft pull of deeper sleep to touch again, to move in ever closer, skin to skin.

"Funny footprints," Nyla mumbled.

"Funny what?" Lucy struggled to stay awake.

"Funny footprints." Nyla opened her eyes as if the ghost of Dru Ketcham had pushed back a lock of hair from her forehead, brushing her again with a touch.

"A beachbum with an alibi. Alibi talks to aliens. A nervous minister. Funny footprints. Surrounded by sea meanies."

"Nyla, are you awake?" Gently Lucy shook Nyla's arm.

They both jerked when the phone rang, its jarring sound ricocheting around the little room. Lucy got up and ended the phone's intrusion.

"Hi Sis, sorry to bother you, I know it's late. Is Perry with you by any chance?"

Lucy shifted the phone to her other ear. She pushed a window closed; the room was cold. "No, he isn't. What's wrong?"

"We were supposed to meet up here at the Lighthouse Inn at nine o'clock. Nothing important—just a beer and some darts. But you know Perry, he's never late. And he'd have called. He didn't show and I haven't been able to reach him at his house. I figured the only other thing in this town that could have waylaid him was you and Nyla Wade."

"We haven't seen him all night."

Moonlight cast a pale wreath over Nyla, who was listening but barely breathing. From both ends of the phone line, a current of worry ran between brother and sister.

"This isn't like Perry," Seth said quietly. "I'm worried."

By morning, there was still no sign of Perry. Nyla and Lucy

hoped that an irresistibly foxy gay tourista had come into the historical society and hit it off so well with Perry that he'd lost all track of time. He'd sheepishly admit his fling and Seth would only tease him unmercifully for a week or two. Nyla kept her secret fear to herself, choking the vision out of her thoughts: Perry on the beach with his flashlight, excited at spotting a float, turning his back for just a second to the treacherous waves; and then that rolling carpet of water hitting him just at the bend in the knees so that he crumpled, gasping, the flashlight slipping from his hand and lying on the beach all night, its light eventually blinking out—like Perry Day Truman.

Seth met them at Amelia's for breakfast but even the fresh strawberry blintzes didn't improve anyone's mood.

"If he did snag himself a catch for the night," Seth said, buttering a croissant, "they better not sleep too late. I'm not in the mood to worry much longer. I'm getting a headache."

Lucy touched her brother's arm. "Did you sleep at all last night?"

"Not much," he grumbled.

"Neither did we," Nyla added. As Seth grinned at her remark, she took friendly exception. "Come on, Seth, we were worrying too! This could be serious."

Still they all smiled, knowing that the first blush of new romance simply cannot be stifled.

Nyla asked Seth, "Hear from your footwear expert yet?"

"I expect to in the next several days. He's running some special tests out of the San Francisco crime lab. They've got every piece of equipment imaginable. If there's anything to find, he'll find it."

Nyla told Seth about Reverend Hammister. "He's just a little more nervous about his previous parish than I think is normal."

Lucy added, "Our little network may solve a murder everyone thought was already solved."

"Our little network," Seth mused, stroking his red beard. "The one that's existed for all time, in every place, every occupation, and every level of money and power. Who would have guessed?"

159

"Who would have guessed Tramp Williams had an alibi?"

The redheads stared at Nyla. Seth asked if someone had responded to her article.

"Oh, there's been plenty of response. Mostly complaints. I think everyone just wrote Williams off as a useless piece of human garbage, just another alkie beach bum. Buried in a pauper's grave without family or friends, especially his one friend—Mitch Masters." Nyla shared with them her conversation with the old man.

Seth said excitedly, "This sounds like Mitch and Tramp were together *past* the time of the murder."

Lucy shook her head. "Yeah, Seth, but who's gonna believe Mitch Masters about anything? Everyone in town thinks the guy's crazy as a loon."

"He can be translated," Nyla protested, thinking of Tony's sea meanies. "Some of what he says makes sense."

Lucy was still skeptical. "The question is, could he ever give testimony in court?"

"I don't know," Nyla answered. "I do know we've got to find out more about Tramp."

"What we need to find out," Seth suggested, "is who picked Williams up that night and drove him into Coos Bay. If people could be located to recount what he had on, if they saw the scratch on his neck—this could be cross-checked with Mitch's story."

"Bums have their belongings stashed in some pretty peculiar places, Seth," Lucy said. "'Burnton was Tramp's hangout—the cops have a definite opinion that he changed his clothes. They might even figure Mitch was an accomplice."

Seth shrugged at his sister, then stood up, stretching. He looked down at Lucy and Nyla. "I'm no one's advocate in this except Joan and Val's. I am a little worried, though—the more we dig into a murder case, the more we'll be stirring up trouble. We're not just a journalist, a construction boss, and a post-woman doing some curious poking. We're gays too and if all we have is maybes to work with, the powerful people in this town can hurt us a lot more than we can hurt them. The murders, the castle, Seascape—it's all tangled up like an angry octopus. Before we start pulling one of its arms I want to be sure we won't get strangled by all the other tentacles. And until

160

I hear from Perry, Tramp Williams is the least of my worries."
He dropped his napkin on his plate and smiled gently at the
two women. "Think I'll buzz the Loop motels. If I find Perry's
car, I promise not to start banging on motel doors to see if he's
all right. The man hasn't had a tryst in so long, I wouldn't want
to ruin his rep."

After Seth was gone, Nyla and Lucy stood at Nyla's car a
moment without speaking. Lucy worked her foot around in the
gravel. Finally Nyla said, "I sure hope Perry's okay. He came
over to the office yesterday to see if I was all right." She looked
at her bandaged hand. "He brought me a book to read just because he thought I'd be interested. He's the most caring man
I've ever known." Nyla sniffed, surprised that two tears had
run down her face. "Damn, I hate it when I cry."

Lucy took her into her arms. She wanted to say everything
would be all right but something stopped her. "Look, I have
the late shift today so let's search for him too. Maybe with the
three of us on the look-out, we'll find him."

Though reluctant to leave each other, they both knew the
logic of splitting up to search for Perry. Nyla headed for
Neptune's Nook, aware that she was reaching out to the one
person who could share her special fear for Perry. Cora Corona
would understand about the sneaker wave and tell her what to
do, where to look.

The venerable beach picker was at her trusty scope. She
and Nyla had coffee. Had Cora seen a flashlight on the beach?
No, nothing had shown up in the scope. But the best thing to
do was take a closer look.

"A flashlight's not too heavy to be pulled under the waves,"
Cora said ominously as they headed for the beach. They walked
slowly along the tidelands, eyes riveted to the finger of sand between the bluff bottoms and the surf. Nyla felt sad to be searching in all the wondrous beach raffle for a sign of death. She
wanted to linger over every partially exposed shell, every clump
of bulby kelp, to concentrate on stepping around the sand
dollars so they wouldn't crumble underneath her toes, to race
the miniature crabs waving their soft pink pincers. Like Joan
Ruddye, if Nyla had had the Wooten desk with all its little compartments, she would have filled them with gifts borne up by
the sea.

Nyla was relieved when the glint of sun on something metallic turned out to be a can, not the flashlight. The two women walked past the castle, until they were at the beach backing Perry's duplex. Seth's truck was there; Nyla and Cora went up to see if he'd had any luck.

When Seth let himself in with the key Perry had given him, the feel of the place wasn't quite right. He walked slowly through every room, unsure what was askew but prickling with foreboding. Things had been moved, he soon noticed, were not in the perfect order for which Perry was known—a vase off-center on the mantel, drawers in the bedroom all open just a little. Clothes in the closet were bunched together on their hangers. The clincher was something incidental—the lid of a brass cigarette box left open. Perry didn't smoke, and kept the box full of perfumed potpouri; he had once told Seth that the scent was too flowery even for him, and they had laughed about it.

Apparently the unwanted visitor had opened the potpouri to mask another scent. Seth recognized the smell as he saw an empty box by the fireplace that made his heart stop.

The box was labeled CASTLE—had held all of Perry's notes and manuscript about the Ketcham's limestone mansion. Now the contents of the box were ashes.

Some of the pages had made poor burning, Seth observed, by someone impatient for their destruction. Several partial pages had not gone completely to ash. Seth took a deep breath, thought of the precious letters from Ketcham relatives and the irreplaceable photographs of Dru and Molly that Perry had been so proud of. He prayed his friend had put a copy of the precious gay history manuscript in safe keeping somewhere.

"Well, they can't burn history," he said to himself. But the pile of ashes made him heartsick. *They've always tried to purge us with fire. Faggots, they call us, like the bundles of sticks piled up around victims of burnings. But we live in every age and no matter what they do, our own flame burns strong.*

For a moment, alone in the duplex, Seth longed for only one thing—to feel the relief of his arms around Perry with a bear hug of welcome-back safe-and-sound.

When Nyla Wade knocked on the door of the duplex, Seth had found the most obvious clue yet that an intruder had been in the apartment. On Perry's desk was a metal box similar to those used for fishing tackle. This had been pried open; the catch broken and the metal on both edges bent back. Papers strewn on the floor included Perry's life insurance policy, a letter from his mother, his birth certificate and high school diploma.

"Whoever did this was a first-rate bungler," Nyla said, looking with contempt at the partially burned pages. "But even for a bungler, they probably remembered to wear gloves." She leaned closer, plucking one of the bottom pages from the ash pile. "Oh no!"

Seth hurried to her. In her hands, half the page badly charred, was one of Perry's petitions. "I wonder what else they burned," Seth said aloud. "Something among his important papers or they wouldn't have bothered with the tackle box."

The two exchanged a glance. Cora Corona watched them quietly. "Time to get Chief Karp over here," Nyla said, picking up the phone.

Walter Karp and Steve Randall arrived quickly. After a brief interview with Seth and Nyla, Randall opened a finger-print kit, dusted the metal box and then went to work around the fireplace.

"I don't think we should be alarmists here," Karp cautioned.

"Yeah," Nyla added, "there's still the hot-blooded Lothario theory." She tried to smile at Seth but they both knew how lame the idea was becoming.

Randall was carefully scooping the ash pile into a plastic bag. "You notice anything missing?" Karp asked. Seth shook his head.

"Actually, this is not all that unusual," the Police Chief told them. "Sure, things look odd here in the apartment but there may be an explanation. With all the pressure Truman's been under with this castle litigation, he might be taking a time-out to think things over."

Karp got no takers for this theory. He shrugged. "Happens all the time."

Seth's tone made Karp take notice. "Not to my best friend."

"Was Truman planning any trip you knew of? Maybe he had a change in his plans?"

Before Nyla could speak what came into her mind, Cora Corona suggested, "Maybe you oughta drag the shallows. Perry's been known to search for floats at night. Sneaker wave coulda got 'im."

Karp raised his eyebrows and looked at Nyla, who nodded. "He's been worried and walking the beach at night a lot."

Seth took a step backwards, his ruddiness draining pale. Karp made a move to reassure him but the gesture faded. Nyla took Seth's arm. "We can't assume the worst yet. That's like giving up." Then she remembered what had come to her earlier. "Perry told me Howard Penn was coming from San Francisco to pick up the petitions. Obviously he didn't get here, and who-ever did burned them. But Howard might know something. Let's see if we can reach him."

Perry's address book was on the floor near the desk with the other scattered papers. "Can I touch this?" she asked Randall. The officer looked over at the Chief, who nodded. She found Howard Penn's number and held her breath as she dialed.

Howard was home. He'd been delayed starting for Port-land and hadn't been able to reach Perry to tell him. No, they hadn't talked since yesterday morning. Nyla explained that Perry was missing.

"I can hardly believe it. He was so high when I talked with him. About the petitions and the White House visit. And about his will."

"What will?"

"He'd just had a new one prepared. Leaving the castle to us—the Gay Historical Society."

ELEVEN

Even Pariahs Want Justice

Chief Karp promised that he and Randall would go over Perry's apartment thoroughly. "But like I said, Truman could come back of his own volition."

Nyla hardly felt able to pursue her assigned football story with Perry on her mind. But she wouldn't find him any sooner by fretting.

She found the Burnton Badgers spiking up clots of grass with their cleats amid the labored impact of shoulder pads and the plodding drag of the tackling sled. But as she watched players juke through rubber tires and run a practice scrimmage, her thoughts were focused on Jim Hammister and Ritchie Dennis. On how right Audrey Louise was—you did have to translate people who talked in a language all their own. Maybe all the alibi Tramp Williams had was from one of the town crazies. Maybe that would be all the alibi Reverend Hammister had as well. Until she talked to Ritchie, she wouldn't know.

After Coach Chuck Sturd sent his boys to the showers and offered an interview about a tough season in a tough league against tough players, Nyla concluded that football was life's first boot camp for boys. She checked in with Gruff. He told her to cover a bake sale featuring the Cranberry Festival princesses and then drop by the festival drama group, who

167

were starting rehearsals for *Gone with the Cranberry*. When she asked if he'd had any more complaints, he seemed glad to report the phone had quieted down. Unfortunately, there was no positive response to the article on Williams either.

"Ante-bellum cranberries," Nyla muttered to herself, wishing Perry were there to share the joke.

The Dennis house looked like it would collapse in one good stiff storm off the ocean. Only Shady Stay was any competition for peeling paint and dilapidation. The porch already had a definite slope and one corner had rotted enough to be sitting on foundation soil. Trusting its sequence of lives, a yellow cat sunned herself near one precarious edge of the porch.

Nyla had been trying to figure out an approach to Ritchie Dennis and his mother but no ruse she could think of quite suited. The direct approach, she had finally decided. She went right up the front steps, which swayed a little. Mrs. Dennis answered her knock with an expression cueing Nyla that no effortless interview lay ahead. The woman had green flinty eyes flecked with grey that Nyla guessed had never trusted. Her face was deeply lined and she coughed with the throaty hack of a long-time smoker.

"Whadyou want?"

I'm Nyla Wade, reporter for the *Beckoner*. I'd like to talk to your son. I'm double checking some facts about the murders that occurred at the limestone castle. I want to know if Ritchie saw anything."

The woman bristled and partially shut the door. "That was over a year ago. I told the police, I'm telling you—he was with me all night from before sundown."

"Yes, yes, I know all that. I'm not here to accuse him of anything. I think maybe Ritchie can help me figure something out."

Mrs. Dennis glared at Nyla. "You know my boy? You sure you got the right house?"

Nyla told the defensive mother, "I know some people think Ritchie isn't right, they're scared of his difference. I also know some people are afraid of *anything* that's different. I'm not afraid. I want to talk to your boy."

168

The hulk of a man-boy was sunk into a beanbag chair in front of a blaring TV. Empty crumpled bags of potato chips and Twinkie wrappers littered the floor around the chair; a Pepsi can lay on its side next to a dried stain. Ritchie's eyes blankly followed the movements of the TV characters. Nyla noticed a bluish bruise on one cheekbone. Mrs. Dennis snapped off the TV set, and Ritchie groaned.

"Show now. Ritchie like . . ." He tried to get up out of the supple chair but its beans whooshed and sifted noisily around his weight.

"Settle down, boy. There's a lady to see you."

Ritchie understood with surprised delight. Obviously he rarely got visitors. When Nyla came over to him, he squinted at her. He didn't know her name, but he did know he'd seen her before.

"Hello, Ritchie. I'm Nyla Wade." She put out her hand but Ritchie only stared at it. Slowly she reached over and picked up his hand and shook it.

He giggled, then quieted, shooting a glance at his mother as if expecting reproach. Mrs. Dennis pursed her lips; she had a permanent look of disdain. "Go on," she snapped at the boy.

"Hello. Nice you meet." He squeezed Nyla's hand, very gently. Again his eyes darted to his mother.

"Ritchie, do you remember the widows? The two ladies who lived up in the castle? Mrs. Prosper and Mrs. Ruddye?"

The boy's eyes brightened but only at Nyla's attention. She tried again. "You know, the big stone house up on Land's End. Clear at the top of the bluffs. Those ladies were killed. Do you remember?"

Still the boy did not respond. Now it was Nyla's turn to look to his mother.

"He never knew their names. All they did was chase him with a broom. Like they thought he was gonna gobble up their damned precious dog."

"Dog! See dog now, ma? Go see dog now!" The boy moved his bulk more quickly than Nyla expected; she was startled. Mrs. Dennis startled her even more with a sharp clap of her hands in front of Ritchie's face.

"No dog! Stop that damned stuff! No dog! Settle down!"

169

Ritchie crumpled back into his chair.

"He liked the widows' dog, I understand." Nyla had to clear her throat to keep her voice from sounding as if she'd been reproved, too.

"He likes all animals. He'd follow a damned stray clear to the next state without knowing it. But dogs are his favorite."

"Dog," Ritchie repeated, and than again, enjoying the round sound. He made petting motions on his leg. "Dog, yes!" His eyes glittered at Nyla.

"Ritchie was on Land's End Road the night of the murders—" Nyla began.

Mrs. Dennis snarled. "I told you—"

"Reverend Hammister told me he saw Ritchie about ten o'clock. Near the castle and—"

"He was mistaken!" Mrs. Dennis's angry tone and piercing eyes made it clear that Nyla had no chance to pursue Hammister's alibi any further.

"All right—the point is that Ritchie's on the road a lot. He might have seen or heard something no one else thought to notice. Please, let me try again, Mrs. Dennis."

Ritchie's mother hunched her shoulders and harumphed. "You'd think from the look of all his pants that he lives on that road. If he's not home on time I always know where to find him. He's got a spot in the bluffs just near the castle, the dirt's plumb flattened down in the same outline as his butt." She pursed her lips again in disgust. "He's no picnic to buy pants for, believe me. Sometimes even the big and tall men's stuff isn't large enough. Funny, he wasn't a big baby."

There was a change in Mrs. Dennis's expression as she regarded her son, but not what Nyla would have called softening. "People think I should've left him in that school," the mother went on. "But the school didn't really help him that much. So I brought him back. I'm all the family he's got and he belongs with me. The Lord made him different and it's been no easy time of it, but still, he's mine."

"Did he say anything unusual about that night? I'm told there was a spooky moon out over the ocean."

"He wouldn't notice nothing like that. Besides, like I told you and everyone else, I had him in here with me before moonlight. And he didn't say nothing. It was just a night like any other."

Ritchie kept his eyes mostly on the rug, with an occasional peek at Nyla or his mother. Mrs. Dennis asked Nyla, "Anything else?" Before Nyla could answer she added, "You want coffee? I've got some hot."

"Yes, that would be nice, thank you."

Mrs. Dennis gave her son another hard glare. "Behave!" she barked at him, and he jerked slightly.

As soon as she was gone, Ritchie wiggled his finger at Nyla to come closer. She wasn't sure she should; she thought about what Loamie had said. He could indeed throw a headlock on her at closer range and snap her neck like a dry twig. Yet everyone else kept saying he was harmless . . . Ritchie's eyes darted to the door and he wiggled his finger frantically. Nyla moved.

"Dogma," he whispered. "Broham nishmon. Like Ritchie —should be onesome when bad boy. Broham nishmon dogma!" He was excited but kept a close watch for his mother's return. "Not onesome Ritchie only. Poor Ritchie."

The large child's eyes actually filled with tears and he grabbed one of Nyla's hands. He held it to his face and said again, "Poor Ritchie." Nyla stared at him, clearly remembering the words Lucy had heard from her stranger in the dark. She realized now that it was Ritchie and the bruise on his cheek must be where Lucy had hit him with the flashlight.

The rattle of china made Nyla scurry back to her seat as Mrs. Dennis returned. "Wha'd he say while I was gone?" Her eyes on her son were harsh.

"Not much. Just a little more about the dog. And something about the brothers."

"Those damned fool priests." Without flinching, Mrs. Dennis took a steep swallow of hot coffee. "They almost ruined my boy. Kept him locked up alone half the time more like a criminal, or worked him on their private docks till he was exhausted. Those brothers live high, I'm telling you. I've been in that place and I've seen what they're up to. They got their own fishing fleet and they make a pretty penny. Ritchie can't stand fish now within twenty feet of 'im and he won't touch a bit of it to eat neither. No reason for them to charge so much to keep a slow boy in their care. They make enough off fishing to build plenty of churches."

"Ritchie," Nyla set down her coffee cup. "Do you remember the rocks? Thrown rocks?" Nyla gestured like she was picking up rocks and throwing them. "At the castle where the dog lived? Just two nights ago, Ritchie—do you remember?"

"Not me! Not throw!" He put up his hands as if someone were about to hit him. He touched the bruise on his cheek. "Ritchie not rock. No nishmon, please! No onesome!" His appeal was obviously meant for his mother, who stood up, spilling her coffee onto the rug.

"What have you been up to now, boy?"

Nyla put a hand on her arm. "Nothing, he didn't do anything. But he was there." She stepped in front of Mrs. Dennis, bent down close to Ritchie. "Who did you see? Who was throwing the rocks? Please tell me."

All the boy's hugeness quivered and tears streamed down his face. Though Nyla did not know what his word meant exactly, she knew to reassure him with it. "No nishmon, Ritchie, I promise. Who did you see? Was it broham? Or dogma?"

He shook his head back and forth, the tears dripping down his shirt front.

"For petessakes, what the hell did he do?" his mother demanded.

At Nyla's touch, the boy lifted his face and for a moment the blank eyes cleared. "Dogma dead," he told Nyla. "Like dead fish."

As with Mitch, to make a translation seemed to require a consistent message to the scrambled sender. Nyla tried again. "All right, not dogma. Was it broham?" Ritchie kept his eyes on her; she wondered what or who broham meant.

The boy sighed. Then said with all the authority he could muster, "Broham not rock. Only two ladies."

Nyla couldn't get to a phone fast enough. To tell Lucy it was Ritchie Dennis in the dark, he hadn't meant to hurt her, was only scared spitless, he couldn't have been the one to dump

172

the dead fish. Furthermore, another *woman* had been throwing the rocks. Who the hell could that be and why?

Lucy reported that Seth was just coming in the door. There was still no sign of Perry. "But we've got a surprise. Can you get right over here?"

"No, I've gotta find out the life goals of Cranberry princesses. Can you meet me? The bake sale's in Old Town."

As Nyla was sampling Princess Becky's cranberry-raisin jello delight, Seth's truck pulled in across the street. He and Lucy headed for her, Seth holding up a manila envelope. "The report from the footwear expert."

Nyla tore into the envelope and read the report to her two friends.

Dear Ms. Wade:

I have examined the size ten Adidas tennis shoe, the footcast, and the rug sample with footprints on it taken from the crime scene. I can report conclusively, validating what is already known, that this shoe made these prints. After microscopic analysis, the shoe and cast match at seventy-seven points of identification. Blood and sand from the shoe also match the scene and the victims.

Now into greyer areas. Though I could not conclusively prove it, based on my twelve years of experience with crime footwear, I suggest that Eugene Williams did not make any of these footprints.

Based on the autopsy report and body measurements, Eugene Williams would not normally have worn a size ten average-width shoe of any type. The footprints made by this tennis shoe are entirely vivid except for a vague impression at the tip of the toe. Had Eugene Williams been wearing the shoes when the footprints were made, an entirely different impression would have appeared because his 23.77 centimeter foot was much too small for this shoe. Movement within the shoe of

173

this smaller foot would have made a less vivid imprint, even had the shoe been packed to make it fit tighter.

I performed a simulation study of ten footprints made in sand with a new size ten man's Adidas tennis shoe. Photos of these simulated prints are enclosed. As you can see in all ten prints, when the shoe is worn by the appropriate foot size, the print is nearly perfect. The other prints were made by a lab employee with a 25.13 centimeter foot length of narrow width. These prints show a vivid heel imprint but from the arch to the tip of the toe, the imprint fades and shows marked irregularity of impression depending on which way the smaller foot slid from side to side or forward to back.

Even though this is only a simulation, I would conclude from my footwear analysis that Eugene Williams was not wearing the size ten Adidas tennis shoes when they made the footprints at the scene of the crime.

I will be happy to review my analysis with Burnton law enforcement personnel should the occasion arise. I hope this information is of some help to you.

> Sincerely,
> Jason Stephens, Footwear Specialist
> San Francisco Crime Laboratory

For a moment Nyla and her two friends said nothing. Finally—something to verify they weren't on a wild goose chase. But so much was still unknown. It was Lucy who broke their silence. "Time to try the cops again?"

Seth answered with a coughed curse word, jamming his hands into his pockets.

Nyla looked at him and said, "They seem like all we've got, I know, and not much at that. But remember we've still got the three of us going strong." With her eyes, she asked Lucy's help.

"Come on," Lucy said. "Let's see if our flatfoots have any brains."

Seth watched them go, his sister and her new lover launching full into the fray.

Nyla took one more look at the widows' crime file. She was right in remembering that the notes didn't reflect Hammister having seen Ritchie a second time on the road. The investigation notes did verify Mrs. Dennis's report that her son was at home from seven-thirty on.

"So who's the trickster? The Reverend or the mother?"

"Maybe both. Or else Ritchie managed to sneak out that night. I think he was in his special spot and he saw the murderer enter the castle. He kept saying something when I was at the house. Broham and dogma, nishmon. Then onesome when bad boy. I'm not sure what it all means but the first part, broham—I think he means Brother Hammister—Jim Hammister's clerical collar reminding him of the priests or brothers at his school."

Lucy and Nyla felt the import of the huge room full of crime files closing in around them. They were out of sight of the file clerk; Nyla stepped into Lucy's arms.

Rusted ball bearings in mud—that's how Walter Karp would have described the aftertaste of the cup of coffee he was finishing when he saw reporter Nyla Wade and postwoman Lucy Randolph push through the swinging doors of the squad room, making for his door pronto. Before he had time to straighten his tie, the two women reached his desk.

"Good day, Chief Karp." Nyla had no hesitance. "I need to talk to you about the widows' murder at the limestone castle."

Karp had the good sense not to be flip and say he could have guessed that much all by himself. "Have a seat, both of you." Though they both sat down in chairs in front of Karp's desk, Nyla Wade was on the edge of hers. "I'm listening," he told her.

"While I've been researching my story on the castle, some curious things have come up. I think you should know about them."

Walter Karp listened and listened close as Nyla Wade reeled out the events and facts involving her with the castle. This included her friendship with Perry, his research on the history of the castle, the incident in the darkened house with the dead fish and the rock thrower, and now Perry's disappearance. Karp did not reveal that Truman's absence had triggered an instinctive alarm in him, like a thumb jabbing his ribcage. He kept his face expressionless except for polite interest as Nyla continued, telling him about the discrepancy of Ritchie's whereabouts on the night of the murder, about Mitch Masters' suggestion that Tramp Williams was with him from sundown until midnight. She finished up with the report and simulation print photos from the San Francisco crime lab.

Karp scratched aimlessly at the copious chest hair visible under his rumpled white shirt; his eyes wandered to a discolored spot of paint on the far wall of his office. With a noisy sigh, he offered both women coffee. They declined. Karp cleared his throat.

"Let's consider the realities here. Some things may have nothing to do with others. In the first place, whoever tried scaring you with the fish may be more concerned about your friendship with Truman, a none too popular figure in this town. Second, we have yet to determine if Perry Day Truman is missing of his own will or foul play, and believe me, you can't imagine how often folks go off for their own little bout of seclusion only to come back perfectly safe."

Nyla tried to interject, but Karp ignored her. "About Tramp Williams' alibi—Mitch Masters is about as reliable a witness as Williams would be testifying against prohibition. We can't be sure if Masters was *really* with Williams or just *thought* they were together. As for Ritchie Dennis, he may have seen something if we can prove his mother lied about his being with her from seven-thirty on, but even if we can, he's another unreliable witness. The boy can barely talk." Karp felt slightly irritated.

"As for the person or persons who sifted through Perry Day Truman's belongings, until we find Perry Day Truman we can't be sure it wasn't himself or someone he allowed into the apartment—jimmy marks on the tackle box or not. We're pursuing evidence with the county crime lab now so you won't feel I'm shirking my duty here." He smiled, to no response. "People *do* forget keys sometimes and get frustrated enough to jimmy their own boxes, containers, safes, et cetera. Sometimes even their own doors. I knew a guy in New York who regularly crowbarred his own doors just to collect the insurance.

"It's not impossible that Truman felt something we don't know about—remorse maybe—or a threat about this manuscript of his and decided to burn it himself or asked someone else to do that for him."

"But not his *petitions,*" Lucy asserted. "They were on their way to the White House, Chief Karp."

The Police Chief looked at her without commenting on this new information.

Nyla asked, "What did you find out about the will? Did you find it in the apartment? It looks pretty obvious to me *that's* why the box was jimmied and that the will must have been burned too."

"As I mentioned, all evidence isn't in yet. We did contact Truman's lawyer to verify the will. And no, we didn't find a copy in the apartment. Which doesn't preclude the possibility that Truman has it with him."

"What about the burned petitions?" Lucy persisted.

Karp ignored her. "Your capper to all this, Ms. Wade, is the independent solicitation of outside criminal investigation." Karp picked up Jason Stephens' report. "Even you, Ms. Wade, cannot be so naive as to imagine bum drunks don't often wear shoes that don't fit them—shoes, clothes, anything the free garbage rewards them with, including someone's last-night dinner. You obtained evidence from a murder case less than honestly, which sits poorly with me. Beyond that, the expert himself says his analysis is not conclusive and is based on a simulation."

For a moment, the Chief and Nyla Wade looked at each other. Then Nyla stood up and pushed her chair back. "I realize you want me to see how easily all that I've told you can be legally dismissed as so much circumstantial nothing. Your points are well taken, but they haven't shaken my resolve. I don't believe Tramp Williams killed Joan Ruddye and Valerie

Prosper. I believe he had on the murderer's shoes when he died in his cell, but he did not have them on when the footprint was made outside the castle.

"You dismissed Mitch Masters as a subject because he couldn't hold his own physically in the struggle with Valerie Prosper. The same might hold true for Williams who was in his forties but had many years of hard drinking behind him. He was small-framed, emaciated, not the best possible candidate to overpower a woman who knew her attacker had just killed her lover. And I think the attempt to scare me and the disappearance of Perry Day Truman *are* connected with the murders, though I'm not sure how. What I do know is we've tried to find Perry and he's not anywhere he should be. Bouts of seclusion or not—please take seriously our concern that something's happened to him. I know he wouldn't burn his own manuscript or his petitions, not in a million years."

Lucy added, "He's not the type to forget his keys—he's the type to have an extra set. Whoever went into that apartment didn't know anything about Perry."

"Why do you say that?" Karp wasn't offended; he was an interested cop.

"Thinking that Perry would keep all his notes and copies with the original. But a friend in San Francisco has a copy of the manuscript and so does Nyla."

Nyla handed the Chief a sheaf of stapled white sheets. "I think whoever killed the widows wasn't after money. And I think Perry Day Truman may have been killed for the same reason."

Lucy gasped; Nyla turned to see her lover's face go pale.

"Go on, Ms. Wade," the Police Chief encouraged.

Nyla touched Lucy's arm, then spoke directly to Karp again. "The widows were killed because they were lesbian lovers adamant about keeping the castle standing. Lesbians built that castle and lived there together and everyone in this town knows it. Perry himself told me he couldn't get any government or agency support for the same reason, because of the castle's suggestive history. And that's what his manuscript is about, the petitions just an extension of that goal. He told me he would use the manuscript however he had to to keep anyone

178

from tearing down the castle. Over my dead body, he said. I'm very much afraid someone took him seriously."

"You're opening Pandora's box, Ms. Wade, and you've got no real wedge, just a lot of circumstantial—"

Lucy stood up. "This damned case was solved in the *first* place with nothing but circumstantial evidence. No bona fide witnesses, not fingerprint one of Eugene Williams in that castle. Just the shoes. Eugene Williams had on a murderer's shoes, all right, that we won't deny. But he wasn't in them when the murder actually occurred. All we're asking you to do is check it out, Chief. We're saying there are too many unanswered questions. Two people were brutally murdered . . ." She shot a glance at Nyla and her voice wavered. "Maybe a third. Members of this community."

"I'm not sure the widows were members of this community."

Lucy's temper flared. "Didn't they shop at the market? Walk the beach every day? Pay their taxes like everyone else?"

"That's not what I meant," the Chief said, knowing his offhand remark had been a mistake. "You just need to know there's a difference between people who live here and members of the community."

"You're telling me about *my* town? *My* friends? They came from money so they didn't rate as real people in Burnton, is that it? Or is it the *other* community they belonged to that kept this town from claiming them or caring about their murder? They were gay so they were expendable—especially if it meant the castle was out of the way of Seascape!"

"Now look, don't make a federal case out of this. They had a distance, see, they lived up in the bluffs, and yeah, they came from money and they were lesbian and they weren't from here. I don't give a damn. I'm not from here either. But lots of people felt that way."

In frustration, Lucy whirled on her heel and smacked the office door jamb with her open hand. For a moment, none of them said anything. Then Nyla charged, "Did you check out *those* people on the night of the murder, Chief Karp?"

"Of course I did. You saw the file—we checked everything."

"You didn't figure out where the dog went, you got no

179

verification that Reverend Hammister went back to the rectory, and he didn't tell you about seeing Ritchie Dennis a second time. You don't know for sure that Mitch Masters and Ritchie can't tell you anything. Do you serve all the people in Burnton, Chief Karp, or just the ones who felt a certain way about the widows and the town crazies?"

Karp picked up the telephone. "Steve, get me the S.P.'s on the widows. That's right. Do it now." Karp looked at both women. "You don't have to live in a place the size of New York to know some murder cases are closed without really being solved. But I don't know if one bit of what you've told me will get us any new answers."

Lucy shot back, "Well you don't have to live in a place the size of New York to know when something stinks."

Karp leaned over his desk. "Don't talk tough to me, lady. I spent eighteen years listening to tough talk. You got a ways to go."

When Steve Randall opened Karp's door, the Chief was backed into his chair but his eyes were still locked hard on Lucy.

Karp took the file and opened a small manila envelope. "I just want you to be sure, Ms. Wade, that you want to remind this whole town. To get everyone stirred up again. This is the raw truth of what happened. This will all be in their faces again."

Karp fanned out the black and white photos—Joan Ruddye and Valerie Prosper laid bare by their intruder.

Closer to the pictures, Lucy saw the details of the first one and closed her eyes. She'd never seen crime scene photos before, photos that left nothing to the imagination, that were ten times more horrifying than murder in the movies.

Nyla stepped up to Karp's desk, picked up a photo and looked at it closely. Karp watched her. She forced herself to contain her revulsion—in black and white photos, blood was black—but no less gory. She put the picture down in front of the Chief and kept her finger on it.

"You'll talk to Mitch Masters and Ritchie Dennis?" Her eyes told him she was afraid of nothing.

"And with the footwear specialist," Lucy added, hearing

her voice break. She wanted to turn all the pictures over. She felt a pang of fear that soon there might be pictures like this of poor Perry.

Karp didn't answer. Nyla leaned in close to him. "Don't underestimate us, Chief. The fact that two lesbians were murdered and one gay boy is missing matters to *our* community, even if we don't belong in Burnton."

Lucy found her voice, and her courage. "Even when lots of places we live in won't claim us or include us in any real sense, don't think we don't have our own network and our own way of getting the word out. People with no civil rights have a historic bonding. They're going to ask a lot more questions than Nyla has."

"We're going to *insist* on answers," Nyla added. "Insist Perry Day Truman be found, dead or alive, and vindicated. We're not going to let the whole town of Burnton be accomplices to an unsolved murder. This smacks of a cover-up and the worst kind: a money trade-off. The money interest of a town being more important than the loss of three gay lives. Oh we'll find out who the ring-leaders are—but the whole town has contributed to letting this murderer go free—all so that Seascape could build over the castle and bury the memory forever."

Nyla wanted to stop, felt she was pressing the Chief's limits, but someone had to break through somehow. "Let me tell you, Chief Karp, this whole town can't keep me or the gay community from finding out who really murdered those lesbians, and probably Perry Day Truman. We're going to raise a stink the size of New York city. We may be pariahs, but we're not expendable. Even pariahs want justice."

181

TWELVE

Sleeping Dogs Don't Lie

Three Bog Road looked much the same as it had a year ago when Karp had been parked in the same spot watching for overloaded trucks from the mill. Today his mind was not on trucks. He was thinking about his confrontation with Nyla Wade and Lucy Randolph. And about Joan Ruddye and Valerie Prosper. And of course, about Perry Day Truman. Sometimes Mindy floated among those faces. He couldn't understand why men took to loving other men or women other women—not more than as close friends anyway—but he did understand the ferocity of their feelings about protecting their own. Out of a similar emotion, he himself had almost killed once. And though it irritated the hell out of him, he knew that Nyla Wade was right to challenge him.

He hadn't liked feeling foolish when she showed him the report from the San Francisco lab. Nor hearing from Lucy Randolph that Truman's petitions were destined for the White House. He had Steve Randall and Van Davidson working overtime on the evidence from Truman's apartment. He wanted to know why the damned petitions had been burned too, and if anything in the ashes looked like Truman's will. And something else was bothering him, something he'd have to ask Bill Prather—the measurement error the coroner claimed to correct. Karp didn't need to be a footwear expert to know Williams' foot was too small to have made that print. If only he'd examined the first report more carefully. But why hadn't Prather caught the discrepancy and why did he lie in the so-called correction?

Nyla's challenge echoed in Karp's thoughts: Did he serve *all* the people or only some of them? Whether he agreed with their peccadilloes or not, he served them *all*.

Smelling the wet air off the recently flooded bogs and eating some of Cranberry Sweet's best jellies, Karp wondered if an innate prejudice had kept him from pressing the Coos Bay boys and the mayor and Strunk, had kept him from doing more than accepting the evidence at face value. Sure, the mayor had told him to lay off, and sure, the Coos Bay boys had taken things into their own jurisdiction, but he could have pulled some weight if he'd really wanted to. As he sat again on Three Bog Road and bit into the warm chocolate, he knew the prejudice wouldn't hinder him again, wouldn't keep him from running down every damned inkling of a fact that Nyla Wade had presented. Nothing and nobody would prevent him.

Before he had come out on his introspective drive, not more than an hour after Nyla and Lucy had visited him, he had looked up from his desk to see Adam Hall leaning in his doorway: the second-term mayor lanky and handsome, his hair long with the look of a modern politico. Karp was forever stifling the urge to suggest a haircut. Hall's suit fit him perfectly, and he knew about image; he intended to be more than a local politician.

"Why is it," the mayor asked his Chief of Police, "that it's never the natives who won't let sleeping dogs lie?"

"Maybe the natives get lazy." Karp smiled.

"Maybe the natives are smarter," Hall countered.

"Maybe the natives know what's good for them." The Chief was no native nor was he the mayor's servant; he was the servant of the people—all of them, as Nyla Wade would be eager to remind him.

"You think letting a stranger stir up old murders is good for anyone?"

"Depends," Karp told the mayor, "on the intent of the

184

stranger and the content of what's stirred up."

"One maybe is as good as another when maybes or what-ifs is all you have to work with, Walter. Seascape can mean new prosperity to this town. If it doesn't go in because the developers get scared off, people may lose their jobs or much of their staff. Even important people, with important services." The mayor looked around Karp's office. "Stuffy in here," he said.

"I guess we're waiting for some of that new prosperity, to fund us some air conditioning." Karp smiled again.

The mayor had replied with raised eyebrows. He hadn't had to be any more specific for Karp to realize his further message: first air conditioning, then squad cars, then officer salaries.

What was the mayor's keen interest in Seascape's success that he would go so far as to suggest muzzling the press? Even in this three-hick Oregon lumber town that was dangerous ground. Karp was beginning to pick up the same stench bothering Nyla Wade and her friends. He'd never been able to ignore it in New York and he wouldn't here in Burnton either. As he started up his engine, he caught his own intense reflection in the rear-view mirror. He didn't say it out loud but he was thinking: *Nyla Wade, go for it!*

Hand in hand, pant cuffs rolled up, Nyla and Lucy were taking in the tidelands without talking, just letting the sea wash away some of the aches. Nyla's thoughts whirled around like a carousel—Joan Ruddye riding the white horse with a garland of flowers; Valerie Prosper on the black stallion, waving to her. And then on the pinkest carousel pony rode Perry Day Truman, but he didn't wave—his expression was fixed and he stared into space. Olympia Swan and Mercy Hayworth stood next to horses going up and down on their painted poles. And of course, at the motor was Druscilla Ketcham. Nyla even saw herself, Lucy, and Seth spinning out of reach, out of focus.

When would it stop spinning and make sense? Would Walter Karp do his duty and shut down the circus, give the widows their rightful justice and find Perry Day Truman?

The two women stopped, looked out to sea, and then

185

oblivious to any watchers or witness, held each other as the chilly water wet their jeans, rolling in over them with all the constancy life did not afford. When they moved apart, Nyla stared down at the sand.

"This all reminds me of that pimp who killed one of his hookers. My friend Sara said he was so slick he could walk in sand and leave no footprints. Ironic—our murderer did leave a footprint, almost perfect—and still it's like he disappeared. And Perry too."

They hugged again, then were startled to hear someone call to them. Jim Hammister jogged up the beach, huffing by the time he reached them.

"Nyla, I thought it was you. And hello to you too, Lucy. I saw Mitch Masters today and he told me something I wanted to share with you. He showed me a spring action rifle loader he'd found. Not still in the rifle, of course." The minister smiled his muskrat smile. "While he was working on the loader, the spring came down on his thumb and left a bruise on the nail. He told me that was where the Iron Worm hit him. Since you mentioned it the other day, I thought it would make sense to you."

"Thank you, Reverend, I'm beginning to think he makes sense more and more."

"Well, I better finish my run before I'm too winded," the Reverend told them cheerily and then ran off down the beach. Nyla forced herself not to clench her teeth when she said, "Call your MCC friend right away, will you, Lucy? I want the scoop on Hammister."

So James Ruddye had money troubles. Who didn't, and furthermore, why should *he* care about it? Jim Strunk wished he'd never met the Ruddyes. Joyce was a first-class social climbing bitch, James a pantywaist gambler. Still, he thought they'd settle up like civilized folks, thought the faggot would give in when Seascape offered him the hundred grand. He'd guessed wrong on both counts.

You didn't win big with bad guesses. And if he lost to weaker people he wanted a second chance to play, to win some revenge at least. Weaker people had no right to win anything.

Yet here he was surrounded by them, and the coup of his career had foundered in their weaknesses and indecision, their petty causes and principles.

Joyce wanted a new start in life with the Seascape money and didn't want her mother's peculiar choices reflected in a state landmark that would forever taint Joyce's future. She'd personally told Strunk to have the dozers grind those limestone bricks into powder. And James Ruddye just wanted to stay alive. He and his family lived out of moving boxes to keep ahead of local creditors and strong-arm Vegas debt collectors.

And then there was Perry Day Truman. Strunk grimaced as if Truman were standing before him making kissing sounds. The guy was worse than a faggot; he was a faggot with a cause. Preserving the heritage of his *people,* for chrissakes. Homos weren't a people—they were a scourge to be eradicated, same as the gooks when he'd been in the Air Force. Just load up a fighter jet with a tank full of radon gas, take a little spin over the Mission district in San Francisco, and bingo, all those homos would have gasped their last.

If they'd been smart, James and his bitchy sister would have had multi-million dollar winnings. Now all those dollars were out of reach as was the deed to the limestone castle, the last link in Strunk's own plans for Seascape.

Few people knew the special genius he had discovered in law school: he could decode government-ese with a snap of his fingers. "Just think in quadruplicate," he used to joke with his buddies. Now he'd applied his genius to a tidy little manipulation of Document F158LG2. A simple scam, really. The Feds were willing to match funds on construction that would net long-term tax return. Strunk had convinced the government that Seascape met the terms; he'd even thrown in an extra goody—claiming Seascape created construction jobs for a certain quota of minorities and females—and so his money-match had been increased.

The Seascape developers didn't know about the matching government funds and neither did the City. They had agreed to split the actual cost of the project. Strunk and his hand-picked stockholders had pocketed a quarter of a million dollars as though the Federal money never existed.

When Burnton residents had begun to grumble about the assessments from the City to fund its share of the construction cost, Strunk had merely offered them stock options. "You're not just buying stock," he'd told them, "you're purchasing a share of Burnton's future." At the same time as he kept an eye on the careful limiting of those stock options, Strunk sold townspeople that dream lingering from Burnton history. He shook their hands, patted their backs, smiled and exclaimed, "Terrific!" as they paid for their small shares in Seascape. Burnton with its new hotel complex might finally realize the long hoped for vision of Burnton as in important sea coast city.

The the plan hit a curve—the scrap between the Ruddyes and Perry Day Truman. And everyone had become a little shaky about having a convention center on the site where generations of lesbians had founded an empire.

The pressure was starting to frazzle everyone's nerves, especially his. He was tired of it, tired of the weaklings. Not just the Ruddyes, but Prather too, and Wasser's constant nettling. The only guy in on the scam with any brains was Adam Hall. Strunk wanted settlement. He wanted to cut the ribbon on Seascape whatever the cost. The longer construction was held up, the more excuses he had to concoct in the quarterly reports to the Feds. One wrong phone call to the wrong person, one letter sent to the wrong office, one government inspector who wanted a little vacation in Oregon—his ass would be in a permanent sling. Construction just *had* to get started.

For once the damned phone had been silent an hour or two. Thank God Prather hadn't called. Death had its place in war time—you sent in a salvo, waited for return firing, and then moved on. But Prather picked in the remnants of violent death like some people picked in beach raffle. And he liked it. So what if he could look at dead bodies like so much driftwood—the dead didn't challenge or fight back. Neither did Bill Prather.

Strunk poured himself a tumbler of vodka. There would be an end to the tension soon, he was sure. And then he could take some time out, go down to San Francisco—no bothersome

188

telephone ringing there, no threat from nosey Feds, no irritation from weaklings or incompetents like Prather, Wasser, or Al Freenan. He could search out the haunts of pleasure that reunited his past with the present.

The phone in Chief Karp's office had been quiet too—it was nearly seven o'clock. He had his shoes off, one socked foot propped up on a wastebasket as he studied the simulation footprint photos and the two versions of the coroner's report. The phone broke his concentration.

Ted Bales was so undone he was stuttering.

"Slow down," Karp ordered.

"Me 'n Randy, you know Chief, just got off duty and were havin' a beer out by the bogs. Just sittin' in the car, listenin' to radio traffic. Havin' an innocent beer. That's all. Honest, Chief."

"I believe you, Ted."

"We started pokin' around by the bog, you know how you do. Just messin' around. Over by the edge. Then we saw it. Floatin' right out there in some tall weeds. A goddamned body. All bloated up and awful."

Chief Karp knew Ted Bales had just found Perry Day Truman.

THIRTEEN

Talking in Tongues

There *was* something about Reverend Hammister—just a rumor, but the most vicious kind, reported Lucy's MCC friend Dora Doonan. A twelve-year old boy in one of the church youth groups had accused Hammister of molestation. The rumor had split the parish; one group, led by the boy's parents, wanting the minister hauled away to jail, the other not so sure they believed the boy, who was spoiled and jealous and known to play pranks. Hammister had denied the charges completely, had been willing to submit to any tests or questioning that would settle the congregation. Suddenly the boy's parents wouldn't let him talk, nor would they agree for him to submit to the same questions as the minister. They would agree to drop the entire issue if Hammister left their parish. Hammister's bishop had reassigned the young minister to a parish at a great distance from his troubles. Still, the matter had never been really settled nor the truth uncovered.

Hammister was popular with the women in the Rome congregation for his patience and sensitivity, Dora had learned. Some of his most loyal parishioners had made him cassocks of Japanese silk to commemorate their missionary tour with him.

"I suppose the cassocks were black?" was Nyla's first

191

question after Lucy had relayed Dora's information. "They were," Lucy affirmed.

Both women were thinking of the unusual black fibers found on Valerie Prosper's body.

"That kind of unprovable lie must eat at one's soul," Nyla reflected.

"Especially Jim Hammister's. The very picture of a man dedicated to God."

"Forever unable to truly cleanse his record. Accused of two crimes, really—child molesting and homosexuality. Trapped in a classic stereotype."

"Vengeance is mine, sayeth the Lord."

"An eye for an eye, a tooth for a tooth," Nyla countered.

"Your bulldog wants to bite down on a motive."

"He's got no good alibi. No one at the rectory confirmed his time of return. He's a jogger with an unexplainable limp the morning after someone tumbles down the beach behind the castle. And why doesn't he mention seeing Mitch Masters? Because both the old man and Cora Corona at her scope saw Hammister looking for something out in the surf—maybe something he left behind in a mad dash out of the castle. He's got black silk clerical clothing that could explain the unmatched fibers. Most of all, he's probably got a gut full of anger about the boy's lie, which forever taints his work for God. *If* the boy lied."

"Even the holy have their monsters, that your angle?"

"He had those beers—maybe they roiled up his monsters. And the widows had rejected him in a way. Like his congregation in Rome had."

"Flimsy, Nyla. Karp will never go for it."

"Maybe not, but what about Ritchie Dennis? He's been trying to tell us something and if I'm right in my partial translation, Hammister is more than implicated. He was *witnessed*."

Brother Damion of Portland's Brothers of Mercy School remembered Ritchie Dennis well. He'd been Ritchie's individual tutor before becoming principal. Ritchie had often scared others with his size but he was seldom a problem for the Brothers.

"Perhaps you can help me understand something Ritchie was trying to tell me the other day." Nyla repeated the unusual words Ritchie had said to her during their interview.

The priest chortled. "He sometimes slurs words together if he can't pronounce them, especially names. Nishmon sounds like part of a mispronounced word, punishment. Slurred and shortened, nishment, hence nishmon. 'Onesome when bad boy' I'm quite sure about. It's a combination of the word lonesome and Room One. The most severe punishment here at the school is to be put alone in what we call Room One, which we sometimes lock. We've found that for our pupils, nothing is worse than to be isolated from the group. Ritchie, when he was occasionally a 'bad boy,' went into Room One, where he was very lonesome. Whoever Broham is, Ritchie is connecting him with punishment or 'nishmon' of some kind. That's what it sounds like to me."

Dogma was not a term the priest understood other than its religious meaning, although he guessed it might have something to do with Ritchie's love of animals, especially dogs.

Nyla shared her new information with Lucy, who offered, "When Ritchie and I collided in the black of night, he screamed 'Broham nishmon dogma!' So he seems to be telling us he saw Reverend Hammister punish dogma. Who is dogma?"

They sat on Nyla's bed and stared out the window, listening to the patient ocean loving its shore. Nyla wanted to escape into the sound, have her thoughts slide out into wet waves instead of roiling over and over all this evidence. She thought of Audrey Louise translating her son's nightmares. Ritchie was having one too and she was sure if they helped translate him, they would help themselves to important answers as well.

Dogs, he loved dogs, and in particular, Dobro, the dog who didn't bark the night of the murder, the dog in Mitch's care. Dog-ma, dog-ma . . . Nyla mouthed the sounds. *Who owned that dog? Val and Joan, the ones who had shooed Ritchie away from Dobro—protecting their precious dog, Mrs. Dennis had snarled. Like mothers protecting their precious . . . babe . . . dog . . . dog-mother, dog-ma: Dobro's human mothers were the two widows but Ritchie didn't know their names so*

193

his word for them must be dog-ma!

Nyla felt her eyes burning; the tears surprised her. "He *does* know," she said to Lucy. "Ritchie really *does* know who the murderer is. He saw him and he keeps trying to tell someone but everyone thinks he's just crazy. Don't you see, Lucy? 'Broham nishmon dogma': Brother Hammister punished Dog Mother—the Reverend did something to those widows and Ritchie saw it. Dobro didn't bark that night—why? Either she was inside the house or gone somewhere. Ritchie was out on the road later than usual and when Dobro didn't bark at him, he went closer to investigate because there was no dogma to chase him away. He got close enough to leave his fingerprints on the window sill when he looked into the widows' bedroom and saw 'broham nishmon dogma': Jim Hammister killing Joan and Val."

With a gentle touch, Lucy wiped away the tears that had rolled down Nyla's cheeks. "Come on, Khaki Girl. Now comes the hardest part—convincing Karp of your translation."

Holding hands, they locked Nyla's door as they left to go see the Chief. They were startled when Dobro barked at them from the other end of the hall. The dog was agitated, barking nonstop, starting down the hall toward them and then returning to the back door. Nyla knew something was wrong. "Mitch is always with her. We better see what's up."

Dobro backed away as they came down the hallway. Mitch was not at the workbench; Dobro bared her teeth, showing no inclination to let either woman enter the lean-to. Mitch's voice croaked at the dog and she shushed just long enough for Nyla and Lucy to rush into the shack.

Mitch was on his cot, coughing and clutching at the covers. Lucy touched his face; the old man was burning up with fever. "Can't let a wave into your feet," he moaned. "It'll burn the skin off the bone."

Lucy stripped his covers back, saying, "I had first aid."

He was covered neck to ankles in longjohns, which he had carefully and painstakingly sewn to the tops of his heavy cotton socks with bright orange thread. Nyla poured the old man a drink of water but he could barely get any down.

"Mitch, you're sick. We've got to get you a doctor."

194

"No doctors." He put one hand up from under the covers to shield his eyes, shocking the women when they saw that it was wrapped in a towel spotted with blood.

"For chrissakes, has this guy been in a gunfight?" Lucy unwrapped the towel. Masters had a nasty cut in the palm of his hand. Lucy inspected the injury. "Looks infected."

"Something rusty, maybe?" Nyla wondered. "Might explain the fever."

"This needs stitches," Lucy told her. "We've got to get a doctor."

As Lucy stood up over the cot, Mitch rolled his head to one side of the pillow, staring at the bloody towel. "Seen blood like this before," he mumbled. "From the Night Rider." He sighed, licked his dry lips. "Ricks, ricks," he said softly. "Relics—from the Night Rider." Painfully he pointed to his three-drawer chest.

Nyla leaned close to him. "Relics? What kind of relics? What do you mean, Mitch?"

Masters slumped against his pillows. "I might be going to die," he rasped. His eyes held her with every ounce of his waning strength. "But not all of me will die. There's the sty of wisdom." He tapped his forehead. "Right there. A little steel ball in there. Ball bearings live forever. You can't melt 'em down."

"You're not going to die, Mitch. You're just sick. I have to get you some help."

"No," he groaned, "wait." He reached out a feeble hand to Nyla. "Remember when I told you about that blue who shot a wave on me and Molly Ketcham? I didn't tell you everything. Molly wasn't scared at all—that's when I knew she was an agent. Only one I seen since I came here. Until I seen you, with that same look in your eye, that nothin' could scare you. You're an agent too and that's why I can pass the relics on to you."

The old man closed his eyes and groaned again, holding his stomach with his wounded hand.

"Nyla, really, I should go for a doctor."

"Wait, wait," Masters gasped. His eyes were wide and wild as he gripped Nyla's arm. "Sit me up," he begged. "Sit me up!"

195

They pushed up his pillows and lifted his light bony frame into a sitting position.

"Give me my gloves."

Nyla retrieved them from a wash stand; Masters pulled them on, wincing from the cut on his hand. Then he gently put a gloved hand on either side of Nyla's waist.

"This is what they call the Vise of Fire. Brings out the core of a wave, you'll be safe if they hook onto you. If I'd given it to Lady Bull, she'd have been saved. I don't know about the magician, but with Lady Bull, she would have."

Mitch pressed lightly three times on Nyla's waist, mouthing silent words to himself. Then he gulped, his eyes wobbled back into his head, and he fell back against the pillows, his gloved hands limp.

Lucy immediately ministered to him. "Dip a rag in some water."

The cool cloth on his face seemed to help. Mitch whispered, barely audible, "The relics."

"Where, Mitch?"

"Bottom drawer."

Scrambling away from the cot, Nyla tugged open the chest's bottom drawer which was squashed full of clothing. As she dug among the musty smelling shirts, socks and longjohns, she felt a shoebox. This she brought back to the cot.

Masters rested one hand protectively on the top of the box and closed his eyes. His voice was fading but he struggled to talk.

"The Night Rider left these. He's the one done them widows wrong. Tramp and I saw him that night from our spot in the rocks. I'da seen him closer when I took the dog but he was invisible then. He had his badge covered."

"You took the dog?"

Mitch nodded slowly. "Did that sometimes. Always brought 'er back. Didn't hurt no one."

Nyla looked at Lucy. "You say the Night Rider had a badge? Like a policeman's badge, gold or silver, and shiny?"

Mitch coughed, shaking deep and congested. His voice trailed into a raspy croak as he answered, "No, no. The Night Rider's badge was white at the throat. Black and white, he was, panting and groaning when he ran past us tearing at his own cape. Ran right into the water, went out to sea and turned into a fish. Only his relics came back to shore. Tramp and me collected them to show what we saw." Masters patted the box.

Lucy dabbed his cheeks with the cloth again and took his pulse. "Open the box." She kept her attention on Mitch, heard Nyla pop the rubber bands around the shoebox and then gasp, "Oh, my God!"

Inside the box, wrapped carefully in newspaper, were the irrevocable clues: a bloody portion of a shirt front, black silk raveling at its edges where it had been torn. Clinging to it was what appeared to be a white clerical collar. The badge—as Mitch called it. Also in the box was a stainless steel kitchen knife with a clear stamp on its handle: *St. John's Episcopal, Rome, Ga.*

Nyla and Lucy could not take their eyes from the contents of the shoebox. Masters said feebly, "There was something else. But I gave 'em to Tramp. No fish needed 'em. Fish got flippers."

His voice was completely gone but Nyla and Lucy saw him mouth the word as he passed out. *Shoes,* he said. *Shoes.*

Lucy had to shake a stick at Dobro to get the dog out of the way for the paramedics. Nyla explained Mitch's circumstances and offered to check on him at the county hospital. As the women watched Mitch being wheeled away, they reached out to hold hands.

When the ambulance was finally out of sight, Nyla said, "Guess I'm headed to see the Chief."

Lucy was going to visit Perry's parents. "They're the one source we haven't checked. However they feel about Perry's life, they have to be upset and concerned, too. I doubt they've heard from him but I love Perry too much not to try everyone."

Nyla touched Lucy's cheek. "It's important, what you're willing to do for him."

"So is what you're willing to do for the widows. Chief Karp may not believe Mitch Masters or Ritchie Dennis, but he can't turn his back on *this* evidence."

Chief Karp was on the telephone when Nyla got to the

197

squad room. Sergeant Allen tried to detain her but as soon as she saw the Chief hang up, she rushed into his office.

"I know what you're thinking—here's Nyla Wade still on her wild goose chase." She held the shoebox out to him. "But this time I have something tangible, something even you can believe in."

"I guess you haven't heard."

"Heard what?"

Karp's expression dissolved her focus on the shoebox. Slowly she sat down.

"It's Perry, isn't it?"

He nodded. She stared at the shoebox, working hard not to let that carousel in her mind spin her into dizziness and hysteria. She knew he was gone, that gentle presence, those eager green eyes. Karp sat down also, cleared his throat.

"Don't." She put up one hand and looked directly at the Chief. "It's just a matter of details now and they don't matter." She swallowed hard. "What does matter is an old murder we can do something about. Perry would want that, I know. Look in the shoebox."

Karp was careful when he pushed back the paper to reveal the knife and the torn clerical collar. Nyla told him where she found them, along with Mitch's story and the information on Hammister from the MCC connection.

"Mitch and Tramp saw someone run down the beach into the surf, tearing at his clothing. When the person was gone, they recovered the collar, the shoes, and the knife. That must be how Tramp came to be wearing the shoes."

Karp examined the black silk. "Interesting piece of material." He turned it over in his hands. "Killed on impulse, then panicked, dropped everything incriminating right in plain sight." He frowned.

"Oh, for chrissakes!" Nyla slapped her hand down hard on his desk. "Are you *still* dragging your feet? It all fits together! Hammister's rage over an unhealable wound, the black fibers, his limp the next day, even what he was looking for, observed by two people. Now Ritchie's gibberish makes sense. Hammister *did* punish the widows—like he'd been punished.

198

They were an easy target, they even left the back door open for him."

"I appreciate your persistence, Nyla, I really do." Karp was thoughtful as he slowly put the lid back on the shoebox. "But this is still circumstantial. These will have to be examined—"

"What *is* it with you? Are you *that* afraid you've made a mistake?" She was nearly screaming. Karp held his temper, keeping in mind the effect of the news about Perry.

"Mistakes scare me a helluva lot less than foolhardiness. We have procedures for good reason. Guesses, assumptions—they don't solve or re-solve anything." They were nose-to-nose, both of them upset. Karp was tempted to give Nyla a lecture on respect. He'd listened and given her her share. She seemed to lack the same generosity. He was also tempted to give her a good hard shaking.

Nyla stepped back, stood up straight. "You're absolutely right. We can't go on accusing. But couldn't we go and *talk* to Hammister?"

He appreciated her yielding but kept it to himself. "*I* could go talk to him."

"Come on, Chief. If something breaks on this, you got it from me. I'll keep quiet, I promise."

They stared at each other, less resistant. Karp half-expected her to try one of her smiles on him, but she didn't. She was serious about much more than a story. Her integrity showed him clearly that his prejudice against gays held no truth.

The church was quiet when they arrived, the sanctuary and the receptionist's office dark. They went down the steps to the basement—no banner painters in the cafeteria but lights were on.

"I'll check the nursery." Karp headed down a hallway.

Nyla thought she heard something and walked toward the back of the basement.

"Three winds to the—no—three shinks to the—let's see . . ." Hammister's voice came from an office doorway. Nyla stepped into it. Hammister was slouched in a chair talking to himself.

An empty champagne bottle lay on its side on his desk.

"Three sheets to the wind—that's it!" He took a noisy swig from another bottle and suddenly noticed Nyla. "Well, well, come on in." He squinted at her. "I'm not surprised to see *you*. Busy little beaver, you are. Made a phone call or two, you did."

He took another swig of champagne. "I'm drinking alone today." He tried to focus on the bottle and mumbled, "This was for a wedding tomorrow."

Nyla wondered where Karp had gone. The minister banged his chair back and stood up unsteadily, nearly shouting, "God told Moses, I punish people for their sins! And the punishment of those who hate me passes to their children, on through the generations." Hammister lowered his voice. "Some irony. I love God *and* children but I'm punished." His eyes narrowed on Nyla. "Did you come to punish me too?"

She didn't answer. He waved a hand at her. "The Lord redeemeth the soul of his servants and none who trust in him shall be desolate." He frowned. "Psalms? Revelations?" The Reverend's chin dropped onto his chest, and he wavered a moment near the chair. "This soul is desolate."

Nyla moved further into the office. Hammister rambled to himself, "Children are God's possessions, to be protected more so than anything on earth. I always did, always, all God's children . . ."

Karp stepped into the doorway but Nyla held up a hand to silence him. The Reverend didn't notice. "I never touched him, it was all a lie."

Nyla came around Hammister's desk. "*Did* that boy lie or did he tell the truth?"

"I'm not a drinker," Hammister said lamely.

"Why did he tell that lie?" Nyla kept at him. "What happened in Georgia, Reverend? And what's happened since then?"

Hammister wobbled a step backward, trying to focus on Nyla. "What business is it of yours? Why are you calling people about me? You have no right to do that. I stood up to everyone, to all of them. I put my head on the block because they thought I owed something. But I did nothing, you understand, nothing!" His voice was hysterical. The bottle dangled limply in his hand.

Nyla kept pressing, hoping Karp wouldn't stop her. "Where did you go when you left the Lighthouse Inn the night the widows were killed, Reverend?"

"The widows?" He looked as if he might fall into a heap on the floor. "What the—I told the police—I came back here and went to sleep. I was nauseous."

"You didn't take a stroll later? Down on the beach? A stroll to the cement steps up from the beach to the castle?"

"No, not until the next morning, like always. My morning run." He massaged his temples.

"You sure you didn't take a run up there that night in the dark, go in the widows' back door and—"

"What? What are you talking about? I saw them earlier in the evening, that was all. I told you this! I told the *police.* What in God's name am I accused of now? Another crime I didn't commit?"

He stared incredulously at Nyla. She caught a movement from Karp out of the corner of her eye. Hammister's eyes glazed. "Lying children who will not hear the law of God," he rambled, raising his voice. "Keep thy tongue from evil!" The minister was shouting. "He lied! I never touched him, all lies!" Hammister jerked and swiped the bottle in the air over his head, staggering toward Nyla.

Karp leaped over the desk, grabbing Hammister in his huge arms like so much playdough. The bottle swung perilously near the Chief's head and he heard it crash. Nyla had scooped up a trashcan to break the blow.

"Good move," Karp sighed, pushing the limp minister into his chair.

For more than an hour, they forced coffee into Hammister. The Reverend began to sober. Karp advised him of his rights. Hammister didn't want a lawyer, he told the Chief, didn't need one.

"I have these . . . blackouts. Kept it a secret. People think you're sick, can't do things. Didn't want to be kept out of the ministry, doing what I wanted most in the world. I've had these migraine headaches . . . since boyhood. Hands go numb

201

sometimes, I get amnesia for an hour or so. Can't remember people I know, where I've been, my own name even. Sometimes with the worst ones, I pass out. Usually I can feel it coming, get to my bed, but not always . . ."

Hammister was shaking, holding out his hands, staring at them. "Both times, the same thing. Back in Rome, the boy came into my office. I was lying on my couch, felt the headache rolling in, waves of pain and nausea. Felt as if someone were stripping off my scalp." Hammister began to sob. "He kept talking to me, asking me questions, but I couldn't answer. Too much pain. He was whining, an angry little boy, and then . . . that's all I remember. All I know is that I would never do such a thing—not to that boy, or anyone!"

He looked at Karp, tears running down his cheeks. "Then that night, I could feel one coming on. Musta been the beers. Can't remember getting home. Woke the next morning and I wasn't in my bed. Things were knocked over and I had a sore leg. I went down to the beach to clear my head, walked right into the surf, cold water in my shoes, I was so groggy. Ran into Masters, he told me what happened. This panic went through me, right through my heart."

He bent over, hugging his knees, his shoulders racked by his own sobbing. "Same thing . . . all over again . . . people would accuse me. Wouldn't believe me. And I couldn't remember . . ."

Karp put a firm hand on Hammister's shoulder. "Reverend, did you bring a stainless steel kitchen knife from your parish in Georgia?"

Still shaking, Hammister tried to wipe his eyes. "Yes, I think so."

"Where is it now?"

Tears kept welling out of the minister's eyes. "I . . . I don't have it. It was stolen last year—the rectory was vandalized and the knife was taken."

Karp nodded gravely at Nyla, then reached for the phone.

"It's the truth, it *is,* it's the truth," Hammister blubbered.

Karp had the minister's story confirmed in a short time. Hammister had filed the proper report after the robbery and the knife was listed. The Chief hung up, he and Nyla glanced

202

at each other. Then Karp said to Hammister, "Stand up and unzip your sweatsuit top."

Hammister blinked rapidly and sniffed.

"I didn't say take it off, just unzip it."

He moved his hand hesitantly.

"Do it!"

On the long thin neck revealed to them, there was only smooth skin never scarred—especially from any violent struggle.

But there was one final proof. Again Karp addressed the minister. "I want to see the special cassocks made for you by the women from the Georgia parish out of black Japanese silk."

Hammister stared dumbly. He was beginning to look less like a weepy hysterical drunk who could have committed murder and more like a puffy-eyed muskrat.

"Do you have the cassocks or not?"

Hammister pulled himself together, leaning against his desk and taking some deep breaths. He looked at the broken glass and mumbled, "Sorry about the bottle. Lost my head. Never would have hurt you."

He took some more deep breaths and shook his head. His eyes were red and bloodshot. He ran a shaky hand over his forehead.

Nyla was seething with impatience when Hammister finally said, "They're hanging right here in my closet."

The cassocks were intact. And looked nothing like the patch of black and white cloth uncovered in Mitch Masters' shoebox.

Nyla felt utterly frustrated. Every possible clue for blaming the murders on the minister had a logical explanation. Even his limp the next day seemed attributable to his knocking over a small table on the landing at the top of the stairs when he finally made it home. Despite her own feelings of defeat, she offered the sniffling man some solace.

"You didn't do it, Reverend. Blackouts or no—you didn't harm those widows."

"I think we can rule out finding any prints on the knife," Karp said as he and Nyla left the church. "But I bet the fibers will match those found on Valerie Prosper."

Nyla appreciated that he wasn't gloating about her misfired hunch.

"So who do you suppose Ritchie Dennis and Mitch Masters saw that night, Nyla?"

Though she was feeling sheepish, she didn't want Karp to think she couldn't admit a mistake. "Whoever it was, it wasn't the Reverend."

Karp tossed aside the toothpick he'd been chewing and smiled. Then he said, "Could be whoever they saw was *dressed* like the Reverend."

"Scotch rocks and a vodka, up, double," Bill Prather ordered at the Wharf Restaurant. Then he chided Jim Strunk, "Little early for a double, isn't it, Jim?" His grin dissolved at the North Bend lawyer's glower.

"You don't have my pressures, Bill." Strunk's tone was edgy and resentful.

Bill Prather had his own pressures, in particular the one he had never wanted Strunk to know about—the error on the autopsy report of Eugene Williams. He'd lied to Chief Karp to protect himself and Strunk—but every day he'd doubted, and the expense of the lie had mounted. Sometimes he just wanted to tell Strunk and get it over with. The lawyer's bid for D.A. had gone bust, none of the politicos so hot to promote Strunk before had shown any interest in a second try. So what did he have to lose by telling him? But there was a look in Strunk's eyes, like he had a spot in him maybe, and if you pressed wrong, he'd strangle you with his bare hands. Prather's gut had always told him to be careful around Jim Strunk.

"It's the Seascape people. They keep calling me, dropping their little innuendos about changing lawyers. I'm sick of them, sick of this whole damned thing. If it's not them calling, it's Adam Hall or Ben Wasser or that goddamned James Ruddye."

Or me, Prather thought. He had his own share of stockholder worries. If a government inspector showed up, found out about the kickback . . .

"That little faggot screwed us all, every one of us." When Strunk's vodka came, the glass barely touched the table before he downed it and ordered another.

The second vodka went the way of the first and a third was on its way when Strunk told Prather, "That little fag bastard isn't going to ruin this for me."

The third vodka came and Strunk sucked it down like water. "This is my shot, Bill. This goddamned dressed-up Howard Johnson's hotel has got to go up—and soon!" His fist clenched his glass so hard Prather thought it might shatter.

This was no time to add to Strunk's agitation—yet somehow, it *was* time. The burr had rubbed him raw for long enough. He couldn't keep the secret to himself any longer.

When Prather finished, Strunk was slumped back against his chair, his face bloodless. When he tried to speak, his voice was an incoherent slur. Then with a yell of frustration summoned from his bowels, Strunk rose up out of his chair and hurled the vodka glass into the mirror over the bar.

"Wait, Jim, please!" Prather begged as Strunk slammed out of the restaurant. But the lawyer got to his car and screeched away from Old Town.

He careened onto the highway, barreling in a blind rage across the lighthouse bridge. His gut burned and he yelled at the top of his lungs.

A car moving toward him honked a warning and he swerved at the last minute, bumping onto the shoulder of the road and slashing sparks on a hundred yards of guard rail before he came to a stop.

The car steamed in the fog. Strunk heard the underbody crack, as if straightening itself from the harrowing stop he'd made. He beat the steering wheel with his fists. His little scam on an easy mark had been perfectly set up, then Truman and the Ruddyes had delayed it. Wasser's stupid moves had nearly uncovered it. Now Prather had toppled everything—Karp would declare the case reopened until the measurement error was explained.

That damned castle, like it has a life of its own . . . Strunk looked up the road, saw the dim halo of a light around a roadside telephone.

FOURTEEN

A Bind in Time

Lucy was on her redwood front porch peeling an apple when Nyla drove up. She could see the gloom in Nyla's face, dropped the apple and the knife to go to her. The raw truth took few words—Perry was dead and the Reverend hadn't killed anyone. They sat down on the porch, not touching, Nyla totally empty. Lucy looked as if she'd had the breath knocked out of her.

They were jolted by the clatter of Seth's truck racing up the road and sliding sideways in the gravel, nearly tipping over as he braked into the yard.

"I can't believe it!" he yelled, kicking open the door. He'd been holding his gut since the call came in, feeling like the huge steel ball on the end of the wrecking crane had pounded into his ribcage and left him cratered and gaping. "I just heard on my two-way radio! Someone's put in a call to Portland for a ball-and-chain wrecker—I think Seascape is going to knock the castle down!"

The news of the wrecker became a secondary shock when Nyla told Seth about Perry. The three of them endured the rest of the evening quietly, eating supper without appetite, listening to music with no joy. Seth wandered the big ranch-style house; Lucy fussed with a fire as night brought in a chill. Nyla watched them both to avoid her own internal wanderings. Grief surrounded the three of them thick as the fog.

It was past midnight when Seth opened the sliding glass doors off the living room and walked out onto the fog-drenched deck. Nyla had been gazing at the embers of the fire dropping from the grate, each with a small hiss. Lucy hadn't turned a page for hours in the book she held. They looked at each other when Seth went out. Nyla sighed; Lucy looked toward the grey mist edging its chilly presence into the room through the slit of the open door.

"I wish to hell I knew what to say to him," Lucy said with anguish.

Nyla looked toward the door and the fog as if she could see Seth's broad back where he was standing and staring into the impenetrable mist, maybe wishing it could carry his grief and pain out to sea. "So do I. To him, to all of us."

Lucy added a log and stirred up the fire, then joined Nyla on the couch. They had curled into each other's arms as Seth stepped back inside. He watched them a moment and then said, "What are we going to do?"

Nyla observed that Randolph brother and sister had the same look about their eyes, a dark storm of defeat and anger. Both seemed to shrink further into the furniture as they sat by the fire. Seth said vehemently, "Whoever's moving on the castle was real sure Perry's out of the way." Nyla quashed her reaction to suggest they call in Karp again. And then in the silence of their grief, she heard the echo of Perry's voice. *I'll fight them to the end . . . I'll keep on using every contact I have . . . only over my dead body . . .*

"That wrecker isn't getting into this town."

Nyla's defiant tone caused the redheads to look at her in wonder.

"I'm calling Howard Penn right now. He can rally people from Astoria to Baja with enough cars to stop that wrecker dead in its tracks."

A slow smile crept over Lucy's face. The storm in Seth's eyes cleared, Nyla saw, as he sat up in his chair. "Get busy dialing," he urged her.

Despite the hour of Nyla's call, Howard Penn rose to the occasion. He assured her they could convene by daylight a blockade of Oregon gays while a California contingent got rolling.

"We can organize faster than we run from a police raid! A tougher bunch of blockaders you never saw. We can walk in, sit in, or outwait the pants off anyone, and we've got signs perfect for every protest occasion. Our persistence makes straight officials cranky as hell. They always think we'll get tired and go home. But we don't."

When Nyla hung up, she kept her hand on the phone for a moment. She worked hard to block the images that swam in her mind of Perry floating in that bog. Perry with his green eyes misting as he talked of his lost friends, Perry as he showed his concern for her cut hand. Now he was lost to them and the wash of feeling was unbearable. She took a deep breath, heard the small sound she couldn't control. And then Lucy's arms were around her and Seth's arms around them both. It was almost enough, their net cast out into the gay family, their unity, their resistance to what threatened the castle. What had been Perry's sign of hope was now their own.

By daylight, Seth had confirmed the radio report—Stadler Construction in Portland was rigging their ball-and-chain wrecker for the road to Burnton. The gay blockade of cars had been activated and the drivers were reporting in by phone. The activity provided respite from thoughts about Perry, especially for Seth. Still their grief was overpowering. Nyla had to get some fresh air, take a walk to clear her head, rest her heart.

Before she left, Seth asked her, "You gonna call Karp?" Lucy was surprised by the sharpness in his voice. Nyla didn't answer. Seth said, "They'll just think we're a buncha queers bent on a demolition derby."

Lucy added, "Or he'll tell us there's nothing to worry about, like he did with Perry."

Nyla looked at each of them and then shrugged. "He'll know soon enough. Besides, Howard just loves reception committees and I wouldn't want to spoil this one for him."

Lucy smiled. "The Lavender Blockade." The two women waited for Seth and finally he allowed the hint of a grin.

The sea wore her cap of clouds but the day was clear of fog, and what sun made its way through cheered Nyla. She headed for the beach, wishing she could quiet her mind. *Wouldn't it be great if I walked up the beach and ran into Perry? Looking like nothing had happened at all, safe and sun-tanned and smiling . . . wouldn't that be something!* He'd wanted the same thing when Joan and Val were killed, to find out it was all a dream, a scare, and that his friends were safe and had come home again.

The pull of the surf lapping the shore that usually seemed irresistible now made her sad. *You can't bring back the dead any more than you can keep the surf from rolling in.* Nyla thought of a painting she'd once seen of wave crests turning into unicorns. The sail-shaped rocks she was gazing at jutted from the water and held their cotillion as if locked in time; the serpent-shaped rock dipped her neck for a dive into the fathoms. So Karp had finally seemed to believe some of what she'd told him—that some other suspect was as likely as Tramp Williams, even though it wasn't Jim Hammister. And Ritchie Dennis and Mitch Masters weren't just crazies with nothing important to say. He was still a cop, though, and had made it clear she should stick to journalism and quit amateur sleuthing. Still, he had come up with no better answers than she had. He might have his procedures, but his answers basically came from instinct, too, and she knew it.

It was time to stop gazing futilely at the ocean. She knew where she was going—to the castle. She'd sit on the limestone steps and concentrate all the powers she possessed. Maybe the

Ketcham ghosts would give her the answers that seemed so within reach and yet so impossibly distant. Maybe Olympia Swan would deliver a message to her.

Nyla was surprised to see a car in the castle driveway and the front door open. She went up the steps and called into the hallway.

Cohista Farrell answered from the kitchen. "Nyla, come in." Cohista was wiping her hands on a towel; she looked first at the open front door and then down the long hallway. "No matter what the weather or time of day, I just have to keep the front door open whenever I'm here alone." She smiled. "I was just dusting and cleaning the windows in the kitchen."

Nyla stared down the dim hallway; a moment of restless silence held her.

"I know about Perry," the housekeeper said softly.

"Yes . . ." Nyla couldn't stop the tears that welled up.

"He was such a gentleman."

Nyla saw that Cohista was tearful too. They stepped toward each other for an awkward hug. They smiled and wiped their faces.

"I was just out for a walk," Nyla said. "Solving the world's problems, you know." Her distracted smile barely peaked before it faded. Again they stood in the entryway without speaking.

"May I?" Nyla asked abruptly, gesturing down the hallway. "I won't disturb anything. I just want to go—"

"Be my guest," Cohista offered. "I'll be in the kitchen if you need me."

The hallway was not nearly so long and forbidding in the daylight as it had been that black night of errant seagulls and chopped fish. Still, there was a dimness in the light that filtered through the shuttered windows, an aura along this path that led back to the place of death. Nyla shook herself and breathed in and out loudly through her mouth, like a runner. She stopped in the hallway at the door to the main bedroom. There was the sleigh bed, a relic of gaiety, rooted here in this gloomy space.

She marched to the windows of the bedroom. Soon the

sleigh was circled by morning rays. Walking aimlessly around the room and then into the bathroom, she sank onto the edge of the tub, chin on her hand. From this vantage point, she could see into the guest bedroom. She stared into that room, her mind jumbled with a torrent of memories about the castle—her first sight of it, her tour through its rooms with Perry—then suddenly a particular memory jogged in her brain, from Mitch Masters' ramblings.

When I worked on the plumbing that day, I looked up and saw something, now. She was there, see, at the window, and she pointed her finger just like this.

From the bedroom doorway, the only windows in view were those in the guest bedroom. Also in sight was the linen closet doorway. What had Val been pointing at from that window?

Crossing to the guest bedroom, Nyla could see nothing unusual about the window; it was covered with yellow transparent curtains to match the brown and yellow bedspread.

She pointed her finger, just like this. The magician's touch, they call it.

Nyla lifted an edge of the curtain, expecting a glass pane marked by nothing more extraordinary than dust. Instead, the lifted curtains revealed six small crystals shaped like snowflakes, each hanging on a nearly invisible thread. They twirled in the sunlight. One twinkled blue, green, red against the yellow curtain.

Looking out the window toward the sea, Nyla wondered where Val might have been pointing. Absentmindedly, she poked each crystal so that it turned and flashed in the sun. What had Val seen out there? What was the real meaning of Mitch's story about a magic room?

Something moved on the carpet near her, a bouncing light reflected from one of the crystals.

Sea meanie, sea anemone . . . magician's touch, magician's blood . . . Nyla slid back the gathers of one of the yellow curtains. One by one, she poked the crystals so that they swung and twirled. The room, the doorways of both bedrooms, the hall were filled with bouncing dots of white light.

Quickly she crossed back to the bathroom doorway; from

there she could barely see the crystals swinging in the window. If Val had stood at the window and poked each crystal, it might well have looked to Mitch with his eighty-year old eyesight as if she was pointing. *Just like this, six stabs in the air . . .*

Crossing rapidly back to the window, Nyla twirled the crystals faster and then rushed back to the bathroom doorway. There was a sparkler effect from the crystals, dots of white light racing across the sleigh bed, up the walls and doorjambs, friendly ghost creatures with no wings or voices, just chubby flat wall dancers. And then Nyla saw it: the linen closet doorway sprayed with bobbing, dancing dots of light. As the crystals moved, the dots flexed wide and small from the center of the door to its edges and the wall beyond it. *Coming out of a sparkler, see, just like the Fourth of July.* As the one colored crystal turned, it prismed red light into some of the dots. Nyla realized this must be the magician's blood, as Mitch had called it.

There *was* a magic room and now Nyla Wade had seen it with her own eyes.

She found Cohista dusting in the office. Nyla touched the polished top of the Wooten. "I think I'll go visit an old friend."

Cohista's expression was an inquiry; her question went unspoken when Nyla said as she went out the door, "My friend's at Peak's Storage."

A dope or a fool could have made better sense of all this than I did, Nyla chastised herself in her room at Shady Stay. She gave a thought to calling Gruff but knew he'd heard about Perry and wouldn't expect her on time. The wrecker would move slowly and was not expected until early evening. She took a quick shower hot enough to sting her skin, then changed into some casual clothes.

There was a soft tapping at her door.

"Who is it?"

"Loamie Newsome."

As the unexpected visitor came in with a shoebox tucked under her arm, Nyla felt a premonition.

213

Loamie's confession had been long held and was known to no one else. On that morning a year ago, Loamie had heard Cohista Farrell scream and had rushed across the gravel driveway into the house. Cohista was in the kitchen, frantically calling Seth Randolph. Loamie saw the open hallway closet door and walked toward it, the door blocking her view of the carnage in the widows' bedroom. Seeing the floor littered with pieces of paper, and soon realizing what they were, out of loyalty to Joan she had quickly gathered them up unobserved and fled back to her own house. Until later that morning, Loamie thought Cohista's discovery of the graphic love poems had been the cause of her scream. Only when she saw the police arrive had she learned that she had been within a few feet of her murdered neighbors and not known it.

"And there's something else too. It was me who stoned the castle that night. I'm sorry. I was hopping mad—about you and Perry going through her things—Joan's things. That was her house and no one else's, not even Valerie's. It made me mad and I blew up. Sorry. Didn't really mean any harm."

Nyla questioned Loamie about the chopped fish, but she knew nothing, had seen no one else until Lucy had come running up the driveway. "Darned near caught me, too." Even remembering how scared she'd been, Nyla couldn't help but smile at Loamie.

"I got to thinking maybe these poems were what you and Perry were after. I got to thinking about who to turn them over to. I don't understand them exactly but I know they're about love and that makes them special. I never cared much for those kids of Joan's so I just kept the poems to myself. Then lately, what with Perry disappearing and all, I got to thinking you weren't so much trying to disturb things as to help. So here I am and here's Joan's poems. Maybe they'll help you."

Loamie put her arm straight out and handed Nyla the shoebox. For a moment, Nyla considered telling Loamie the news about Perry but could not bring herself to do it.

"Thank you for bringing these to me. Perry was so worried the Ruddyes would use them in court—make them into something awful."

Loamie gave Nyla a curious smile. "They're just love poems." As she was about to go out the door, she said, "Joan and me were the same birth sign—Taurus the Bull. Stubborn, hot-headed sometimes." Loamie stopped talking for a moment to remember. "One birthday we had to laugh. We gave each other the same thing—a little necklace with the bull design. Joan was a great lady. And what a heart. You can tell that from her poems."

Loamie had verified Nyla's translation of Mitch Masters' Lady Bull—she'd guessed he meant Joan Ruddye and now she was sure. Taurus the Bull—Mitch had seen Joan wear Loamie's zodiac necklace. And Loamie had seen the truth of Joan—the graciousness of a kind and loving personality in their nine years as neighbors. How ironic that the magic room had revealed the love poems. There had been some very important magic in that closet after all.

Visualizing the nude portrait of Valerie Prosper, Nyla could see both women as she read their poems—poems of initial separation and eventual consummation. All of this Joan wrote to Valerie. From the devotion in the verses, it was clear how Valerie had evoked Joan's passion. The poems contained what Perry had feared—what could be distorted to show them as women willing to break taboos.

"I dreamed all the first times were gone for me
Till your scarf bound my wrist, yet still I was free.
Till your scarf was my blindfold, yet still I could see.
Every binding of my soul that you devise
Makes me dive toward the trust I find in your eyes.
Others may not understand our care.
No others see the power we share.
I loved you when first I heard you sing
And love still the soft touch you bring."

Only a scarf—a silken touch to entice a lover, to hold her back with softness in love's challenge, to bind her for a private exchange. It was only a scarf, Nyla thought, and nothing done against any will.

Thinking of the Ruddye children, she carefully put the

poems back into the shoebox. Only a scarf, not their mother pilloried and chained. How different fearful people see the same signs of those who love unafraid.

She sat alone in the quiet, decaying motel. Once again she joined lovers' ghosts from another time and knew them by what they had written, just as with Mrs. Porter's letter. Once again they gave her their trust from beyond life, from the other side of the fragile tissue separating souls alive from souls in memory. She was a kind of guardian.

Nyla sighed, got herself up from the bed and headed for a stiff belt of scotch. She wasn't sure she wanted to be so chosen.

Lucy would have thought the warehouse was empty except for the pale shimmer of one bulb at the far back corner. The silence in the huge building surrounded the collection of hulking shapes, all manner of oddities stored under tarps. Cohista had told her where to find Nyla, and as she walked down a row of tall boxes toward the meager light, she saw Nyla sitting up on a box, her feet dangling. She was softly tapping the box with her heels, seemed to be staring at something. As Lucy came to the end of the boxes, she saw the tarp pulled back from the golden oak desk.

"Hi," she said softly. The space demanded quiet. Nyla lifted a hand in greeting. "This is your old friend?" Lucy indicated the desk.

Nyla nodded, then slid off the box. "Here she is, safe and sound. The movers were careful—didn't set any boxes on her. And this place is pretty clean." She pushed the tarp back further.

"I don't know . . ." Nyla touched the wood of the roll top. "I thought maybe I'd open a drawer and presto, some answers would come to me. But just like with Joan's Wooten and all those little compartments, I've got all these questions and no answers . . ."

Lucy came up close to her, put an arm around her waist and rested her chin on Nyla's shoulder. They stared at the desk in silence. When Nyla sighed, Lucy turned her around so they faced each other.

"Your Eastern mystic types talk about the void. Some

think it's outside us, some think it's within. Right now I feel like it's everywhere except the part of me . . ." Her eyes met Nyla's. "The part of me that loves you."

She reached into her pocket and pulled out a tiny seashell white as bone that had been in one of the Wooten compartments. "Your faith in what we can do is all that's keeping me going, Nyla. When I saw you sitting here, I felt like the entire void of pain and sorrow that surrounds us can shrink into this one tiny seashell. And leave only an echo."

They held each other. Nyla felt Lucy's tears against her neck and took her lover's face into her hands. "We *are* magic," she said. "Magic and faith and will. We *are*."

Nothing out of the ordinary. No matter how many times Walter Karp had walked through the rooms of Perry Day Truman's apartment, nothing had stuck out like a sore thumb, yelled "Foul!" or prickled the Chief's antennae. He finally slumped down on the couch and stared into the fireplace.

The lab results were in—Truman had been struck by a blunt instrument here in the apartment and dumped unconscious into the bog. A section of the carpet had showed microscopic traces of Truman's blood and scalp tissue. And paint samples revealed someone had tried to wash his blood off one wall. Bill Prather had pronounced the death an aggravated drowning, saying Truman would have died anyway from massive cerebral hemorrhaging. But nothing was simple—there were no unusual or unidentified fingerprints in the apartment. Might have been some at the door but those were smudged into oblivion. Karp sighed loudly, then coughed, aware of how loud his sounds were in the empty, cold apartment. He kept his topcoat buttoned.

He was frustrated—by evidence that didn't tell him anything, by incidents that seemed unconnected, by the ratio of questions to answers. Did the same person or persons who scared Nyla Wade kill Perry Day Truman? And who was it that wanted Truman dead? How would his death affect the litigation with the Ruddyes, who would now be dealing with Truman's executor? That would probably be his parents, native Burnton citizens with great loyalty to the City and none for their son's lifestyle. No doubt they would be happy to settle out of court with the Ruddyes and allow Seascape to raze the castle. Yet if they'd known about his will, they'd also have known, as Karp now did after talking with Truman's lawyer, that Seth Randolph was executor of all Truman's worldly possessions *except* the castle, which had been clearly designated the property of the Gay Historical Society.

From the lab analysis of the partially burned pages, the will, the petitions, and the manuscript had been burned. What Karp couldn't figure was why anyone would bother to burn the will. Anyone with common sense would know Truman's lawyer had a copy. Unless . . . supposing it was burned because it had been touched. Or simply burned in haste, thrown in as an after-

218

thought. Karp's instincts told him this crime had not started out to be murder but a simple B&E, to get the petitions. He couldn't tap a specific suspect but it would have to be someone with an interest in protecting Seascape or the City. Certainly neither would profit from petitions presented at the White House and possibly making national news.

To Karp, the jimmied tacklebox and half-hearted burning suggested a person without much savvy. Yet fingerprints had been eliminated or smudged. Whoever dumped Truman in the bog had hoped his head wound would appear to be accidental, caused by his fall into the water. And the evidence of the struggle in the apartment had been cleaned up, except for what the microscope had revealed. Karp didn't like the hodge-podge of facts nor his feelings about them. How could anyone know where the petitions were or when Howard Penn was due to collect them, or that Truman had written a new will? He'd only told Nyla Wade about the petitions on the morning of his disappearance. The only other person who'd known about the will was his lawyer, who, of course, declared that he certainly would not broach client confidentiality by discussing it with any of his associates. The new papers were still in a locked file in the lawyer's private office. Karp believed him and he didn't think Nyla Wade would discuss Perry with anyone who might want to do him harm. So how did someone find out?

The Police Chief worked his hands in the pockets of his coat, glanced around the cold living room. *Strange colors for a man, all this lavender . . .* He ran back over the statements of Nyla, Seth, Lucy, the lawyer. *"He told me he'd been on the phone all morning to Howard Penn . . ."* Penn was the odd man out but surely he wouldn't be in on the killing of one of his own. *"He told me he'd been on the phone all morning . . ."*

When you were a small town Police Chief and no longer a big city detective, no longer working streets full of New York's lowlifes, pimps, and cheap operators, instincts got less sharp, sometimes you forgot routine things. There'd hardly been a Brooklyn case Karp ever walked in on that he hadn't checked for a phone bug, especially with all the protection rackets and bookie joints he'd busted. Even the pimps made tapes, thought it was some kind of defense. Funny how that worked out—sometimes it was other people getting dirt and sometimes it was dirty people collecting their own. Karp was still shaking his head when he picked up the receiver. But even he was a little surprised when he unscrewed the mouthpiece and found the disk microphone.

FIFTEEN

In Jeopardy

Nyla and Lucy agreed that work was the best therapy for grief. Seth was busy keeping tabs on the blockade drivers. Four carloads had already arrived, along with a semi-cab which was stashed at the construction yard. Howard Penn had reached Eureka with another four cars and two trucks. The latest on the wrecker was that it had left Portland but was moving slowly. Seth's ETA was 10:00 the following morning.

At the *Beckoner* office Nyla found only a note from Gruff. He'd dashed over to Coos Bay and Jean was taking the day off. The stringers' columns and some other items for her to edit were stacked neatly on her desk underneath his note which closed with, "Sorry to hear about Perry."

She sat down in her chair, rolled aimlessly to and fro on its wheels as she wondered what Perry's folks would do about a funeral and if Reverend Hammister would organize another memorial service. Her musings were interrupted by the ringing phone.

"Burnton *Beckoner*. Nyla Wade speaking."

"Miss Wade, you're just the person I wanted to speak to. I'm Mr. Avery from Oceanview Rest Home. I thought you'd like to know we'll be holding a special sunset service tonight. Many of our residents knew Mr. Truman and so the service

221

will be dedicated to him. I was sure you'd want to know, both for yourself and the paper."

"Why yes, of course."

"We thought we'd van the seniors over to the little roadside park at the end of the Loop for a change of scenery. Will we see you there?"

"Certainly, Mr. Avery. Thanks for letting me know."

There was something comforting in the quiet office and Nyla made headway with her stack of work. Until her growling stomach got the best of her, she was unaware it was well past two o'clock and she'd skipped lunch. She ran next door to the grocery store for a microwaved cardboard-tasting burrito.

She went back to her desk and wrapped up everything Gruff had left her. The last sheet of paper in the stack was yet another note: "If you've finished everything else, you're in for a treat. *Gone with the Cranberry* is running a dress rehearsal today. 4:30 at the high school." He'd even made an attempt at drawing a smiling face with his signature.

Nyla gave Seth a quick call, told him she'd be at the sunset service and would join them afterward. He reported that the Lavender Blockaders were in high spirits and huddled with him around his two-way radio when they weren't raiding the Randolph fridge.

Ben Wasser shifted the weight of his gun belt below his doughy waistline, then locked his patrol car. He took a healthy swipe at his face with his handkerchief, heard himself wheeze as he went up the few steps of City Hall. Christ, he wished he didn't sweat so much. What the hell did Walter Karp want? They weren't what he'd call bosom buddies. City cops and county cops were fairly territorial . . . still, he held the larger jurisdiction, with three solid terms to his credit. But Karp wasn't just any bothersome small town Police Chief. Wasser knew his background, knew Karp was smarter than the job he held.

The Chief smiled broadly when Wasser arrived. "Phil, get Ben some coffee," he called, offering the sheriff a handshake and a seat in his office. "How's the county holding up?" he asked.

Wasser just nodded and squashed down into a chair. He eyed the coffee Allen delivered but didn't drink any. He shifted onto one hip in the chair and twirled his hat around in his hands.

"I appreciate your stopping by, Ben," Karp began. "Some pretty strange things have been happening around town. I thought maybe city and county ought to cooperate, see what we could come up with. You know—two heads better than one . . ."

As he talked, Karp's voice became a drone. Wasser sweated, his mind reeling back over recent events. Had he wiped away all the prints? Did Karp know something, find something they'd missed? Or maybe he'd been double-crossed . . .

"You take this Truman thing. Not a clear-cut murder, not exactly a drowning," Karp was saying.

He does *have something. What the hell could it be? Only Strunk and I know* . . . And there it was. Strunk, with everything to gain and no compunction about sacrificing him or anyone else. *Penny ante swindler, just his word against mine, and he's a guy people remember* didn't *get elected. Karp, though, not penny ante anything. If he's got something, I'll be swimming upstream without a* . . .

"We found that someone had made a poor attempt to burn some petitions, Truman's will, the manuscript he wrote on the gay history of the castle."

Wasser's eyes flickered at the word. "Christ, Walt, can you believe this, in a town this size?"

Karp paused but didn't respond to the sheriff's comment. "I think it was an accident, Truman wasn't expected, he came back early. There was a struggle and he got bashed. Then here's the dilemma—a B&E turns into an assault, Truman's seen the person or persons, they've gone too far. He gets dumped in the bog and now we're up to Murder One." Karp stopped talking, waited for Wasser's affirmation.

The sheriff just stared at him. *How does he know that's the way it went down? Christ, I never figured Strunk would talk! No one else could have told him. What kind of story has he cooked up? A sure bet something digging me in deep* . . .

The Police Chief went on. "I got it figured two guys, think

223

they're doing a duty for Seascape and the City."

Wasser swallowed. He stopped twirling his hat. He felt numb.

"I couldn't find any fingerprints in the apartment so they knew what they were up to, but I figure we'll recover the weapon when the bogs dry out after the harvest . . ."

My whole career, toed the line pretty good, nothing too far afield. Then Strunk comes along, I figure I can work him at his own game, make myself one easy score, a nest egg . . .

When Karp pushed his chair back and stood up, Wasser flinched, squinting at him.

"But you know how it goes, there's a body to be dumped, the pulse rate's up, the guy's in a hurry, something gets forgotten." The Chief walked around the desk toward Wasser.

The sheriff pushed back against the chair and felt his soaked shirt. Karp stopped, leaned against the edge of the desk, one hand in his pocket. Wasser was staring at him, a little wide-eyed, holding his breath.

"All those years in New York weren't for nothing." Karp was smiling but Wasser saw him almost in slow motion—his hand coming out of his pocket, holding a little plastic evidence bag and inside it, the familiar round black disk.

Wasser's hat fell to the floor, its stiff brim making a small sound. He heard the Police Chief ask him, "Did Truman really have that much interesting to say, Ben?"

Lucy felt she'd run her entire shift at top speed. She tossed her boots on top of her crumpled uniform—she'd worry about getting everything cleaned tomorrow. With a bang of her locker door, she jogged out of the post office toward the high school, using the last of her energy. Seth had given her the message of Nyla's activities and Lucy hoped she'd catch Nyla before she left for the sunset service.

At 6:45, she found Scarlett O'Cranberry delivering a smarmy soliloquy in front of a huge stage flat depicting the regal columns of Tara, but painted cranberry color. She had just missed Nyla. She decided to walk to the roadside park—the activity would do wonders for her restlessness despite her tired muscles. Searching for Nyla was far preferable to waiting for her even if it meant a walk in the dark.

Odd, not a soul around. Nyla checked the note she'd made when Mr. Avery called. At seven o'clock, the sun was dipping fast—but not a senior was in sight at the roadside park. Nyla opened her car door, stepped out to look around. Only one other car, and no one in it—they must be down at the beach sightseeing.

She turned at the fast slap of footsteps but the two men were there before she could scream. The big one clamped his hand over her mouth and the skinny one grabbed her hands. Together they wrestled her into the Mustang.

The light was giving way and Lucy could barely see the center line on the Loop. Headlights splashed yellow in front of her and she stepped to the side of the road as the vehicle passed. Then she heard the horn beep twice. The hodge-podge truck that Cora Corona drove seemed to be the parts of many past vehicles welded together. Strips of silver glittered down each side and glowed in the dark. Lucy ran up to the slowing truck. She told Cora about the sunset service.

"I think I'd have heard about that," Cora said in a crusty tone. "Well, we'll see." They headed toward the roadside park.

Randy Petrowski had lost count of the pots of coffee he'd brewed. Ted Bales yawned and looked at his watch. Sergeant Allen was on the phone, and Steve Randall, rubbing his lower back, had just escorted Ben Wasser to supper in the holding cell. Chief Karp was keeping everyone late, but the afternoon parade had been exciting.

The sheriff had tried a shaky bluff with Karp, admitting to planting the tap. "You know as well as I do, Walt, you've got a troublemaker, you think you need an edge to see what he's up to, he might even come to no good. And that's just what happened." But when Karp pressed Wasser, there were too many unanswered questions about Truman's last conversations concerning the will and the petitions, some difficulty

with Wasser remembering where he was at crucial times. Eventually, he spilled the beans on the government scam. Then lots of prominent names had been called to Karp's office. Bill Prather; the head of the Chamber of Commerce; the bank president; the Seascape developers. Jim Strunk had been called also but Karp hadn't been able to reach him.

The final visitor was Adam Hall. He emerged from the Police Chief's office looking sheepish, and he exited quickly.

For a moment after they were all gone, the Chief stood in his office door meeting the stares of his officers. As usual his tie was yanked down, his sleeves rolled up and he scratched at his chest hair. Then he went back into his office, dropped the blinds on his windows, slid off that left shoe that was squeezing his arch, and opened his bottom drawer for the fifth of Southern Comfort. Crass whiskey with a bite that seared the throat and numbed the tongue—just the relief he needed before he'd question Wasser again. He would bet his next pay check that Ben Wasser had been in the apartment when Perry Day Truman was assaulted.

Her hands tied behind her back, the slight figure of Nyla Wade was no problem for the two men. They pushed her out of the Mustang behind a beach house under construction. She couldn't tell that she had been driven only a short distance from the park. The men pulled her into the darkened house. She could see nothing but heard them clatter around trying to find a light.

"Over here, Max." Heavy footsteps lumbered away from her, then she saw a match and a slow halo spreading from a kerosene lantern.

"Heard you been causing lotsa trouble for some friends of mine," the skinny man said. The two of them stood facing her. The larger man had a puffy face, a week's worth of stubble, an ample beer gut. He wore a black T-shirt that was unraveling at the neck, rumpled grey pants and tennis shoes. The skinnier man was also unshaven, needed a haircut. Thin black hair was slicked back off his face and he sported one of those too-bright Hawaiian shirts so popular with tourists. He picked up the lantern and walked over to her, held the light up close to her face. He reeked of alcohol.

"Heard you want to write a big story about the castle, dredge up a lot of old history." He grinned, breathing into her face. When he walked around behind her, she shivered. He jerked the bonds on her hands.

As he moved away from her, she saw cartons stacked on top of each other. She heard the swish of liquid and the skinny guy spit out a cork. She saw his head jerk back as he took a quick swig. Then he handed the bottle to the big man.

The skinny guy stared at her, leering. Beer Gut kept watch at a window, his huge body blocking the light from the lantern. When the skinny guy started to move toward the cartons, Nyla jumped and he laughed. "Little nervous, sister?" He dragged an empty carton to her. "Sit." She sank slowly onto the wooden box.

Skinny went back to the stack of cartons and pried open the top one, then pulled out a dusty, corked bottle. When he turned to Nyla, he was grinning again. "Just a little side business me 'n Max got." He brought the bottle back with him, walking up close to her again. "We coulda come forward for that easy five hundred you offered. Cuz we're the guys picked up Tramp Williams that night." He shook the bottle in front of her. "But now we can have some fun with you."

No event had been planned by Oceanview Home and there was no Mr. Avery there. Lucy knew something was wrong. As she and Cora drove back to the roadside park, she could hardly breathe.

"We oughta get the cops." Cora kept her eyes on the road.

"Not enough time." If only she had run, Lucy thought, got to the park sooner, Nyla would be safe.

They swung into the park, Cora's truck lights illuminating a battered brown Chevy. Lucy jumped out—but there was nothing to see in the Chevy except springs popping out of the seats. She ran the perimeter of the park, yelling for Nyla. Her voice was swallowed up in the noise of the crashing surf. She ran back to Cora, stood beside her glittery truck.

"What's near here? I can't think—a motel, a restaurant?"

"Seaside Motel's up about two miles, the Jason Maxwell place a little beyond that. Then nothing until you hit town."

Lucy groaned, stamping her feet in the night chill.

"Oh," Cora remembered. "There's a beach house down a quarter mile. Nobody lives there. It's only half built."

"Come on!"

Skinny's name was Al, and he liked to talk as much as he liked to drink. Bragging mostly, about his days in the Air Force, about the big shots he supposedly knew. "And some of 'em want you shut up pretty bad." He was in her face again with that awful grin and his stinking breath. He nudged her with his knee, ran his finger down her jawline. "They want your pretty trap buttoned all right."

When she leaned away from his touch, his expression soured. "Not just a snoop, are ya, you're a snoot too. Think you're better'n the rest of us, do you? You got problems, lady, *real* problems." He jerked back another swig of whiskey.

"If I don't write the castle story, someone else will." Hearing her own voice comforted Nyla.

Al was right back at her, too close, snarling, "Not likely—not when they see what happens to you. Reporter found drunk on main street. We're gonna treat you to a taste of our homemade. A nice *large* taste." He was close enough to touch her face with his own. He lowered his voice and she felt his hand. "We'll dribble a little in your lap, too." He laughed, moved back to the opened carton.

"Ole Tramp Williams liked our hooch plenty, didn't he, Max? Drank it all the way over to Coos Bay."

Max turned from the window and grunted. Al was working the cork out of one of the bottles of bootleg. Nyla knew if anyone coming by on the road was to see the flicker of light, she had to get Max away from that window. She tried frantically to think what to say that would distract both of them.

The cork popped out of the bottle Al held. His laugh fit his weasely appearance. "I'm no reporter but I got some good stories of my own. 'Bout things we've got away with. You wanna know about Tramp Williams? You oughta pay me a real reward for what I know about some of our *local* citizens, like my ole Air Force buddy Jim Strunk for instance." Al sniffed the bottle. "Real vintage." His eyes glittered at Nyla and he turned to look at Max. In that moment, Nyla jumped up and ran directly toward the stacked cases of bottles.

"Hey! What the—Max, grab her before she breaks those bottles!"

The big man lunged toward her but not before she had drawn him from the window, not before she felt her shoulder crack in pain as she toppled the cases, the bottles and glass crashing loudly.

"What was that?" Lucy pointed to the left of the road.

"Nothing. Couldn'ta been. That's the beach house. Under construction but they stopped building when Seascape was delayed."

"Stop the truck. I saw some light."

The redhead was out of the truck and running up toward the house before Cora could put the brake on. Cora followed, but not before she reached into the back of the truck and pulled out a rusty speargun.

From the driveway, they crept up to the side of the house. Lucy heard scuffling sounds and cursing. Cora pulled back the spring of the speargun, which looked like it could pierce armor. She nudged Lucy and pointed to a pile of two-by-fours. Lucy picked up a short length. They were just steps from the back door.

"Gonna dose you up good, girlie, and dump you. All the right people will see what a hot shot reporter the *Beckoner* got themselves." Max was holding her on her back; Al had a knee on her shoulder. He pinched her cheeks hard until her lips opened. "Open wide, you . . ." She felt the liquid splashing on her, stinging her eyes.

The back door crashed open as Lucy and Cora burst in on them. Max ran at them, his huge hands ready. Cora stopped him with her speargun in his gut. Al threw a bottle at Lucy. She dodged it, then whacked him a good shot with the two-by-four. He went down with a groan and stayed down.

Suddenly the shell of a house was silent, except for Al's moaning and Lucy's panting. Holding the two-by-four with both hands, she glared at Max. Cora gave him a threatening poke.

"It's over, buddy," Lucy told the big man. "It's over."

As she untied Nyla's hands, Lucy kept repeating, "Thank God, thank God you're all right." She helped Nyla to her feet. Nyla clung to her, crying with relief.

"Anything broken?"

"I don't know. I can't feel my shoulder."

The three women looked at each other in the light of the lantern. Though she was shaking, Nyla wiped her eyes, kissed Lucy loudly on the cheek. "You're becoming indispensable!"

The Burnton police officers thought Walter Karp's parade of suspects had been lively enough until Lucy Randolph and Cora Corona brought in their captives—the huge, glowering Max prodded by the speargun, and Al holding one elbow and moaning. Nyla Wade followed them all and it was obvious from her torn and dirty clothes that she'd been in a skirmish. She was also favoring her right shoulder.

"We'll be pressing charges," she said to Ted Bales as she headed for Karp's office. He clambered out of his chair all rattling keys and handcuffs as he took charge of the two prisoners.

The blinds were up in Karp's office. Everyone in the squad room watched the Chief and Nyla conferring. A few phrases floated within hearing. "You said he might be dressed like the minister . . ." "Wasser's the one who did the fish . . ." "Something *was* taken from the castle that night and I know . . ." "Mrs. Dennis gave in, was afraid her boy was somehow involved . . ." "Explains the footprints . . ." "Picked up Williams, his hair wasn't wet, got the scratch in a scuffle with Max when he couldn't pay his bar tab . . ."

Nyla gestured to the terrible twosome. Karp touched Nyla's shoulder gingerly. Then he walked quickly into the squad room.

"Steve, get me a search warrant! Phil, I want to talk to Doc Stressand at county hospital. Randy, bring Wasser back in here on the double! And Ted, book these two." He jammed a finger at Al and Max, frowned fiercely at them. "Bootlegging, kidnapping, assault, attempted murder."

With his officers scrambling to carry out his orders, the Chief turned his attention to Lucy and Cora. His face had cleared with relief as he asked them, "You sure you ladies are all right?"

SIXTEEN

It's Your Story, Khaki Girl

Though it was Walter Karp's voice on his phone recorder, Jim Strunk dubbed it bad luck all the same. He'd just hung up from a hasty call to Bill Prather so he knew the reason for the Chief's call. He drank down his vodka without tasting it, wondering what else Karp knew, and began to form a plan for beating the rap. He had enough of city powers implicated with him—so whatever strings they could pull had better include him. They could say he was the mastermind but he would name Adam Hall as the ringleader.

He'd missed dinner—fresh lobster—and he felt irritable, hungry, the same kind of pre-flight scared and excited he'd been in the service. The challenge of combat, not knowing the enemy's strength, the fly-boy confidence that his wits were stronger. His gut burned and not from the vodka or the lack of food. *Too many weaklings, in war and life, only a few good men . . .*

Strunk remembered riding toward the castle that day a year ago with Prather, who always smiled that dumb-ass smile like he was going Christmas shopping instead of looking at corpses. They'd heard Randall radio Karp. Prather laughed, said they could beat the Police Chief to the scene. "He's getting slow in his old age!" And the coroner slapped him on the leg.

Strunk had some hope then for getting out of this three-hick town, getting himself a desk at the capitol in Salem. He'd be out of the field and away from two-bit adventure types like Prather and Wasser. He'd get away from being the D.A.'s errand boy. Luck always seemed to hang on his coattail. Adam Hall's backers liked him, thought he had a good chance, let it be known they'd get him the campaign funds. The Seascape developers liked him, thought he could walk on legal waters for them. He was in a position to deliver Burnton's destiny and deliver himself a shoo-in in the election.

The memory grew sweeter—that trip over to Coos Bay to rescue a crony the D.A. owed a favor—and then his joke about the tennis shoes had been no joke but a godsend, making him into a local hero before he'd even started to campaign. His fake-out about those poor murdered Burnton ladies and their horrible injustice made him smile even now. He poured himself another vodka.

The mental savoring of the past began to sour. Wasser with his sweaty grin, Prather's paltry smile fading before it started, just like his nerve. Adam Hall's backers spending less than they'd promised in both votes and bucks, the election a quiet failure and Strunk finding himself in the same spot, surrounded by the same weak-willed locals. The political route was a bust—no one had come back to him for a second round. Seascape was all that was left, a score that might be big enough to pull him some new contacts, some hope for notice by a sizeable law firm, even out-of-state. And then Perry Day Truman had thrown a wrench into everything.

At the thought of Truman, Strunk slammed his empty glass onto his desk. He could see that yielding too-soft face, interspersed with Wasser's, both of them floating in ugly deformity. "Goddamn sonofabitch!" He pushed a bound legal dictionary angrily onto the floor, hearing it smack against the tile.

Not a backbone between the two of them and they've crushed my efforts, my future!

The Assistant D.A. clenched his fists, closed his eyes to try and push away the faces that haunted him. He wondered how fast he could pack, where he could go, and if they were on their way to him already.

Nyla asked the Chief as they sped down the highway, "You think we'll have any trouble getting Al and Max to testify?"

"I doubt it. When Van Davidson analyzes their moonshine, I think we'll have them dead to rights on those alcohol poisonings. Add that to your own testimony and they'll plea bargain like crazy."

Nyla was so excited and nervous about the mission ahead that she could barely breathe. The ghosts who had chosen her to solve their secrets once and for all echoed around her. She thought of the poems, the search through the castle, the painting of Valerie Prosper. She knew now that there was proof the murder of Joan and Val had been no disturbed robbery—but something had been taken from the castle that night. She and Karp were betting the murderer still had it.

Her shoulder ached but her heart was afire. Justice was at hand and nothing could stop her seeing it through.

"You're better than I thought, Wade," the Chief told the reporter as they drove into North Bend.

"Me 'n my sidekick," Nyla wanted to say, wishing Lucy were with her. But she and Cora had other business—the wrecker had speeded up and might hit town before daylight. They had gone to join Seth in the highway blockade.

"I'll be with you anyhow, babe," Lucy had told her. "Take it from here, Khaki Girl. It's your story."

Jim Strunk showed considerable reserve, masking any panic, when he opened the door to Police Chief Karp and reporter Nyla Wade. Karp apologized for the lateness of the hour and then asked Strunk if he could account for his whereabouts on the night Joan Ruddye and Valerie Prosper were murdered.

"Christ, Walt, that was over a year ago. I'll get my calendar and see where I was, but what's the reason for these questions?"

"No need to get defensive, Jim. We've got new information and the case's reopened."

Strunk rummaged in a file until he found his calendar. "I was with Bill Prather that night. Talking politics, no doubt." The lawyer seemed calm. "You can call him to verify that."

Karp's voice was steady, his presence imposing. "I don't think Bill will help you out on this one."

Strunk closed the calendar slowly. He cleared his throat. "What do you mean?"

Steve Randall stepped in the front door. "You know what to do," Karp said to Nyla and then motioned to his officer. "She'll tell you what to look for." The two headed toward the back of the house.

"What the hell are you up to? You've got no right to—"

"Relax, Jim, I've got a warrant." Karp dropped the white rectangle onto Strunk's desk. "You want to call a lawyer?"

"What the hell for?" Strunk gave Karp a scornful look. "What's up, Walt? Someone downtown gunning for me?"

The Police Chief forced a smile.

Strunk said, "Christ, you bring a warrant in here and you haven't even charged me with anything."

"I will."

"Fine, take your best shot. I'm not saying another word."

"Okay, Jim. Then I'll do some talking." Karp walked over to the fireplace, stoked a heap of glowing embers and helped himself to one of the logs in a nearby basket. He waited until the log began to flame before he turned back to Strunk. The lawyer's color had begun to fade.

"Nice digs you got here, Jim. Befitting a District Attorney, or an *almost* D.A."

Strunk remained silent, his eyes hard and hateful upon the Chief.

"A guy wants to run for office like you did, Jim, he's got to sever all ties with anyone questionable. Lowlifes have a way of making more trouble than they're worth, you know what I mean, Jim?" Karp slid into one of the chairs facing the fire; its leather squeaked against his back.

"Join me over here, Jim."

Strunk moved into the chair opposite the Chief.

"Now you take a guy like Al Freenan—there's a lowlife who's nothing but trouble." Karp saw the lawyer go white.

236

"Freenan's a thief and petty burglar who tells us he some-times did jobs for you, Jim—rifle someone's office, bug their phones. An old Air Force buddy, he says. One time he pulled a freelance job at the Episcopal rectory. He needed to stash what he'd taken and you volunteered your garage. Poor choice of friends, Jim, very poor." Karp leaned toward the fire to warm his hands. "There was a knife with Al's stuff in your garage. Reverend Hammister reported it stolen. Unmistakable marking. That knife was used to kill those widows up in the castle."

Karp leveled his look on Strunk. "I've got the weapon traced to you, Jim. Witnesses who saw you enter and leave. The shoes, your blood type, even a patch of oriental black silk—it all fits you. You sure you don't want to call a lawyer?"

Strunk blinked, cleared his throat again and then asked softly, "What witnesses?"

Karp told him about Ritchie Dennis being within a few feet of the back door and Mitch Masters down on the beach. Strunk gave a hoarse cough of a laugh.

"*Those* are your witnesses? The town loonies—an obese retardo and a senile schizo. Garbage pickers, both of them, and you're slinging garbage too, Walt. I could bring you up for libel." Strunk shook his head but there was a wildness in his eyes. "I can't wait to hear what you've cooked up for motive."

"That . . ." Karp put his two palms together and spread his fingers. "That isn't simple to explain, but it got easier once I had a look at your Air Force personnel file."

Strunk said nothing, stared at the Chief for a moment. Then he stood up unsteadily and headed for a cabinet. Karp stood up too, watching the lawyer. Strunk banged open the mahogany door and grabbed for a bottle.

"You had quite a time in Japan at the end of your Air Force tour. Al Freenan remembers it clearly. Kinky Fly-boy he used to call his captain, who took to wearing a black silk Nehru jacket with white at the collar, spending his nights in brothels. Liked to hire three or more girls to have sex with each other. He watched mostly, liked them to tie each other up." Karp reached into his inner coat pocket and pulled out a notepad. He flipped through several pages.

"Here it is in Freenan's own words. 'Them slanty-eyed girls thought he was a priest by that coat of his. Sometimes Jim got real wild and beat them. I thought all that tying up was his main pleasure but he could flare up, too. Kinda scary, you never knew what he might do. After awhile, I didn't go with him any more.' " Karp closed the notebook.

"There was more in your personnel file. Seems the MP's were called one of those nights you went out to play." Karp kept an eye on Strunk, aware he might spring any moment, aware of the force that seethed very near the surface. "Seems you roughed one of the Japanese hookers up pretty good, Jim."

"You're reaching, Karp. Your case is weak and you know it. So I roughed up a Japanese prostitute once—that doesn't make me a murderer. Your witnesses are borderline, even Freenan. They won't hold up past preliminary. Give it up, I'll forget what you said."

Karp moved closer to him, picked up the phone receiver on the desk.

"You better call your lawyer, Jim. I'm going to read you your rights."

Strunk's eyes flashed fear. "You're not going to make any headlines off my back, Karp, no way! I'd have thought you got your fill of that when you lost your temper in Haver Square!"

Strunk didn't expect the Chief to get around the desk so fast. Karp jammed his square face into Strunk's, resisting the urge to grab him by the tie.

"I've got a case all right. And plenty of *reliable* people willing to talk. Adam Hall in particular."

Karp moved in closer, saw Strunk's irises shrink down like camera shutters. "I know all about your shitty little government scam. Funny thing, everyone will probably get off. But you, Jim, you've got a much bigger rap coming. Ritchie Dennis thought you were a priest in that jacket, just like those hookers did. Mitch Masters called you the Night Rider with a cape—because as you ran down to the water that black jacket was flapping, you were tearing at it, it was covered with blood, you wanted to get it off you. You wanna show me that jacket, Jim? I'll stop all this right now if I see it's intact."

238

Strunk remained silent. Karp's closeness made him bend backward and his neck ached, his collar felt too tight.

The Chief continued. "You were fighting your demons that night—those from Japan, the memory of that hooker you nearly strangled with the scarf used to tie her up. And your Burnton demons, pressures for money and status. You walked right into that open back door and killed those poor women who did nothing to you except want to stay in their castle together. You're a first rate monster, Strunk, a goddamned walking Frankenstein, and I'm going to lock your ass up for good."

Karp straightened. He lowered his voice, casually brushed one of Strunk's lapels as he said, "Bet you were praying, weren't you, that you'd find everything when you took that walk on the beach while Prather was with the bodies. He was the perfect way for you to keep tabs on what we'd find. You couldn't really believe you'd just thrown the shoes and the knife into the water. You couldn't remember if the tide was going out or coming in. It was coming in, and it all came in, right into Mitch Masters' hands."

Strunk moved away from the Chief, taking the vodka bottle with him. At the fire, he poured another drink and said, "I'm not making any statement. I was with Prather. He's your liar."

"He's lied, all right, and owned up to it. Along with another of your victims, Ben Wasser. Ben made a bad liar and a worse accomplice."

The vodka sloshed over the inlaid tile of the hearth.

"It was an accident! Goddamned faggot walked in on us. Wasser got there first, found the will, and went nuts. Started burning things half-ass as if no one would see the smoke in the middle of the day. I was trying to stop him when Truman came back, went crazy when he saw what we were burning. Climbed Ben like a damned maniac, scratching and biting. In defense, I had to—"

Karp felt his temper boiling. He moved toward Strunk at the fireplace. "Cut the crap, you caved half his damned skull in. Dumped him unconscious into that bog to cover your tracks."

"We found it, Chief."

Karp turned at Nyla's voice. She held up the white scarf

with the tiny holes in it, the one Cohista thought Valerie had discarded, the one Valerie had gently tied on Joan Ruddye's wrist that night.

Karp grimaced at Strunk. "Couldn't leave it behind, could you? Had to bring some sign of your perverted—"

Strunk swung the vodka bottle squarely at his head but Karp dodged and the bottle bashed against the Chief's shoulder. Strunk scrambled to the desk and yanked open a drawer but Karp wrestled him until they fell over the desk, crashing books and files to the floor. Strunk scooped up a ceramic ashtray and took another swipe at Karp before Steve Randall subdued him with a chokehold. In the partially opened drawer, Nyla spotted a revolver.

After Steve had cuffed Strunk, Karp jerked him to his feet. Then Karp slowly loosened the lawyer's tie, slowly unbuttoned the top buttons of his shirt and with a snap of the material, yanked open the collar. There for all to see was the jagged pink scar, the mark of death Valerie Prosper had left behind.

On the way back to Burnton, Chief Karp told Nyla, "Strunk almost had me with that round house swing of the bottle. I needed your trashcan trick." Nyla's smile told him she was glad he was all right.

The squawk box rattled in Walter Karp's unit. It was Officer Ted Bales, reporting they had one helluva mess just outside Burnton. Someone had ordered a ball-and-chain wrecker in from Portland to knock down the limestone castle and a whole lot of angry folks had stopped the huge machine at the edge of town.

"They've got the sucker surrounded like a goddamned war pack!"

Nyla Wade was grinning when the Chief gave his ten-four.

"Don't s'pose you know anything about this, do you, Nyla?"

All the reporter gave him was her famous smile, and he couldn't help but respond in kind.

SEVENTEEN

Finding Love Anew

The scene at the edge of town seemed like a replay of David and Goliath—the massive wrecker lay on a flatbed trailer pulled by a huge, two-stack semi-cab with tank tracks, the entire rig stretched across the highway. Nyla imagined the wrecker's huge hydraulic arm swinging like a giant-sized medieval weapon, smashing against the castle. She shuddered.

Floodlights attached to the top of the blockaders' semi-cab bathed everything in glaring white light. Engines steamed, horns honked, people were yelling and waving signs. When Nyla and Karp drove up, she caught sight of Lucy and Cora Corona sitting in the blockaders' semi-cab, high up over the crowd.

Karp led the way among the cars toward the front of the caravan. Nyla could see Seth up ahead, like a red-bearded Ulysses. A short bald man was yelling in his face, poking him hard in the chest.

"You got no right blockin' us out! Get these cars movin'! What's with you jerks anyway? We got orders!"

Howard Penn suddenly leapt onto the hood of one of the cars and started a chant, "So we're gay, here we stay!" His fists upraised, he jumped gingerly from car to car like an elfin ballet dancer, fueling the chant to a fever pitch. Others climbed

241

onto their cars, began to stomp as well as shout until the cacaphony was overwhelming.

The bald man was screaming, "Get the hell out of here! I gotta job to do! I'll call the cops!" Finally, just as Karp and Nyla reached them, the bald man took a swing at Seth. Ulysses blocked Baldy and spun him around as easily as tossing a pillow. Seth held the man up on his tiptoes kicking and cursing.

"The cops are here, settle down!" Karp yelled, flashing his badge. "What's going on, Seth?"

The bald man scrambled away when he saw the badge. Seth tried to fill Karp in but they could hardly hear each other. Howard Penn was now perched atop the semi-cab in between the floodlights, waving with fervor as the stomping and chanting continued.

"Who is that nut?" Karp yelled but before Seth could yell back an answer, Baldy in the wrecker cab blasted his horn to which Lucy in the blockaders' cab replied with her horn. They went on blasting back and forth, behemoths arguing in ear-splitting decibels. Karp signaled to Seth and they split up, struggling through the crowd and cars, many of which now also contained curious townspeople. Karp managed to wrestle Baldy away from his horn while Seth subdued Lucy.

The Randolphs made their way back to Karp. As soon as they were within reach of each other, Lucy and Nyla embraced. With a faint smile, Karp stepped away from them. He was considering running his sirens to quiet the crowd when a Stadler Construction car flashing hazard lights braked next to the wrecker. A man emerged from the car who was as big as Seth and had his own full beard, crisp and curly black. Both men looked like stars of a gladiator film.

"What's the trouble?" Blackbeard's voice boomed.

"Had to stop your boys," Seth yelled. "No one touches that castle."

Blackbeard held up a piece of paper. "We've got a legit order."

"Maybe so," Seth shouted. "But our castle stays, order or not."

"Hey, don't I know you?" Blackbeard called to Seth. "Forty-Niners, wasn't it? Fullback or tackle?"

242

Seth grinned. "Tackle."

"Me too." Blackbeard stuck out his hand. "Deacon Robinson. I used to be with the Raiders."

They shook hands. Seth said, "Didn't we play against each other in the pro bowl?"

"Oh yeah, I remember you now. You could give a hit as well as take one."

Seth's eyes twinkled as his memory came clear. "I remember how you played *after* the game."

They both roared with laughter and slapped each other on the back.

"You were with Vince Parker, weren't you? I couldn't believe it. I didn't even know about him."

Blackbeard nodded, grinning. "Quarterbacks are shy, you know." And they both laughed loudly again.

"So what're we gonna do about all this?" Blackbeard shouted.

"Whad'ya say we park your wrecker at my construction yard, then go have a beer and get this all sorted out?"

Blackbeard gave a thumbs-up sign. Seth conferred with Karp, Nyla, and Lucy about dispersing the crowd.

Everyone attended the party at the limestone castle: Nyla and Lucy, Seth and Deacon Robinson, Cora Corona, Chief Karp and Cohista Farrell, Officer Steve Randall, Howard Penn with most of the blockaders, and two reps from Seascape, one a new lawyer. Jean Thomas was taking pictures. Gruff Hamilton was bragging about his reporter and his layout to Jim Hammister as they looked at the extra edition of the *Beckoner* with Nyla's front page story on the re-solved murders. Even Mitch Masters was there, like a puppy freed of a paw burr now that he was out of the hospital and cured of blood poisoning. Ritchie Dennis and his mother were there as well, Ritchie gazing at everything as if he might coo. Loamie Newsome was heartily downing champagne, sashaying among the guests in a new fur coat and sunglasses. Seascape had bought her out but she was going to rebuild up the Loop where all the tourists would pass.

The Ruddyes and the Seascape developers had immediately settled out of court with Howard Penn and the San Francisco

Gay Historical Society. Everyone would see a pretty profit and the castle would stay, to be incorporated as a historical site next to Seascape.

"Well, you can't fight progress," the new Seascape lawyer said as if he had an original idea. "Who knows?" he added, toasting Howard Penn. "Controversy may make for good commerce. People pay to get in, we profit. The castle stays, the town gets Seascape. Everyone gets something."

Jean took their picture. It was Howard's idea that Seascape and GHS sign the agreement in the now famous castle on Joan's now famous Wooten desk. He knew he was considerably more comfortable than the Seascape people and he was loving it.

At one point, Chief Karp put an arm around Nyla and gave her a friendly squeeze, careful of her still aching shoulder. Looking at her and Lucy, he told them, "I thought about awarding you an honorary badge. But I don't want to encourage you. That kidnapping was a close call." He winked at Lucy. "Keep her behind the typewriter, will you?"

To great applause, Nyla and Lucy and Seth announced that the repaired portrait of Valerie Prosper would soon hang in the great hall dining room.

Nyla managed to slip upstairs for a more peaceful view from the second story terrace under the blue window. The single pall over her contentment was Perry's absence and she felt it keenly. He was missing the celebration he'd made possible with the giving of his life.

As the sun set over the ocean, Nyla felt the ghosts leaving the castle. She'd done their bidding and they were at rest; Druscilla and Molly Ketcham, Mercy Hayworth, Olympia Swan, Joan and Valerie. She'd been guardian and translator again, in ways she hadn't entirely understood. And she'd also found the beauty of casting out the net into the gay family, of which all her ghosts were a positive part. For a moment, she wished they were closer, these ghosts of the past who had so affected her present, and the others too: W. Stone, Cybil Porter, and Sara, who had disappeared from her life but never from her thoughts.

She consoled herself, knowing loved ones may leave us in the death of love or even in death, but we find them anew. She had a marvelous life ahead, of possibility, discovery, and adventure with Lucy. Lucy, who could stomp and blow like Bogart in a big screen shoot-out but who was as silky and soft a lover as Valerie Prosper's favorite scarf.

"You left this book on the table, babe." Lucy joined her on the terrace. The book was *Pioneer Women.*

"Perry loaned it to me from Joan's library. I didn't get to read it and thought I should return it now that things are settled."

When Lucy opened the book to thumb through the pages, a small faded piece of flannel in the shape of a star floated to the terrace floor. Nyla picked it up, knew at once it was part of Rose Ketcham's prairie quilting. Her eyes filled with tears.

"This book was meant for you, Nyla. Perry knew that when he gave it to you." Lucy held her lover as the sky burned blue-orange, and the soft queer blue of Dru Ketcham's window wrapped around them. "That's my Khaki Girl," she whispered, kissing Nyla's hair. "I'm so proud of you, and your story. I loved that line you gave Karp about pariahs having their justice."

"That was no line, schweetheart, that was serious business." Nyla wiped her eyes, then took Lucy by the hand. "Come on, let's get out of here. Go take a walk on the beach, like our first date."

They escaped the party, slid hand-in-hand down the sand at the end of the castle's funny sidewalk. The sun glanced its final dancing rays off the water. They walked among the trailers and ribbons, sea kelp in knobby wads or ribbon-thin and shining silver from the water. The descending sun settled a notch, a starfish scuttled in with the tide. The lovers watched her spin around in the foam like her own compass.

"Looks like she's doing the jitterbug," Lucy said softly.

As they walked on further, Nyla's thoughts were filled with dancing starfish, dancing dots made by twirling crystals, needlepoint designs, footprints disappearing in shifting sand. As she held the warmth of Lucy's love in her heart and clasped between their two hands, she held those women lovers from the past who had also claimed this beach, claimed their passion at no small cost.

She reached into her coat pocket and pulled out a crumpled piece of paper. "One of Joan's poems. I wanted to read it to you."

Lucy's eyes showed her open and ready heart.

> "Peel down my barriers,
> Find my true heart—
> An endless well
> To drip passion
> Upon your thirst.
> I gladly give it up to you
> Even as it stays my own."

The tide splashed past them in a surge, filled their foot-prints as if healing the sand.

What would you do for me in this world, Joanie?

Anything, Val, anything you asked.

Nyla and Lucy both turned at the echo, as if they heard.

ABOUT THE AUTHOR

VICKI P. McCONNELL talks to plants and cries at the ocean. She used to do the hand-jive and Elvis Presley imitations. She still loves gay pride marches and believes something *did* happen when she turned thirty. She is thirty-four years old with a Bachelor's degree in Theatre/English, hails from Kansas, writes her first draft in longhand, and names Lillian Hellman, Alice Walker, Dorothea Brande, May Sarton, and Lily Tomlin as some of her sheroes.

"I believe we need ideals more than ever. I find them in the writing of other women, I show my own in my characters. I don't know whether I found Nyla Wade or she found me, but I'm proud of her. She fights fiercely for her ideals."

Other books written by McConnell include her first novel *Berrigan* from Naiad Press, Inc. (1977), *Sense You*, poetry from Gena Rose Press (1979), and Nyla Wade's first mystery adventure, *Mrs. Porter's Letter*, also from Naiad (1982).

ABOUT THE ILLUSTRATOR

JANET FONS has a B.F.A. from Michigan State University in Print Making and Graphic Design and has done graphics and illustrations for more than ten years. She is currently a freelance art director for a major Denver ad agency. Her work appears in Chocolate Waters' poetry book *Charting New Waters,* The Word Is Out newsletter, Vicki McConnell's first Nyla Wade mystery novel, *Mrs. Porter's Letter,* and McConnell's short story, "The Improper Ladies." She also does graphics for Antelope Press.

A few of the publications of
THE NAIAD PRESS, INC.
P.O. Box 10543 • Tallahassee, Florida 32302
Mail orders welcome. Please include 15% postage.

The Burnton Widows by Vicki P. McConnell. A mystery novel. 272 pp. ISBN 0-930044-52-5 — $7.95

Old Dyke Tales by Lee Lynch. Short Stories. 224 pp. ISBN 0-930044-51-7 — $7.95

Daughters of a Coral Dawn by Katherine V. Forrest. Science fiction. 240 pp. ISBN 0-930044-50-9 — $7.95

The Price of Salt by Claire Morgan. A novel. 288 pp. ISBN 0-930044-49-5 — $7.95

Against the Season by Jane Rule. A novel. 224 pp. ISBN 0-930044-48-7 — $7.95

Lovers in the Present Afternoon by Kathleen Fleming. A novel. 288 pp. ISBN 0-930044-46-0 — $8.50

Toothpick House by Lee Lynch. A novel. 264 pp. ISBN 0-930044-45-2 — $7.95

Madame Aurora by Sarah Aldridge. A novel. 256 pp. ISBN 0-930044-44-4 — $7.95

Curious Wine by Katherine V. Forrest. A novel. 176 pp. ISBN 0-930044-43-6 — $7.50

Black Lesbian in White America. Short stories, essays, autobiography. 144 pp. ISBN 0-930044-41-X — $7.50

Contract with the World by Jane Rule. A novel. 340 pp. ISBN 0-930044-28-2 — $7.95

Yantras of Womanlove by Tee A. Corinne. Photographs. 64 pp. ISBN 0-930044-30-4 — $6.95

Mrs. Porter's Letter by Vicki P. McConnell. A mystery novel. 224 pp. ISBN 0-930044-29-0 — $6.95

To the Cleveland Station by Carol Anne Douglas. A novel. 192 pp. ISBN 0-930044-27-4 — $6.95

The Nesting Place by Sarah Aldridge. A novel. 224 pp. ISBN 0-930044-26-6 — $6.95

This Is Not for You by Jane Rule. A novel. 284 pp. ISBN 0-930044-25-8 — $7.95

Faultline by Sheila Ortiz Taylor. A novel. 140 pp. ISBN 0-930044-24-X — $6.95

The Lesbian in Literature by Barbara Grier. 3d ed. Foreword by Maida Tilchen. A comprehensive bibliography. 240 pp. ISBN 0-930044-23-1 — $7.95

Anna's Country by Elizabeth Lang. A novel. 208 pp.
ISBN 0-930044-19-3 .... $6.95

Prism by Valerie Taylor. A novel. 158 pp.
ISBN 0-930044-18-5 .... $6.95

Black Lesbians: An Annotated Bibliography compiled by
JR Roberts. Foreword by Barbara Smith. 112 pp.
ISBN 0-930044-21-5 .... $5.95

The Marquise and the Novice by Victoria Ramstetter.
A novel. 108 pp. ISBN 0-930044-16-9 .... $4.95

Labiaflowers by Tee A. Corinne. 40 pp.
ISBN 0-930044-20-7 .... $3.95

Outlander by Jane Rule. Short stories, essays. 207 pp.
ISBN 0-930044-17-7 .... $6.95

Sapphistry: The Book of Lesbian Sexuality by Pat Califia.
2nd edition, revised. 195 pp. ISBN 0-930044-47-9 .... $7.95

The Black and White of It by Ann Allen Shockley.
Short stories. 112 pp. ISBN 0-930044-15-0 .... $5.95

All True Lovers by Sarah Aldridge. A novel. 292 pp.
ISBN 0-930044-10-X $6.95

A Woman Appeared to Me by Renee Vivien. Translated by
Jeannette H. Foster. A novel. xxxi, 65 pp.
ISBN 0-930044-06-1 .... $5.00

Cytherea's Breath by Sarah Aldridge. A novel. 240 pp.
ISBN 0-930044-02-9 .... $6.95

Tottie by Sarah Aldridge. A novel. 181 pp.
ISBN 0-930044-01-0 .... $5.95

The Latecomer by Sarah Aldridge. A novel. 107 pp.
ISBN 0-930044-00-2 .... $5.00

VOLUTE BOOKS

Journey to Fulfillment	by Valerie Taylor	$3.95
A World without Men	by Valerie Taylor	$3.95
Return to Lesbos	by Valerie Taylor	$3.95
Desert of the Heart	by Jane Rule	$3.95
Odd Girl Out	by Ann Bannon	$3.95
I Am a Woman	by Ann Bannon	$3.95
Women in the Shadows	by Ann Bannon	$3.95
Journey to a Woman	by Ann Bannon	$3.95
Beebo Brinker	by Ann Bannon	$3.95

These are just a few of the many Naiad Press titles. Please request a complete catalog!

WHAT THE CRITICS SAY ABOUT *MRS. PORTER'S LETTER* BY VICKI P. McCONNELL

IF NANCY DREW HAD COME OUT —A NEW LESBIAN MYSTERY writes Alden Waitt in OFF OUR BACKS. "Vicki P. McConnell has helped launch a new genre of lesbian literature—the lesbian detective novel—and her audience will soon be clamoring for more. In Nyla Wade, McConnell has created an intelligent, credible, and life-sized woman who discovers herself while she solves a mystery. Join Nyla Wade and treat yourself to a remarkable, well-written story and a memorable mystery with a modern, original heroine who will not disappoint you."

"If you love women and you love mysteries, you're in for a real treat when you read *Mrs. Porter's Letter.*" Stephanie L. Gotlob, PLEXUS

". . . deliciously intricate plot and sub-plot . . . so vividly written it works like a good movie." Nancy Walker, GAY COMMUNITY NEWS

"*Mrs. Porter's Letter* starts with a bang and ends with a wonderful surprise . . ." Sue Williams, PHILADELPHIA GAY NEWS

"Telling her own story, Wade is the upbeat female voice of Dashiell Hammett. She likes her Scotch in quantity. Of special note are the illustrations by Janet Fons. Now that I've met her gumshoe and found her to be a gutsy woman with perseverence and wit, I can hardly wait for McConnell's next mystery." Joyce Bright, THE ADVOCATE

"A mystery that is both an engaging whodunit and a spiritual and lyrical tale." Lynn Weaver, BAY WINDOWS

"Superb . . . a real page turner . . . a jewel . . . who wants to help organize a Vickie McConnell fan club? I do, I do . . ." Yaraich, WOMEN'S PRESS

$6.95 plus 15% Postage from NAIAD PRESS
P.O. Box 10543, Tallahassee, Florida 32302